Alfred Duggan was bor
American descent: his m
was born in Illinois in 18
(born in Argentina of English par....,
General in Brazil. Duggan was taken to England at the age of two. After his education at Eton College and Balliol College, Oxford, he worked for the British Natural History Museum, collecting specimens. At the age of twenty-one he sailed in the 600-ton barquentine, *St George*, from England via Madeira, Trinidad and Panama to the Galapagos Islands, pursuing his job for the museum. In later years he travelled extensively in Greece and Turkey, studying Byzantine monuments, and in 1935 helped to excavate Constantine's Palace, Istanbul, under the auspices of the University of St Andrews. From 1938 to 1941, when he was discharged as medically unfit, he served in the London Irish Rifles (TA) and saw active service in Norway. For the rest of World War II he worked in an aircraft factory.

A prolific writer, Duggan turned out more than one book a year. His first was *Knight with Armour*, written in 1946 and published in 1950. Next came his novels *Conscience of the King* and *The Little Emperors*, the latter dealing in lively fashion with the decline and fall of the western Roman Empire as it impinged upon the life of a British civil servant. 'As one novel follows another in pleasant succession', wrote Thomas Caldecot Chubb in the *New York Times*, 'it dawns upon this constant reader of historical fiction that in Alfred Duggan he has found an extremely gifted writer who can move into an unknown period and give it life and immediacy'. 'A specialist in decline and fall', in *Lady for Ransom* he dealt with one of the great crises of Byzantine politics. 'Mr Duggan's characters are sharply drawn', wrote Chubb, 'and, as always, he keeps his eye on the flow of history'. His 'cheerful cynicism' and satirical view of men and politics 'have introduced a refreshing new element into current historical fiction'. Orville Prescott wrote in the *New York Times*, 'Mr Duggan looks upon the past with a connoisseur's relish of villainy and violence'.

Alfred Duggan died in 1964.

CONSCIENCE OF THE KING

ALFRED DUGGAN

PHOENIX

A PHOENIX PAPERBACK

First published in Great Britain in 1951
by Faber and Faber Limited
This paperback edition published in 2005
by Phoenix,
an imprint of Orion Books Ltd,
Orion House, 5 Upper St Martin's Lane,
London WC2H 9EA

1 3 5 7 9 10 8 6 4 2

A CIP catalogue record for this book
is available from the British Library.

ISBN 0 304 36646 3

Typeset by Deltatype Ltd, Birkenhead, Merseyside
Printed and bound in Great Britain by
Clays Ltd, St Ives plc

www.orionbooks.co.uk

CONTENTS

PLACE NAMES IN THE STORY

Anderida   *Pevensey*
Aquae Sulis   *Bath*
Arelatum   *Arles*
Armorica   *Brittany*
Augusta Treverorum   *Trier*
Calleva   *Silchester*
Corinium   *Cirencester*
Demetia   *South Wales*
Deva   *Chester*
Dumnonia   *Now Devonshire, but then including also Somerset, Cornwall and Dorset*
Durobrivae I   *Caistor-next-Norwich*
Durobrivae II   *Rochester*
Durovernum   *Canterbury*
Eboracum   *York*
Elmetia   *West Riding of Yorkshire*
Glevum   *Gloucester*
Lindum   *Lincoln*
Loidis   *Leeds and district*
Londinium   *London*
Noviomagus   *Chichester*
Otadini   *A tribe of the eastern lowlands of Scotland*
Portus   *Portsmouth*

Ratae   *Leicester*

Regni   *Name of the British tribe living in Sussex before the Romans came to Britain*

Regulbium   *Reculver*

Sabrina F.   *River Severn*

Sea of Vectis   *Solent*

Sequana F.   *River Seine*

Sorbiodunum   *Salisbury*

Valentia   *Uncertain, but probably in South Wales*

Vectis   *Isle of Wight*

Venedotia   *North Wales*

Venta   *Winchester*

Verulamium   *St Albans*

I

451–469

CHILDHOOD IN THE KINGDOM
OF THE REGNI

I have attained a very great age, more than eighty years, and my exciting and various life is closing in great prosperity. It would be a pity if my adventures were entirely forgotten; but to preserve the memory of them will be a difficult undertaking, for my grandsons and their followers are quite uneducated, and I should be surprised if their children are ever taught to read. Yet learning is still preserved in the eastern parts of the world, and surely, after many generations, it will creep back to this island. Therefore I have decided to write the story of my life. When it is written down I shall seal it up in a stout metal box, and arrange to have it buried somewhere; not I think in my own grave, for my son will put a respectable amount of treasure there, and one day robbers will break into the mound; but in the foundations of a ruined church, for I think that these will presently be repaired.

So here is the story of my life, told in Latin as accurate and elegant as I can make it after all these years of speaking another language; though here and there I have been compelled to use barbarian names for barbarian things.

At the very beginning I am faced with a difficulty. At the present time we have no proper framework for dating events; our ancestors dated official documents by the names of the Consuls, though very often the year was quite old before we learnt here in Britain who the Consuls were. Or one could use the regnal years of the Emperors; I generally know who was reigning in Constantinople a few years ago, but I don't know the date of his accession, and I might easily miss out some Emperor altogether; in my lifetime their reigns have often ended unexpectedly. There are other ways of naming the years, for example from the Creation of the World or the Foundation of the City; but people disagree about when the World was created, and I am not sure that the City is still standing. I shall reckon from the Incarnation of Christ, as I believe some holy men have done; if anyone wants to compare this system with his own different calendar, please note that the third Consulship of Aetius, which is still remembered in Britain, is the equivalent of 446 by my reckoning.

I shall have to tell at some length the story of my family, for it explains how I am at the same time a citizen, descended from citizens, and yet quite genuinely Woden-born. My great-great-grandfather was Fraomar King of the Buccinobantes, a tribe in the great confederation of the Alemanni of Germany; of course he was Woden-born, like all German Kings. Fraomar's land had been so devastated in war that his people decided to emigrate, but they were too weak to win new fields by the sword; accordingly they petitioned the Emperor Valentinian I, who allowed them to settle in the southern part of Britain, about the year 370. Fraomar's own estate was near Anderida, the great fortress on the Channel, which he helped to guard from pirates. His son, Fradogild, was Woden-born on both sides, but he was brought up a Christian, and married the daughter of a citizen. Their eldest son was my grandfather, Gaius Flavius Coroticus. His first two names are not important; no one uses the praenomen except in legal documents, and nearly

2

every citizen in Britain is either a Julius or a Flavius; but it is worth noticing the cognomen. It came from his mother's side of the family, and shows that they liked to think of themselves as descended from some ancient British chief before the coming of the Empire. In fact, there was quite a revival of old British names at that time, when everybody looked back regretfully to the good old days. My grandfather was a boy when the Germans crossed the Rhine on the ice and swept south-westward through Gaul; next year Constantine III was proclaimed Emperor in Britain, and invaded Gaul with all the troops he could collect. He took with him the garrison of Anderida, and my family began to treat that fortress as their private property. We have had no Emperor in Britain since; nor have we been able to attach ourselves to the Emperors in Italy, since the barbarians in Gaul cut us off from Ravenna.

My grandfather grew up with one curious advantage; his grandparents, proud of their descent, had taught him to speak German as well as Latin. He realized that an educated man, who really knew both languages, would make a better interpreter than the average German who can grunt a few Latin words for things to eat, or the Roman officer who knows some barbarian war-cries. During most of his youth he was used by the governors of the different cities of south Britain to negotiate with German pirates about ransoms for prisoners and payments to make them go away, and when Vortigern King of Demetia was entrusted with the defence of the east coast he joined the King's court as interpreter in German. He arranged the treaty by which King Vortigern settled Hengist and his three shiploads of Saxons on an island off the Kentish coast, where he was to protect south Britain from the pirates.

You may think it odd that Vortigern should be a King, only forty years after the last Emperor had left Britain; but his office was quite regular. His ancestors had ruled a tribe of Britons north of the Wall, and had been brought down into Valentia to chase out the Irish. Unfortunately his splendid title set a bad example. All over Britain the municipalities had fallen under the rule of the local honestiores, the wealthy landowners whose evidence was officially regarded by the law courts as outweighing that of any number of coloni settled on the land; these men began to imitate his grandeur, more especially as Kingship is obviously a hereditary distinction, and they wanted their power to descend to their sons. Soon the whole country was a mosaic of little Kingdoms.

When my grandfather Coroticus decided to follow the fortunes of Vortigern he turned over the management of the family estates to his only son Eleutherus, my father, who was three-quarters Roman and married to a Roman wife. So when I was born in the year 451, and christened Coroticus after my grandfather, the position of affairs was fairly complicated, but peaceful. My father Eleutherus was living with my mother on the family estate, between Anderida and the Great Forest; my grandfather Coroticus was with Vortigern, who lived mostly at Durovernum in Kent, where the danger from the barbarians was greatest; Hengist and his followers dwelt in their island and kept the pirates away; and considering the state of the world at that time we were on the whole prosperous. If you had asked a colonus in one of the villages who ruled him, the answer would have been my father Eleutherus, the owner of the fortress. If you had asked my father who ruled him, he would have said that he had to follow King Vortigern in war, but that in the lands round Anderida he had no superior. There were no law courts for the whole island, as there had been fifty years before, but each man did justice for his coloni, whether slave or free.

I was the third child of my parents, and the third son. My eldest brother, Constans, was six years older, and my second brother, Paul, two years; my mother had thought it her duty to suckle my two brothers, but she went through a bad time at my birth, and I needed a wet-nurse. My grandfather found a healthy young Saxon woman; according to the laws of the barbarians she was unmarried, but she had been seduced by a chief; his wife, who was childless and jealous, murdered the baby, and the mother fled to my grandfather in fear of her life. I mention this to bring out several points about the Saxons; the lack of supervision of their virgins, the power of their married women, and the rather insulting habit of the chiefs, who insisted on marrying wives of their own race, though they would amuse themselves with captive Roman women. The result was that I was suckled and brought up by this Saxon woman, who had been christened at my mother's orders and was always called by her Christian name, Ursula. My grandfather encouraged her to talk German to me, and gave me lessons himself when he was at home, so that I grew up bilingual in Latin and German, but with hardly any knowledge of Celtic; while my brothers spoke Latin to their parents and the other gentry, but Celtic to the servants. Three languages are too much for anyone to learn at once, and I have always spoken Celtic badly, with a strong German accent.

Quite naturally, I grew up to dislike my brothers. There was no settled future for me; my father, who dreamt of turning Anderida into a Kingdom, was determined to leave everything to Constans; my mother had vowed Paul to the Church, and he was brought up with the idea of becoming a Bishop one day; it was frequently pointed out that I was an unwanted extra, and would have to make my own way in the world.

My earliest memories are of the villa we lived in, north of Anderida. It was a great rambling place, with stables and granaries stretching on both sides of the dwelling house, and ranges of wooden cabins for the slaves. There had been an upper storey once, but only traces of it remained, for the whole establishment had been sacked and burnt in the great barbarian raids about eighty years before my birth. The ground floor of brick and rubble had survived the fire, and my great-grandfather had put a roof on it; every year we had to patch some part of the walls, so that the house had a curiously particoloured appearance, but so had all the other large villas in the neighbourhood. What is the use of building an expensive house when it will soon be sacked? In all my life I have never seen anybody begin to build in proper masonry from the ground up. But though the house was only the shadow of what it had been, it was still the largest and most impressive in the neighbourhood.

We were all Christians, my mother especially so, and I was brought up to despise the western Britons who still sometimes propitiate Nodens of the Silver Hand; though looking back it seems to me that they have had more help from Heaven than my devout family ever received. There was a chapel in the villa, and occasionally Mass was said there; I know my mother would have liked to have a chaplain staying in the house, and my father would also have liked this extra dignity. But the Bishop of Noviomagus would not allow us to keep a private chaplain, on account of the great shortage that prevailed of secular clergy.

That Bishop was rather a tiresome man anyway. He held the theory that although we were cut off from the Empire Roman law was still in force, and he was always expostulating with my father for arming his slaves. He pointed out that the fundamental regulation of the Empire

6

was that workers on the land must stick to their hereditary task; it is an unattractive life, that no one would choose for himself if he had the chance of anything better, but we should all starve if no one ploughed. That of course is perfectly true, but we would never have gathered our harvest if we had not guarded the crops from raiders. My father could easily provide both plough men and armed guards; his following increased every year, as the poorer citizens of Kent fled through the Forest to escape from Hengist's foraging parties or Vortigern's tax-collectors.

I suppose I can say conventionally that my childhood was the happiest time of my life. My brother Constans bullied me sometimes, but he spent most of his time out in the fields, while I chattered German to Ursula at home; Paul's future was all mapped out; one day he would be Bishop of Noviomagus, and he was already preparing for the part, with his face fixed in a smile of neighbourly love. There was plenty to eat, and we were growing richer and more powerful every year. My father was at home most of the time, and was quietly engaged in recruiting his guard, so that one day he would have a real comitatus.

I remember a long visit from my grandfather when I was six; he looked very grand and impressive, with his hair and beard worn long in the German fashion, and a beautiful silk cloak that was a present from King Vortigern. He was delighted to find how well I spoke German, and used to tell me in that language long stories about his dealings with Hengist. I remember another visitor about the same time, and a rather ominous one. This was Viriconius, who had been the largest landowner near Regulbium in northeast Kent, and in practice the ruler of the district. But King Vortigern had given his lands to Hengist, and he was now a pensioner at the court of Durovernum. I know that my father was depressed by this reminder of what might happen to us one day, but he trusted to my grandfather's influence at court.

When I was seven, that would be in the year 458, there came the first sudden upset of my life of sudden upsets. One summer evening an excited messenger rode in from the Forest, we spent all that night packing our clothes and plate, and next morning I was sent to Anderida, with the rest of the women and children. The able-bodied men stayed behind to dig defences. What had happened was this: Hengist had quarrelled with King Vortigern, and the Saxons had attacked Durovernum. The King, who was more of a politician than a soldier, had fled to his hereditary dominions beyond the Sabrina, but his son Vortimer was trying to raise an army to keep the raiders in Kent. All this was happening just the other side of the Forest, which a man can cross in three days; but it is tangled and roadless, so we did not expect the main army of the Saxons to come our way. Nevertheless the women and children were safer behind walls.

Of course, when we arrived in the fortress we children expected desperate and bloody fighting at once; Constans was allowed to carry a sword, though the hilt was kept sealed to the scabbard so that he could not draw it without the knowledge of the grown-ups; and I was disappointed that I was not given one too. Paul hung around the church, and carried doles to the poor; he never was a fighting man. But as long as there was a hostile army in the field the Saxons were afraid to plunge into the Great Forest. We heard very little accurate news of what was happening, though there definitely was a war, with pitched battles, not merely casual raiding. Perhaps I know more about it than anyone else, for I was told the Saxon side of the quarrel as well as the Roman. There were many stray Germans dotted

8

about the countryside as slaves or hired guards, and they told the news to Ursula, who passed it on to me.

This is roughly what caused the war, as far as I can make out from the abuse each side directed at the other. King Vortigern was a tough old politician, and his private life was pretty scandalous; one day he saw Hengist's daughter, the child of his Saxon wife, and therefore a Saxon virgin of high lineage. She was attractive, at any rate to one used to seeing Saxons in the mass and the King asked her father if he might take her into his household. Hengist was quite agreeable, presents were exchanged, and the girl came to Durovernum. I have already told you of the high position the Saxons give to their well-born virgins, and Hengist thought that King Vortigern would make her his consort (of course there could be no question of Christian marriage); but King Vortigern kept a large establishment of concubines, and he installed this girl among them, in rather a lowly place. The new concubine managed to send a complaint to her family that she was being despised and insulted, and the Saxons flared up at once. They are always on the look-out for Romans to treat them as an inferior race. Hengist was in a strong position at the time, for not long before he had been joined by his son, Oisc, with sixteen shiploads of reinforcements; he sent a very rude message to the King, and marched on Durovernum with his whole army.

Although the King at once set out for his dominions in the far west, ostensibly to raise reinforcements from the mountaineers of Valentia, there was, as I have said, much more real fighting than in most of the wars of my manhood. Young Vortimer and his brother Categirn led the royal comitatus and the local militia in three pitched battles that summer, and in the first they were fairly successful; Categirn was killed in it, but so was Horsa, the brother of

Hengist. Then more and more Saxons came to join the army in Kent, some from other settlements they had on the east coast of Britain, some across the sea from Germany; while Vortimer's forces dwindled. The King, though he raised an army in the west, kept it about him for his own protection; and the petty rulers of the southeast, such as my father, were reluctant to send their men to serve under a rival. Nevertheless the second battle was fought right on the coast near Regulbium, and at the end of the day the Romans held the battlefield. But Hengist was a most persistent man and so well known among the Germans that he could always gather fresh recruits; he tried again, and in the third battle Vortimer was slain and his army scattered.

We had been camping out in Anderida all that summer, expecting to go home to the villa when the war was over; but the news that the Roman army in Kent had been destroyed meant that the open country would be unsafe for a long time, and my father decided to live permanently in the fortress. He set about building a town house; it was only timber-framed wattle and plaster, and it contained no bath, because a hypocaust is such a tricky thing to make; but it was roomy and gaily painted, and it looked quite smart when it was new.

No one could tell how long we would have to stay behind walls, and we settled down to live as we thought townsmen should. All the gentry for miles had come in to take refuge, and there were plenty of children of my own age and class; my mother thought it a splendid chance to start a school that would give us a really good education, but the difficulty was to get hold of a competent teacher. My father offered a large salary, and Gaul is always full of unemployed rhetoricians, but though a fishing-boat made the daring voyage across the Channel with an invitation, none of them would face the danger of the journey or the uncertain life in such a frontier town. In the end my mother had to fall back on a Dumnonian named Peter, who had been trained for the Church, but had never been allowed to take even deacon's orders because he was accused of being a Pelagian heretic; I don't think Master Peter had the strength of character to be different from his neighbours, and if he had ever been a Pelagian it must only have been because he found himself among heretics. Like most Dumnonians he had been brought up to speak nothing but Celtic in the home, and this was an advantage; a man who has acquired Latin only as a learned language usually speaks it more correctly than a Gaul who has picked up slang and bad constructions in his cradle. He was very firm with us if we used barbarian words or dropped our case-endings, and I learned from him to write elegantly.

The poor man was always telling us that it is the duty of the rich and well-born to serve the state; that is an excellent piece of morality, handed down to us from pagan Greeks, but when I was a boy it was rather difficult to apply. In fact, you might say that no state of any kind existed in Britain, and certainly none that had any claim to my allegiance. There was no Emperor nearer than Constantinople, and our fathers had given up the farce of proclaiming a local Emperor for Britain; if they did, he always took all the troops and treasure he could collect, and went overseas to enlarge his dominions. We had to obey King Vortigern if he really insisted on anything, but no one could love or honour that tough old intriguer from the western mountains. I grew up without any loyalty to anything outside the family.

That winter the condition of things in Britain got very much worse. King Vortigern had stayed in the west while Vortimer was alive, for he knew that his heir would dethrone and imprison him if he stayed within reach. Now Vortimer was dead he came back with a small comitatus, but found his only course was to fix up some arrangement with Hengist. He ostentatiously gave his Saxon concubine the position of a queen, and kept the rest of his playmates out of sight in a remote castle of the west; then he opened negotiations by recognizing Hengist as King of Kent. At Christmas in the year 458 there was a great feast to celebrate the new alliance, but unfortunately fighting broke out when everyone was drunk. All were supposed to have come to the dinner unarmed, but the Saxons had brought the little seax-knives which they use for eating, and for other purposes as well; these are sharp iron knives, pointed and with a cutting blade on one side, though the other is thick and quite capable of parrying a sword-cut. The Saxons say that their tribal name comes from these knives, which are sacred objects that they must always carry. Anyway, these sacred objects came in very useful at the party, and though Vortigern's comitatus put up enough resistance with benches and cutlery for the King to get safely away, for the rest of his life he was nothing more than the petty ruler of a castle beyond the Sabrina. Naturally, the official story that all Romans still believe was of a treacherous Saxon plot, but I heard from Ursula that it was a spontaneous and unpremeditated quarrel; King Vortigern had begun to make advances to a handsome Saxon youth, who presently struck him. It is very easy to anger Germans in this way.

No one succeeded immediately to Vortigern's position, and southeast Britain found itself without a leader. The Saxons began to raid far and wide, though they had neither the engines nor the patience to besiege walled towns. Nobody nowadays likes living in a stinking and crowded town, where there is no sport, and the presence of the clergy makes most people lead a far more Christian life than they are naturally inclined to; in consequence, those who had large sums of gold in their possession crossed the sea to Armorica, and the craftsmen who can earn a good living anywhere did the same if they could escape from their masters; but my father, whose property was in immovable land, stayed as near it as he could with safety.

The Great Forest saved the country round Anderida. It is not an impassable barrier, but the roads through it are few, and so rough and narrow that pirates find it difficult to get their plunder back to Kent. The sea was open to Saxon ships, and they sometimes went down Channel, but our coast had been fortified by Stilicho; these forts were less than a hundred years old, and still quite defensible; in any case our land is rather a backwater. We heard terrible stories of the destruction in the midlands and the west, but only a few Saxon foragers and scouts occasionally found their way south from Kent. In the spring of 459 we expected to hear of the gathering of a Roman army, and of more hard-fought battles, but nothing of the kind happened, and the stupid wasteful raiding continued unchecked.

I was learning to like town-life. Of course we were not cooped up inside the walls all the time; the ironworkers of the Forest sent us word if there were raiders about, and usually it was safe to go riding among the marshes near the town. Apart from my schooling, which I enjoyed because I was a quick learner, I was also being taught how to handle my weapons. My grandfather Coroticus undertook to teach me warfare; he was now living with us permanently, since Roman and Saxon were not on the sort of terms that needed an interpreter at treaty makings. Constans was at the age when he thought he knew it all already, and Paul intended to be a man of peace, but I liked my grandfather,

I enjoyed learning, and I had the patience, unusual in a child, to practise as much as he told me. He had been a good fighting-man in his youth, and he had thought out his own views on the best method of self-defence. In the first place, he favoured the Saxon equipment. These barbarians use no body-armour, except a helmet and a round shield, and their swords are of the pattern called scramaseax, a heavy single-edged sabre with a sharp point; in fact, a bigger edition of the sacred seax-knife. It would seem as though warriors armed like this would not be a match for loricated Roman infantry, but you must remember two things: competent smiths were becoming very rare, so that many Romans had in fact no cuirasses, and though our men were trained to fight shoulder to shoulder, they were very badly trained. The Saxon method of fighting was quite different; they did not try to keep in ordered ranks, but charged independently as fast as they could run, knocked an opponent off his feet with a blow of the sword, and then jumped on him and cut his throat with the seax-knife. Half-trained men do not trust the comrades beside them well enough to stand firm against this charge. No wonder the barbarians usually beat us in pitched battles.

My grandfather took great trouble with my training in single combat, though he did not try to teach me tactics; for he said that anyone but a fool could slink into a safe place in a set battle, but no one could prevent a treacherous assault when he was alone, and the important thing was to grow up to be a difficult man to murder. He taught me to go in hard, using the sword not to pierce but to knock the other man off his balance, and to strike with my shield at his face. I grew strong and active, for we had good food and plenty of exercise, and thanks to my town life I escaped the shambling clumsiness that so often mars the muscles of country-bred youths.

Meanwhile I was doing quite well at school, though this was more because I had a quick brain and managed to get on the right side of Master Peter than because I worked hard at my lessons. I learnt to speak and write good Latin with ease and fluency, and history also interested me, since it has a bearing on present politics; but theology left me cold, though we had to study a great deal of it. I should also have liked to learn something of geography and where the different tribes of barbarians lived, but what was taught seemed to be out of date and unconvincing. I did not see much of my father, who was now governing the fortress; my mother had taken to her bed as a permanent invalid, and when I was not at school or military exercise I was talking to Ursula about the Saxons. She made them out to be a very fine people, and the best of them were the Jutes, who were her own ancestors and also Hengist's. If I sometimes wished I had been born a barbarian who didn't have to go to school she would remind me that I was Woden-born, and as good a German as any of them. I owe a great deal to Ursula.

All this time we were living as though on an island, for no one friendly ever came to us through the Great Forest. The Saxons were plundering all the open country as far as the banks of the Sabrina. In 463, when I was twelve, we heard one piece of really shocking news: the townsmen of Calleva, a strong town among the forests south of the upper Thames, had grown tired of living permanently inside walls with Saxons watching them from behind every bush; they had decided to emigrate, and when their ruler tried to stop them they murdered him and went off to Dumnonia all the same. Their town was left empty, a standing invitation to any band of robbers who wanted a fortified base; they might at least have broken down the walls before they left. I remember hearing my father discuss it with my grandfather, for he feared our citizens might follow their example; but my grandfather pointed out that our men could not march anywhere safely by land, and we could stop them emigrating by sea if we kept a guard on the fishing-boats.

Children accept the world as they find it; I took it for granted that all civilized men hid behind walls, and that the open country belonged to barbarians; but I also took it for granted that barbarians could never get inside the walls. Master Peter taught us that everything would come right soon, and then holy men would travel safely to Rome and back; but Ursula told me differently, and I secretly thought that she had more sense than the schoolmaster. In any case, things suited me very well as they were, and my father would not be such a great man if a Vicarius of Britain came back.

Our followers now liked living in a town, and the coloni at the villa had grown used to their hazardous life; they ran into the woods so fast that the Saxons did not often catch one. Of course, every time they rebuilt their miserable huts these were more squalid and poorly furnished; but I suppose they were used to that also, and in any case there was nothing they could do about it. If things had stayed as they were I would have lived a prosperous and uneventful life in Anderida. But the world changes a great deal every year.

In 465, when I was fourteen, my grandfather died. Luckily he had already taught me single combat and the German language, and I don't think he knew anything else that was at all useful. I suppose he had led a fairly successful life; but I don't think he had made the most of his opportunities. A man who was the go-between in all the negotiations of Vortigern and Hengist ought to have been able to grab something substantial out of the mess that they made. There was a splendid funeral, and the Bishop of Noviomagus made the dangerous journey by sea to conduct it. That was only decent, in spite of the old man's descent from Woden, and my mother was very angry when she caught Ursula trying to smuggle his best sword into the coffin. She threatened to have her exorcised by the Bishop if she practised any more of this heathen nonsense. Ursula subsided at once. The poor woman was always terrified of anything that looked like Christian magic; most Saxons are, for though they have a lot of spells of their own, they always think other people's are more powerful. Otherwise the funeral was a great success.

My brother Constans was now nineteen, and he had finished his education. My father made him second-in-command of our armed forces, and he led a raid through the Forest and took some pigs from the Saxons of Kent without losing a single man. He knew a lot about the drill and tactics of our Roman ancestors, though that knowledge did not help him to lead our undrilled levies, and he was not particularly handy with his weapons in single combat. My second brother, Paul, at sixteen was nearly ready to begin his career in the Church; the Bishop took the opportunity of my grandfather's funeral to ordain him deacon, although he was still under age according to the Canons. It was understood that he would be the next Bishop of Noviomagus, so that he had no desire to enter the priesthood just yet; it is much smarter to go straight from deacon to Bishop, without having the care of a parish. I never understood Paul; no one could be so unselfish and law-abiding as he appeared to be, certainly no member of my family; yet I could never catch him out in hypocrisy, and he really seemed to enjoy distributing alms to talkative and smelly old women. I could only suppose that he was far-seeing and had himself very well disciplined, with the intention of eventually becoming a Bishop of great temporal power; such Bishops rule many cities in Gaul, but I could see no opening for them in the present state of Britain.

As for myself, at the age of fourteen my mind was as active and mature as it is now, and I had already decided on my future; I would become a ruler, with no superior at all, free to give my wishes the force of law. This was an ambitious goal for the third son of a petty tyrant, master of a single little town, and it needed very careful planning. I would have to get hold of some trustworthy followers from somewhere, but the fighting-men of Anderida were all attached to Constans and my father; I should have tried to win them over, but I was still too young to impress them by feats of arms; also a boy of that age has not got his desires under proper control. At about that time I seduced the daughter of one of my father's best soldiers, and the man took offence; he was only a colonus by origin, but he had carried a sword for so long that he felt himself free, and complained to my father in open court. It was all very embarrassing, and the family were very nasty about it. Only Ursula admired my spirit, for the Saxons always blame the girl in these cases. She was quickly married off to an ironworker of the Forest, where women are scarce, and now I have even forgotten her name; but the whole episode showed me that I must practise self-control. After all, my ambition was not overweening and inordinate; I did not want a wide Kingdom, only an absolute one.

Meanwhile the Saxon raids continued, all over Britain north of the Forest and east of the Sabrina; Hengist's men in Kent had begun to plough the land and build wooden huts, as though they intended to stay for the rest of their lives, but everywhere else the barbarians wandered about the open country, laying waste the villages and spoiling much more than they consumed. They would have done better for themselves if they had come to some arrangement with the terrified villagers, and drawn a regular tribute, but then they would have lost the reputation for savagery which made them invincible, so perhaps they acted wisely.

In 466, the year after my grandfather died, my father decided that the time was ripe for him to assume the title of King. He collected a large comitatus, several hundreds strong, and set off westward by land to return the visit of the Bishop of Noviomagus. That city was in theory governed by an ordo of curiales, that is hereditary town-councillors; but in fact the Bishop was much the greatest man in the place, and any agreement that he made would be ratified by his colleagues.

After a short stay my father came back safely, and summoned his three sons to decide on the way he should proclaim his new dignity. It was the first time I had been asked to attend such a council, and I was delighted with this new sign that I was to be taken seriously in future. There were only six of us in my father's office, the four members of the family, the commander of the comitatus, and the steward, who knew all about money and food supplies. I remember it vividly. The room was partitioned off from the sleeping apartments, under the gable farthest from the street; it was autumn, and there were some bits of charcoal in a bronze pan on the table, which was much more pleasant than the open fire in the middle of the floor which filled the big living-room with smoke; charcoal was rather a rarity, since it was made in the dangerous Forest; we felt very civilized with it glowing there wastefully in the middle of the room. When we were settled, and

Maximus, the captain of the comitatus, had barred the inner door, my father began to speak:

'The Bishop is a reasonable man, and he sees that he must accept my protection. Now what I propose is this: I shall give a great feast at Christmas to all the comitatus and as many of the citizens as I can feed. (That is why I want to consult you, Sergius.) At the proper time, when plenty of beer has been drunk, you, Maximus, will raise the cry, "Long live Eleutherus Rex", and the citizens ought to join in if the feast has been good enough. Then the comitatus will raise me on that old legionary shield with the embossed decoration, and you, Paul, come forward, bless me, and sprinkle me with holy water. The drinking will presumably have sent Father John off to bed before that. He is the only man who might make a fuss; he wants us to join up with Noviomagus, but he would prefer the Bishop to be the head of the new state. If he is still there, that's where Coroticus comes in. Keep near him, my boy, and have a group of your young friends round; if he begins to speak in favour of the Bishop, jostle him and shut him up. I suppose I can rely on all our comrades of the comitatus, Maximus? You, Sergius, build up the stores so that I can give a really lavish feast. Has anyone anything else to suggest?'

I was still very young, young enough to want to show myself cynical and disillusioned; also I wanted to make a speech of some kind in my first council. Foolishly I broke in:

'What exactly do you expect to gain, Father, by this interesting ceremony, which may very likely go wrong if someone has too much to drink? Will you wield any more power than you do now? It seems to me nothing but a waste of good food.'

Constans took me up at once, and I have always

remembered his words. 'You must understand, little brother, that names are real things. Our father will continue to rule Anderida and Noviomagus as he does now, and so far you are right. But at present any of the honestiores might take it into his head to start opposition, and it would look bad to have him murdered; also the Bishop has never said publicly that he will take our orders. When King Eleutherus has been proclaimed things will be very different; everyone knows that it is rebellion to disobey a King. I am sure that you yourself will feel more powerful when you are Prince Coroticus, although the only change will be in your name.'

'There is another point also,' said Sergius. 'Noviomagus would not be willing to take orders from Anderida. But they will not be insulted if they obey the King of the Regni, which I suppose will be your title, sir. I am all in favour of the change. I myself shall be a greater man when I am a King's minister, than I am now as the steward of an honestioris.'

'One thing we haven't discussed so far', said Constans, 'is the effect this will have on our neighbours. Nothing comes from the sea except pirates, and the Saxons to the north and east don't know or care what we call ourselves; but there must be some ruler to the west. Will he acknowledge you as his equal?'

'There is no ruler immediately west of our territory,' answered my father. 'The lands round Portus were so ravaged by the Irish that they still lie desolate, though that was more than fifty years ago. King Constantine of Dumnonia is our nearest neighbour in that direction; he is a powerful monarch, but there is a wide belt of no-man's-land westward from Noviomagus before you come to the first of his subjects. I shall send him an envoy, of course, but I don't anticipate any trouble from him.'

At Christmas everything passed off as had been planned, and my father was now a King. The title of the new state was Civitas Regnorum, from a people who had been under a foederate King of their own in the days of the Emperor Claudius; it was purely an antiquarian name, for we had been Roman citizens for two hundred years, and our ancestors had come from all over the Empire. But it was a natural unit, all the same; the two cities, Anderida and Noviomagus, are separated by a stretch of open, well-drained country, two long days' march in extent but of no great width, hemmed in between the Forest and the sea; the coast is defended by cliffs for most of its length, and the only harbours are at the mouths of the short rivers that flow south from the Forest; there is always a fishing village and a hill-fort at each of these harbours, so that the Channel pirates usually pass us by, and try their luck on the open beaches farther west; our only dangerous frontier was the passage along the western coast, where the Forest does not quite reach down to the sea. For this reason, and also because the citizens might otherwise try to set up a leader of their own, Constans and half the comitatus were sent to garrison Noviomagus, with sentries in the hill-forts round about.

I must explain about these hill-forts. They were made by our forefathers before the Emperor Claudius civilized the land, and were deserted when the Romans built walled towns in the valleys; but the earthen ramparts remain, and a wooden palisade on the bank and a little spadework in the ditch make them as good as new. Of course, they cannot stand a long siege, for as a rule they have no water supply; but pirates don't like long sieges, they are always anxious about their ships and in a hurry to catch the next tide; these forts can be defended for a couple of days, which is usually long enough.

To my extreme annoyance, this foundation of the Kingdom seemed actually to decrease my importance. Constans was heir-apparent, with a territory of his own to rule; presently the Bishop of Noviomagus would die, when Constans would come back to Anderida, and Paul would take his place as guardian of the city and Bishop as well; but what future was there for me? I could not even poison Constans, the obvious solution, as long as he lived at the other end of the country.

However, I was only sixteen, and there was plenty of time, for somehow I always seemed to know that I would live to a great age. Meanwhile my mother died of the illness that had kept her so long in bed, which gave me rather more scope in my private life. No man is quite without affection for his mother, and I was slightly sorry; but she had been ill for so long, and kept such a careful watch over my morals, that I chiefly associated her with lengthy moralizings on the subject of chastity and sobriety.

My great support at this rather objectless period of my life was the sympathy of old Ursula. She was convinced that one day I should be a great King, and she was willing to help me against Constans. I had decided not to plot against my father's life; he was thirty years my senior, and British Kings do not live long.

I settled down to make myself popular with my fellow-citizens, and to learn all I could about the fortifications of the countryside and its strategic points. I also practised hard with my Saxon weapons; I did not bother about drill, for I never intended to wage a regular campaign against my brother when he succeeded to the throne, but rather to seize his person by surprise. For this I needed, more than anything else, faithful followers; but I did not seem able to win anyone to my side, and of course I could not be too open in my efforts at persuasion. Looking back now, I see that there was no reason why the comitatus should have preferred me to Constans, who was handsome and gallant, cheerful and amusing; while I was rather solitary and introspective, and preferred lording it over the peasants to being the life and soul of the party with my father's war-companions. I think, also, that even the stupidest people divine more of our motives and characters than we ever allow for, and in my secret heart I was not the type of man these tough soldiers admired. Ursula impressed on me that it was no use attempting any move until I had at least three companions who would follow me in anything, even to murdering my father. As yet there was no one I could rely on utterly, so there was nothing for it but to bide my time.

All these years while I was growing up the Saxons were still raiding Britain. From a mere stupid hatred of civilization, and to increase the terror of their name, they killed every man, woman or child that they could catch. North of the Forest, as far as the upper Thames, not a field was sown and not a hut left unburnt, and the rulers round the headwaters of the river had to hire other Saxons, enemies of Hengist, to garrison the riverside villages; farther north all was a blank from which no news came, though we heard in a roundabout way that the sons of Vortigern and the descendants of Cunedda of the Otadini had chased the Irish out of the land beyond the Sabrina, and were ruling there with strong armies. To increase our feeling of isolation, we could learn nothing about what was going on in Gaul; when I was five years old a delegation of Gallic churchmen came to tell us about the new method of fixing Easter that had been decided on at the Council of Arelatum; but since then the pirates have made their lairs on the Gallic coast opposite us, and that was the last news we had from overseas. I don't even know whether a Bishop reigns in Rome.

At seventeen I was in a rut. I never had an opportunity of distinguishing myself, for my father kept me always in his household, and I was given no troops of my own. When raiders were off the coast I would have to ride in his following, and keep behind him when we dismounted to form our ranks. When they saw us, as a rule the pirates made off; they wanted plunder, not battles. Very occasionally they stood, but that is not my sort of fighting, in close ranks where a comrade can so easily let you down, or make sure on purpose that you are killed; I would not lead a charge to win glory for my father.

There was very little else I could do to increase my reputation. My father, who saw that I was at a loose end, offered to turn over to me the management of the estate, but I have never been interested in farming, and in those days we could not plan ahead; we grew everything possible, reaped what we could, and the raiders took the rest. I was allowed to judge a few lawsuits, but an appeal lay from me to my father and no one was ever satisfied with my judgement, so it did not save him as much time as he had expected. Presently he stopped it, for I was making him unpopular; I suppose this was because I took bribes, for that has always seemed to me the obvious function of a judge; the silly fools of litigants did not realize that my father took bribes also.

If I just hung about my father's court with nothing to do, an obvious focus for any discontent that might arise, Constans would see to it that I ate something that disagreed with me; he was a well-behaved young man, but he wanted to make sure of the succession. There was only one field of activity that my family had left clear: the sea. Fishing was carried on all along the coast, but with little coracles and rowing-boats that could only carry two men; these took out the nets in a semicircle, and were beached while the net was drawn in from the shore. No one went more than a few hundred yards out to sea, for fear of the pirates. Now I reasoned that pirates at sea would behave like raiders on land; they would not be particularly anxious to attack a boat filled with armed men, which would cost them loss and yield very little plunder. So I had a big boat built for me, and made it long enough to hold twelve armed men. It was a difficult thing to construct, but even in this Ursula helped me; she had come over from Germany in a war-boat, and remembered what the inside of it was like; she said that she had only to feel her ribs to recall the pattern of its timbers, and she insisted on coming out with us to see if it felt the same. The boat had a mast and a big sail, and the first time we went out I nearly drowned us all; but here again Ursula gave me her advice, and once I had learnt the force of the wind, which no landsman can ever appreciate, I picked up enough seamanship to be able to get about safely. Of course, we could only go out when there was a steady breeze, for the pirates in their oared boats would have caught us in a calm, but even so we were able to bring in more plentiful and more palatable fish than Anderida had enjoyed for many years.

From my point of view, the great advantage of this perilous occupation was that I was able to pick ten comrades of the comitatus to accompany me; naturally I always chose the same ten and I had a chance to get them accustomed to taking my orders.

By the autumn of 469, when I had passed my eighteenth birthday, I had a definite position in the state. I was the recognized authority on everything connected with the sea, and my little comitatus of ten men would probably follow me if I was attacked, though not if I began the quarrel. It was such a convenience to have a sea-going boat that my father became ambitious, and put his carpenters to building a real long warship; but they had no experience of such work, the tree that they chose for the keel was not strong enough, and the new ship broke its back as it was being launched. Then the new developments which I will relate in a moment put it out of his head, and I never had the chance to command a British-built warship.

For in December of that year a message came from Constans in Noviomagus, to say that envoys had reached him from the west, and that he would bring them with him to Anderida for the Christmas feast. My father gave out the news in open court, and it caused tremendous excitement; we had been isolated for more than ten years, but this meant that there was a Roman ruler somewhere who wanted at least to trade with us, and perhaps to make an alliance. Father John was the most excited of us all, for now he might get good wine from Gaul; at present he was using the produce of a little vineyard outside the walls, which for lack of sunshine had a most vile taste.

Two days before Christmas Constans arrived with half his comitatus; there was no great danger in weakening the garrison of Noviomagus at this season of the year, since the Saxons keep a mid-winter feast called Yule, and during that time they get just as drunk as Christians do in honour of the Nativity. We were pleased to see our friends again, but the crowd thronged and stared round the three envoys, forgetting to cheer my brother as loyal subjects should. The messengers were people very like ourselves, and obviously understood both Celtic and Latin; but though they were very like us, they were not quite the same. They wore tunics of unbleached wool, as we did, but instead of the sleeved and hooded cloaks of thick felt which we used in bad weather, they had loose garments of white wool wrapped round them, and they were bare-headed. My father welcomed them in a rather bad Latin speech, for as the peasants and most of the soldiers spoke nothing but Celtic he rarely had to use grammatical Latin with the correct case-endings. Then they all three were brought into the private office at the far end of the house; my father, Constans, Paul and I came with them, and Maximus and two comrades stood behind with drawn swords, in case of treachery. The senior envoy drew a rolled-up paper from the breast of his tunic, and my father gave it to Paul to read aloud.

'To Eleutherus, King of the Regni, Greetings from Ambrosius Aurelanius, Comes Britanniarum,' he began; and then came to a full stop, as we gasped in astonishment. For we all knew what that resounding title meant; the Count of the Britains had been commander of the field army in the old days, but as far as we knew the last one had been deposed when the cities rose against Constantine III sixty years ago. Had the Emperor sent an army from Italy, and if so how could it have landed without us hearing about it? The envoys said nothing, but motioned for Paul to continue.

'Next spring, by the first of May, I shall be with my troops at the source of the Thames. I know you have the Saxons on your frontier, and I congratulate you on your stout resistance to their encroachments; but bring to my muster all the men you can spare, and we shall free Britain of these barbarous invaders once and for all. My messengers will give you the details, and bring back your answer.' That was all that was written in this laconic despatch.

Obviously the first thing to do was to find out more about this mysterious Count, and we all began asking questions at once. The questioning was a slow business, for everything had to be translated into Celtic, so that the comrades should know what was going on; it is most important that your comitatus should not get the idea that you are planning a campaign behind their backs, but dignity demands that negotiations should be carried on in Latin. At first the envoys merely repeated that Ambrosius was Count of the Britains, and that it was the duty of loyal citizens to obey his lawful commands. They were reluctant to tell us how he had risen to that exalted position; in fact, Maximus had to suggest the advisability of torturing them to get at the truth before they would tell us about his origin and appointment. Eventually the chief envoy promised to answer all our questions.

The story he had to tell was not as romantic as we had hoped. The Count had not brought an army from oversea; in fact, he had been born the son of a curialis of Corinium, in the uplands between the source of the Thames and the lower course of the Sabrina, and had assumed command of the militia of that city when the raiders first appeared from the east. Apparently he had done well in some small engagements, and his comitatus thought highly of him; then he had entered into an alliance with the Kings of Dumnonia and Demetia, and supported by their contingents he had done even better; now he had given himself this splendid title, and was issuing orders to all the Kings of Britain. It seemed to me a very impudent proceeding, but I had never forgotten what Constans had said at the time our father assumed his crown; undoubtedly names are things, and quite possibly the self-promotion of Ambrosius would make him the ruler of Britain.

The envoys were dismissed, and the five of us crowded round the table to discuss what answer we should make. Of course, it would be very nice indeed if the Saxons were finally driven out of Britain. Yet that meant putting ourselves under the rule of Ambrosius, and naturally my father, and Constans as his heir, did not wish to lose their independence. Maximus also was not anxious to serve under a stranger. At first those three were in favour of sending a refusal, though a polite one.

Paul, however, begged us to answer yes; he made a little speech about the duty of all Christians to defend their religion against the pagans, and how St. Germanus had set us the example at the Alleluia Victory. They had been speaking in order of age, and now my father asked for my opinion, which was only fair, for I would have to risk my life if we fought, and as a King's son I would be in the forefront of the battle. I did some quick thinking; on the one hand, if Britain came under the rule of one man, there would be no chance of the independent position I longed for, and I did not like what I had heard about the pettifogging restrictions of Imperial rule; on the other hand, if Ambrosius succeeded in gathering all the Christian forces of Britain he might very possibly beat the Saxons; if he was to be our future ruler it was only common sense to join his side while our support was still valuable. I began to speak very politely, in a humble voice.

'Of course, Father, you are quite right. It would be silly to give away our freedom to a self-appointed ruler, of whom we know nothing except that he has three messengers to follow him. But we don't want to antagonize a chief whose strength is unknown to us. I suggest a compromise. Get Father John to write a polite letter to the Count, saying that we think a united campaign against the Saxons is a splendid idea, and that we will send him all the men we can spare; but that will not be a very large force, as the enemy has begun raiding through the Forest. (He won't know what the real conditions are, unless we are foolish enough to tell him.) Then send me and my ten companions, with a few other men you can trust, and perhaps some half-armed peasants, to show you have levied every man you can raise. If we find the army too small when we get there we can slip away as the battle is joined; otherwise we can send home for reinforcements. Then we are not risking too much; but if we take no part in the war your reputation and your power will surely dwindle.'

If they agreed to this plan I would have an independent command, though a very small one; I might be able to seize a little hill-fort somewhere, and set up as a ruler by myself. But my father was not a fool; he was not going to let me lead a party of his soldiers out of reach, and then throw off my allegiance. But he was a great believer in keeping the family united, and therefore he did not squash my suggestion.

'That seems a sensible compromise,' he said. 'It is never prudent to return an unqualified refusal to a peaceful envoy. But I think, Coroticus, that you are too young for such a responsibility, and a campaign in the valley of the upper Thames will not call for the skill in seamanship that you undoubtedly possess. I shall send a small contingent, and Constans will lead it. Thus he will get to know the other rulers, and may confirm some friendships that will be useful when I am gone. But we can't leave Noviomagus without a garrison next summer, when the pirates sail again. Maximus shall hold it until Constans returns. Has anyone any objections to that plan?'

I had a great many, though I thought it wiser to keep them to myself. It was obviously intended to leave me without any troops under my command; and that Maximus, the leader of the comitatus and the grandson of a slave, should be preferred to me as regent of Noviomagus was positively insulting; but I did not dare openly to complain. I must go to this war, if I was to earn the reputation that I needed among the comrades. I spoke humbly:

'Dear Father, I have my own way to make in the world, and I shall probably settle down as a sea-rover; but I have never seen a bigger army than our comitatus, or been present at a battle with more than three shiploads of enemies. Let me go on this expedition, merely as one of the comitatus, and I am sure I shall learn things that will be useful to me in after-life. Here is a splendid chance to see how great armies are drawn up for the encounter, and I am quite old enough to bear my part as a warrior.'

I think my keenness pleased my father, though Constans frowned; he always suspected me of trying to take his place, and it is easy to arrange a fatal accident in the heat of battle; I had already noticed that he never turned his back on me when we were alone together. But my father, who liked all his sons equally, was too slow-witted to realize the state of feeling between us; he agreed that we should go together to join Ambrosius.

That evening the envoys were sent for to receive their answer, which Paul had written out for them on a precious sheet of clean parchment. It said that King Eleutherus would send two of his sons with a band of picked men to the muster that the Count had commanded; but the envoys had to listen to a long explanation by word of mouth as well. It is so difficult to write down all you want to say, and if you make a mistake in the Latin case-endings it is so easy to be ambiguous, that a verbal commentary always accompanies a despatch; that is why messengers have to be intelligent men, with good memories. My father dwelt on the great danger to which his Kingdom was exposed, from pirates by sea and raiders through the Forest, and offered to show them the ruins of the villages that had been burnt last summer; all this as an excuse for not coming in person with his full levy. The chief envoy was not impressed, and answered that there were burnt villages in every part of

Britain, and that the only way to stop them being burnt was to send all the help we could to the Count; but my father had a great flow of words when he wanted to persuade anyone, and the envoy could not give him the lie direct, if he wanted any help from us at all. He was a very dignified, I might say pompous, man, who had probably been chosen rather for his impressive bearing than for his skill in argument. Eventually he gave in to our clamour, and promised to tell his master that we were truly sending him all the help we could spare. I made up my mind that if ever I was in a position to send ambassadors of my own I would choose a clever talker, even if he was round-shouldered and squinting, rather than an impressive and dignified man who could not argue.

The envoys only stayed one night, and rode off the next morning on their dangerous journey round the western edge of the Forest. They reached Corinium safely, as we heard later.

We had four months to prepare for the expedition, and as soon as he had recovered from the Christmas drinking Constans began to choose and organize his following. The whole comitatus was about three hundred strong, and we could call on about ten times as many untrained and shieldless peasants in an emergency. But my father decided that fifty comrades and one hundred of the bravest and most active peasants were quite enough to send. Naturally Constans wanted to take the best men, but my father was worried about the safety of his two cities, though he liked Constans too much to fear lest he was making his heir stronger than himself, as many other Kings would have done. Maximus, who was absurdly loyal to his master, was aware of that danger, and he helped to arrange that some of the best and most influential warriors stayed at home; also it was his influence, I think, that prevented me from taking my own ten comrades, who were split up and packed off to the different hill-forts round Noviomagus. It began to look as though this war would not help me to gain my independence, after all.

The peasants presented no difficulty; if we were going to take any at all we might as well take the best. There were plenty of volunteers, only too eager to risk their lives if it meant a holiday from never-ending toil, and they were promised that any one of them who got hold of a shield and proper equipment on the field of battle might become a real warrior and live in idleness for the rest of his life. Of course, while they were unarmed they would carry the baggage and stay in the rear ranks.

So we settled down to the dullness of Lent, and the feasting of Easter. I was very excited about seeing strange lands, and the journey promised to be so interesting that I hardly thought about the battles that would follow; I had never been north of the Forest in my life, and I wondered if I would see real towns with properly roofed houses, and glass windows, and amphitheatres, and all the wonders of civilization that I had heard about from my grandfather. Or was the rest of Britain even more ravaged than our own land, sheltered by the Forest? In any case, I ought to get some advice about how to comport myself in foreign lands, and I turned to old Ursula as the most travelled person I knew. Unfortunately she was not a very intelligent observer, and what she told me, though sound enough, I could probably have guessed for myself: to give my name and rank to my host as soon as I entered a strange house, and eat something of his as quickly as I could so as to put myself under his protection; never to boast in front of warriors I didn't know, nor to start a fight if I could possibly avoid it; to beware of bored and discontented housewives; to make very few promises but to keep those I had made: that was all the counsel she gave me, and it left me no wiser than before. But if poor Ursula had been prudent in the ways of the world she would not have ended up as a servant in a Roman household.

My brother Constans also thought I needed some advice before I set out on my first campaign, and on the afternoon of Good Friday, when we were all sober from fasting and full of serious thoughts, he took me aside and gave me his views on my behaviour.

'Dear little brother,' he said, 'remember that I shall have my eye on you all the time, and that I don't trust you a yard. I know you hope that I shall fall on this campaign, and that with Paul a Bishop you will find yourself heir to the Kingdom. I wouldn't put it past you to assist any bad luck that may be coming to me. Well, bear in mind that the comitatus I have chosen is absolutely faithful, and that if there is anything suspicious about my death they will cut you down at once. Conan will be your orderly, and will guard your back in battle; his orders are that if I meet with an accident, you don't survive me ten minutes; he will report to me on your conduct from time to time. I tell you of these precautions to keep you from the sin of fratricide. But now that you see how well you will be looked after, why not be friends? Make up your mind that there is no throne waiting for you here, and I am sure you can win glory in this army. You are of noble birth, and a good swordsman; some great King will be glad to have you in his comitatus.'

I was annoyed to see my hopes dashed like this, but I controlled my face, and answered with a sad smile:

'Dear Constans, I cannot blame you for your suspicions; I know the heir must always fear his younger kinsmen. But the thought of replacing you has never crossed my mind, and my highest ambition is to succeed Maximus as captain of your guard. Please don't exile me to a foreign comitatus; I love Anderida and this countryside, and I will help you to make it the foremost state in Britain if you will allow me to live in my home.' Of course, while my father lived he had no power to send me away, but this supplication flattered him. He graciously consented that I might return with the Regnian contingent, if I behaved myself.

When I thought over this conversation, I decided that I had better show myself loyal and trustworthy during this first summer that we made war together; I was still very young, there was plenty of time, and it would be easier to arrange for Constans' death if he regarded me as a friendly supporter. I worked hard at the fitting-out of the force, but took great care to ask his advice in everything.

II

470–474

CAMPAIGNING WITH COUNT
AMBROSIUS – MY BROTHER MEETS
WITH MISFORTUNE

On April the 15th we paraded in front of a cheering mob of peasants and took leave of my father. Constans rode in front, on the best horse in the Kingdom, which was decked out with an ornamental saddle; he wore a steel helmet and an ancient cuirass covered with steel plates, with a long red woollen cloak flowing from the brooch at his throat to the horse's quarters; on his legs he had woollen trousers, cross-gartered, which was rather a barbarian touch, but bare legs are uncomfortable for riding; there was in the baggage a pair of military boots on the Roman model that he could wear for state occasions. Behind him marched the comitatus; all were armed with Roman thrusting-swords, and oblong Roman shields, but their body-armour was made of bronze, for most of the old steel helmets and cuirasses have rusted away by now.

Between the trained soldiers and the peasants I rode by myself, with Conan walking at my bridle. I also had a comfortable saddle, though it was not so richly decorated as my brother's, nor was my horse quite so handsome; I had a steel helmet and a red cloak, but I carried the Saxon arms that my grandfather had taught me to use. My little round shield was of wood instead of leather, and it was painted bright red; my sword was the heavy scramaseax, a sabre for slashing with, unlike the straight Roman thrusting-sword; on my right thigh hung the murderous little seax-knife; I wore no cuirass, and on my legs were thick red trousers. Although my hair was short and I had no beard as yet, I looked a thorough barbarian.

Last of all came the peasants, half of them leading pack-horses; they carried spears, and a knife of some sort in their belts, but they had no helmets, armour, or shields. So equipped, they would do to fill up the rear ranks, unless they ran away when they first saw the enemy. My brother had placed me at the back of the comitatus, partly to annoy me and partly as a reminder that I had no friends among the comrades; but to the onlookers it seemed that I was leading the largest contingent, and some of the more foolish gave me a specially loud cheer. The peasants of Anderida did not understand politics.

We only marched a few miles that day, for the feast we had eaten was a burden to our stomachs. In the evening we openly lit fires, and slept well in our warm blankets after a hot meal.

Four days later we started to skirt the western edge of the Forest. Now we were entering unknown and probably hostile land, and we marched slowly with all military precautions. Constans gave me command of the rearguard, for I had shown myself zealous and he was beginning to trust me. I had never been more than half a mile into the Forest before, and I was very interested in all that I saw. The stories I had heard from the old women were not exaggerated, though it is false that it sprang up in a night when Constantine III left Britain; Master Peter swears that it has always been there, even when our Roman ancestors first crossed the Channel. But every year it spreads a little farther. No one lives in it permanently, except the rather

uncanny ironworkers, who have their own secret incanta-
tions; for it is infested with demons. Luckily the Saxons
don't like it any more than we do.

We did not have to go through this awesome and
tangled tract of country, since the western end of the
Forest does not quite reach the sea, and half a mile of open
chalk is the only gateway to our land. But we rode very
close to the verge, for it is always better to avoid the sea-
shore. The men, who should have been excited at leaving
their native land for the first time in their lives, were
depressed and apprehensive. We made a long day's march,
and reached open country in the evening.

We had been going slightly north of west, by the sun,
with the intention of striking the road between Portus and
Calleva. Master Peter had told us of the existence of this
road, and had sketched a rough map, which Constans
carried. Master Peter himself had come from Dumnonia by
very much the same route that we were travelling, but he
was too old to guide us, and there were no other travellers
in the Kingdom. We would have to pick our way by the
stories we had been told, unless we met friendly natives.
However, we knew that the road ran north from Portus to
Calleva, and we could hardly walk over it without
noticing.

All the same, on the fifth day we nearly did so. We were
in open country except for a few patches of gorse, and the
scouts were well out on the front and flanks. We had seen a
few peasants in the distance, digging up their little patches
of ground with spades, for raiders had long ago taken their
oxen; but they had run away and hidden in the broken
ground before we had a chance of asking them any
questions. Suddenly a man stumbled, and then began
scratching at the earth with his hands; he called out loudly,
and showed me what he had uncovered, the unmistakable

pavement of a main road. Twenty years' disuse had let the grass grow over it, but it showed as a clear green alley through the scrub. There need be no more arguing about where the north lay when the sun was hidden behind a cloud.

An hour before sunset we turned off the road, and hacked a way into the middle of a thick wood. The horses were muzzled so that they could not neigh, then we ate dry bread, and wrapped ourselves in our cloaks for a cold and miserable night. The ground was so wet we could not light a fire at the bottom of a pit, and it would have been madness to let one burn where it could be seen. We dared not trust our peasants to keep watch, for they are apt to cover their heads with cloaks so that the ghosts of the night will not recognize them; as we had to have sentries on every side it meant that the comitatus got very little sleep. That was my first experience of a night spent in hostile country, and I remember the uneasiness and discomfort to this day.

Next morning we heard cocks crowing in the distance; that should mean that Venta was inhabited, and by peasants, for robbers do not keep poultry. But peasants cannot settle anywhere for long without attracting soldiers to take tribute from them, so we went cautiously. Soon we topped a rise and looked down on the city.

Venta is the very opposite of a hill-fort, though there are hill-forts round it. It lies in a marshy valley through which runs a little stream, and its defences are wet ditches rather than walls; no Saxon raiders would have the patience to destroy an embankment, so that the town was still as strong as it had ever been, though unroofed buildings and smoke-blackened walls showed that it had been sacked not long ago. The moat was held by a small garrison for the King of Dumnonia, and their commander refused us leave to enter. We were all disappointed, for we had been looking forward to seeing a strange town and comparing it with Anderida; but we could not complain of such a sensible precaution. I have seen the inside of Venta all right, but that was many years later.

Next day we rejoined the road to Calleva, and marched along it without incident. This was the most ravaged district in the whole of south Britain, and the people fled from armed strangers; we saw only a few patches of cultivation and no cattle at all, but that evening, on the outskirts of the Forest of Calleva, we had an unexpected piece of luck. A little band of peasants manned a stockaded hill-fort when they first saw us, but as we drew nearer their courage failed and they bustled out with their women and children to take refuge in the Forest. We walked into the fort, lit fires, and spent the night in safety and comfort.

The road was now very bad, for bushes had encroached on it, and swamps had formed in every hollow. Next day we made very little progress, since the pack-horses caused us endless delay; their loads kept on being caught by the branches, and as they had no more sense than any other horses, the stupidest animals I know, instead of standing quietly to be disentangled they would struggle forward to get free. We made an uneasy and fireless camp a few miles short of Calleva.

In the morning we sent forward an intelligent scout to examine the town; he came back to say that no one had replied to his shouted challenge, though the gate was blocked by a barricade. We found a way in where a stream had undermined a portion of the wall; then Constans put a sentry in the top of a tree, and told us we could scatter to rummage in the houses. No matter how often a town has been sacked, you will usually find something useful lying about.

What made Calleva such a queer place to wander in was that it had been abandoned while it was still a going concern. The streets were overgrown, and most of the roof-beams had been stolen by people who were too lazy to cut timber even in that thick Forest, but many house-walls were intact. In sheltered corners you could trace frescoes on the plaster, and mosaic floors glimmered through a layer of mud. For the first time I could visualize what Britain must have looked like a hundred years ago, when the Emperors still ruled undisturbed in Augusta Treverorum. Some of the frescoes were very curious indeed, and so lifelike that they had probably been made by wizards; at least Conan thought so, and would not let me look at them for long, in case they cast a spell over me. Nowadays we don't like our designs to be too lifelike; no one can work a charm into a pretty pattern that means nothing.

Before the citizens finally despaired and emigrated to the west, they must have called on every Power for assistance; the church was in ruins, but we found a large pillared building still carrying its stone roof, and in it a statue of Mars, upright behind an altar. The Saxons love to desecrate churches, but they had evidently taken this figure for their war-god Seaxneat, and had left his temple unharmed. Constans thought that as Christian warriors we ought to overturn it, but our peasants would have liked to make an offering, just in case; so we compromised by doing nothing at all, and left him brooding over his deserted city.

As a matter of fact, it was not quite deserted; one of our men caught an old woman who was too weak with hunger to run away, and Constans ordered that she should not be harmed. When she found that she was safe, and that we didn't even want her cloak, she bubbled over with gratitude, and told us the recent history of the place. She had been born a colona near by, but had moved into a good town house when the citizens went away; she had lived there ever since, with occasional excursions to the Forest when raiders were about. She said that robbers, both Roman and Saxon, often settled inside the walls, which seemed such a perfect base; but they soon found the neighbourhood too poverty-stricken to support them, and moved to better hunting-grounds. She told us we were unlikely to meet anyone in the Forest, if we stuck to the main road to Corinium, although she knew nothing of the open country to the northwest. Constans gave her a piece of salt beef, and we left her building a fire on her marble floor to roast the unexpected feast. She was a living warning of what happens to peasants who try to live without the protection of trained and well-paid soldiers, as the comitatus took pains to point out.

We had picked up very little of value in the town, apart from a few bronze building-clamps prised out of the walls, but I think the experience had given us a new determination. If someone didn't do something soon about the Saxons, Anderida would share the fate of Calleva, even though her inhabitants had shown greater stubbornness. We rather hoped to meet a party of barbarians, so long as it was small and badly armed.

We had not gone a mile from the town when we crossed a little stream, and saw that it flowed northeast; I had never in my life seen a stream that flowed in any direction except the south, and I was thrilled to realize how far we had travelled. All that day we marched to the northwest, and in the evening we camped by the roadside and lit fires, as an earnest of our new resolve not to give way to the Saxons.

Next morning we came into open and well-tilled country. The peasants did not hide, for they were used to seeing Roman troops. When we halted for our midday meal a number of them came out of the nearest village bringing jugs of beer and great round cheeses; their spokesman, who wore a cloak draped toga-wise over his leather breeches, told us that we were now in the territory of Corinium, and he had orders to supply food to the Count's foederati. The men were delighted; it was quite a new experience for them to find villagers giving food willingly, without a foraging expedition waving drawn swords; but Constans grumbled that we were free allies, not foederati bound to follow the Count of the Britains.

If the countryside was a revelation of what Britain could be like under a strong government, the City of Corinium quite took my breath away. It was a good deal decayed, of course, for there is really no function for a city when traders dare not go fifty miles from their workshops to sell their goods; but the walls were not only undamaged, but newly repaired with well-squared freestone, and only one of the three gates had been blocked up. Since they had never been burnt the houses had kept their red-tiled roofs, and this gave the city a very strange appearance to our eyes, accustomed to the untidy bundles of thatch in Anderida. The streets themselves were not in very good shape; a few fallen columns had been left lying about, half-buried in the clay and gravel with which the stone pavement had been repaired; but the market-place was full of well-dressed citizens, and in the shops traders were selling for silver money a surprising assortment of well-made goods. We stopped to sell the bronze we had pulled out of the walls of Calleva, and though there was no time to haggle we received a parcel of minute silver coins in exchange. The smith just scooped them out of a drawer and put them in a little linen bag, without worrying whether they all contained the same amount of alloy; evidently a man could trust this coinage, tiny though the

44

individual pieces were. So this was what a city looked like, when it was well governed and secure.

The next day we marched into the camp of Count Ambrosius, on the bare hills above the source of the Thames. As soon we had chosen our camping-ground Constans took me with him to call on this mysterious general, who had appointed himself Count – and made others recognize him. I was very glad that Constans took me along; it showed that my good behaviour had produced its intended effect, and that he now regarded me as his second-in-command. Conan was left behind, and I began to feel myself free.

I had expected to find the Count a mighty warrior, seven-foot tall and covered with hair, the type of man to win obedience from the fighting Kings of Britain; and I got a surprise when the guard led us into his tent. I saw a wiry little man sitting behind a table, leaning forward on a folding stool ornamented with ivory, and dressed just like the pictures of the Emperors on the old coins; he wore a bronze breastplate, the front all in one piece and decorated with images of the gods, and a long red cloak hung over his shoulders; his arms were bare, except for bronze wrist-guards, and so was his head, though a handsome bronze helmet with a horse-hair crest stood on the table beside a short Roman sword; on his legs were greaves and ankle-boots below bare thighs. If he dressed like this on a cold hill-side in April, I reflected, it could only be for effect; I determined not to be impressed.

He was beardless, except for a grey stubble, and the hair on his head was also short and grey; his face was deeply lined, and from under thin eyebrows large brown eyes looked out sadly; his fingers were long and well-kept, as though he had not handled his sword as often as his pen.

He looked like a wise old steward dressed up as a statue of Mars.

He did not rise as we entered, which made Constans speak very loud and haughtily. He listened to the formal account of who we were, where we came from, and what force we brought; then he squared his shoulders, wrinkled his brows, and looked my brother full in the face.

'Eleutherus should have sent his whole army,' he said in a stern, rasping voice. 'But I suppose your little comitatus is better than nothing. Now, young sir, fifty men are too few to form an independent command, but as you are all well-armed I shall put you in a good numerus, and you can be a captain; your young brother must serve in the ranks, for such a small force does not need two officers. Of course you don't know any drill as yet, but you will pick it up quickly if you train hard, and that's just what you shall do. Go now and report to the Tribune Aurelian, then see that your men are comfortably encamped. Lights-out is an hour after sunset, and they must make no noise from then until the trumpet blows at dawn. You will draw bread and beer from the central store, but there must be no waste, and any extras you must pay for yourselves. That is all. No, come back. It is the custom in this army to salute before you leave my tent.'

We were both glad to get outside, for the Count could be very frightening. It was, however, a manner that he put on and took off like a cloak, and he really preferred to be friendly with his subordinates, once he had got them into the right frame of mind. Constans went off to see his superior officer, who was the nephew of Count Ambrosius, and I returned to the comrades, to tell them that we were in a Roman army now, and that life promised to be dull and strenuous. Nobody liked the prospect.

The actual training was not as bad as we had feared; we

were pushed into a line, three ranks deep, along with a lot of other well-armed soldiers, and practised for hours advancing and retiring together at the word of command. It was hard on the legs, but restful to the brain. Yet Constans and the other officers found it very exhausting, for they had to learn their drill and teach it to us at the same time, and the Count was always riding up on his big black war-horse to criticize them. Our numerus was made up, apart from ourselves, entirely from the very large comitatus of the King of Dumnonia, so all the men in the ranks were socially my equals and pleasant people to be with, though I could hardly understand their speech; but some of the other first-line formations contained shepherds and foresters, for west of the Sabrina every man is a warrior, and they have no servile coloni. That explains the great size of the army, which was larger than I had supposed all the Kings of Britain could put into the field. Besides the Count's own followers we had the whole levy of Dumnonia and Venedotia, the eighteen grandsons of Cunedda each with his comitatus, and a sprinkling of the Irishmen they had conquered. There was also a small band of Saxons from the upper Thames, settlers who lived among the peasants by leave of the Count, and defended his borders from their cousins. These last no one attempted to drill; they were surly brutes, who would soon have murdered any officer who tried to push them into line.

But it was these savages who gave me my chance to get out of the ruck. I was not enjoying my service in the ranks; it seemed all wrong that Constans could sit up drinking all night, and have a servant to wait on him, while I, his brother, had to polish my own arms, and go to bed when the trumpet sounded. One day, about a fortnight after we had arrived, I was standing idly on the parade-ground. A young officer had just tried to march his men in column slap through our line, and we were fallen out until the confusion was righted. A hundred yards away some Saxons were throwing spears at a mark, and the Count, cantering up with his eyes on the mess we were in, nearly rode over one of them. The man jumped round angrily, drew his scramaseax, and trotted after the horse. I saw what was happening and shouted to him not to be a fool, for the general had never meant to insult so noble a warrior; these Saxons are absurdly sensitive about their prestige, and the only way to deal with them is to apologize quickly when they take offence. The man calmed down when he saw that he had attracted sufficient attention to his wounded honour, and put up his sword; but Count Ambrosius had seen what was going on, and he beckoned me to him.

'Well, young man,' he said kindly, 'you seem to speak very fluent German for a Roman soldier. I won't ask you where you learned it, in case the answer shocks my grey hairs, but your talent is wasted in the ranks. I want to split up that band of Saxons, for they may change sides if they act in one body. Can you look after ten of them if I make you a decurion? I see you carry Saxon arms yourself, and that makes it easier.'

I explained that I was of German descent and was brought up by a Saxon nurse, though I was also a true Roman. I was dismissed from my numerus, and as soon as I had taken my barbarians aside I proceeded to get on good terms with them. I said that we would take mutual oaths, and they would be my comitatus, so that they need feel no indignity in obeying my orders; I admitted that they were probably more experienced warriors than I was, but reminded them that it was the Count himself who had put me in command, and promised always to respect their honour; they were very easily flattered, and swore to live and die with me.

Now I was much better off. As I could not possibly live with my men, whose manners were frankly disgusting, I had to be treated as an officer in spite of the small size of my command. The only things that Saxons ever keep clean are their swords, so I persuaded one of them to look after my arms, and as we did not attempt any drill I was free to wander about the camp.

That camp was a curious place. There was all the dull housekeeping work to be done that is necessary when a lot of men are living together, but apart from that we all seemed to be acting parts in a play; everyone was seriously pretending to be a Roman of a hundred years ago, and the Count dealt sternly with anyone who forgot his part. The commands had to be given in Latin, and they made a tremendous business of posting sentries every night, and saluting the standards in the morning. Men who came drunk on parade, or kicked up a row when they should be sleeping, were flogged, and one who punched his officer on the nose was publicly hanged. Everyone drilled all day long, and Count Ambrosius lectured the officers on tactics in the evening.

He was a man of remarkable force of personality. There was no real reason why we should obey him, but we did; and I confess I jumped to it just as smartly as the rest. After a month we began to believe that we were the invincible troops of Constantine or Theodosius, and that it would be an easy task to drive the barbarians out of Britain. The Tribunes could even move the whole army together, without different detachments getting in one another's way. It had been a great strain, and sometimes I wanted to burst out laughing, but by the end of June we were ready for battle, and no one had defied Ambrosius.

On July 1st we left camp and marched eastwards, keeping to the bare hills that enclose the Thames valley on the north; no army could march through the tangled woods and swamps of the valley itself. Though we had been gathering for more than two months the Saxons had no force in the field to meet us. They are an independent lot of savages, and they would not give up their pleasant life of plundering in small gangs because of a rumoured danger. Consequently we were able to march eastward without a serious battle, and we caught and killed several small parties of the enemy. Our scouts swept the country far to the north, but my own little command was kept on the southern flank, squirming through the dense woodland of the river-bank. Saxons are good at getting through forest, and my men were not afraid of tree-devils, as civilized Romans would have been. I had to send my horse back to Constans, for no horseman could have followed where those Saxons went, and though I was young and fit I found it hard work to keep up with them. Luckily my equipment was as sensible as theirs; without a cuirass I could bend down easily to get under a branch, and the little round shield, slung low on the back, did not catch in the twigs as a square Roman one would have done. There was nothing much worth stealing in the almost uninhabited valley, but the plunderers made it their base for raids to the north, so we had to move carefully, expecting to meet them at any moment.

Count Ambrosius was sensible of the danger that my men might decide to go over to the raiders if they were left on their own; I had instructions to send for reinforcements as soon as I bumped into anyone, but sometimes things happened too quickly, and we had to fight by ourselves. I was pleased to see that my men followed me willingly, and fought bravely against their cousins, though I had to risk my life more than was prudent. For a man of my station in life to be killed in battle is a natural death, but it seems to me an admission of incompetence, and I have always tried to avoid it in any way consistent with my prestige. Unfortunately, it is no good standing still and ordering Saxons to charge; they expect their commander to lead the way.

The secret of the Saxon method of fighting is to go into your man very hard, not bothering about his head and shoulders, which any cripple can guard, but stabbing him low in the belly with an upward thrust. I had been well practised in this by my grandfather, but the first time we cornered six raiders with their backs to a swamp I wondered how it would work out in reality. I ran up to the biggest of them with my shield held low, and when he levelled his spear at my head (he was too poor to carry a sword, like many of these wretched foragers) I did not raise my guard. As I had expected, his first thrust was only a feint, and as I jumped forward he stabbed at my bowels; but my shield was there, waiting for his spearpoint, and next moment I had my scramaseax in his throat. It is a nearly infallible way of dealing with Saxons, although it needs a steady nerve.

These particular robbers must have been amateurs at their job, perhaps newly landed from Germany, for they had nothing on them worth taking; but there was always a chance of meeting a chief laden with gold, and we continued our scouting zealously. I knew my men would follow where I led, so long as the enemy was weaker; and I had no intention of leading them against odds.

By the middle of August we had marched without a battle to the neighbourhood of Londinium (our general caused some confusion by referring to it in orders as Augusta, the old official name which nobody now uses).

We stayed there for a week, as a challenge to the barbarians; but no one came out to fight us. I could see the walls of the city in the valley below, and they looked to me undamaged. But the position is too near the permanent Saxon settlements in Kent, and the Count could not persuade any craftsmen or traders of Corinium to come and live there. It requires too big a garrison to be held merely as an outpost, and in the end we had to leave it desolate. My brother went inside to have a look, and found no one but a handful of squatters, who fished in the river and stole pigs for a living; all the houses were in ruins, and their metal clamps had been removed already. But I was busy scouting, so I did not see even the wreckage of what was once the mightiest city in Britain.

In the beginning of September we marched northwestwards to Verulamium. Here again the Count offered to refound the city, if people would come to dwell in it, but again with no success; even the squatters who were living there already said that they would move out if he tried to make them pay taxes. We went on northwest along the great road, and left the splendid flint-and-brick walls ungarrisoned, and the mighty gateways yawning open. It was a great disappointment to us all, for we had hoped to restore the forts and blockhouses along the Lindum-Londinium road, and confine the barbarians to the east coast of our island.

As it was, we marched northwest to Ratae, which was still an inhabited town, and then northeast to Lindum. We caught many little gangs of raiders, and chased others away; but we knew they would start to creep back as soon as our backs were turned. Nevertheless our unopposed march had been so successful that we were in very high spirits, and expected, sooner or later, to free the whole of Britain from the invaders. Then Ambrosius would be

Emperor of the Diocese of the Gauls, and we should be his trusted Counts and the rulers of his cities. Even I, who valued my independence so highly, would have accepted a really good subordinate position under that great man.

We managed to restore Lindum, for the Saxon raids had not been very bad in that district and the people were warlike. At the end of October we set our faces for Corinium and our winter quarters; the Count meant to keep the army together all winter, for he knew that the war would begin again in the spring. In November we dispersed to the hutted camps that had been built round the city, and carried on with our training for the next campaign.

The army began to exercise as soon as the days grew longer. This drill was beginning to bore us all, for we subordinates could learn our simple part in it very easily, though I see now that the senior officers needed all the practice they could get; in any case we thought it a waste of time, if the barbarians were not going to face us in a pitched battle. But somehow we paraded every morning to the sound of the trumpet, and ran about the drill ground under the eyes of our leader; no one thought of deserting and going home, though there was really nothing to stop us.

I wish I could explain the remarkable ascendancy that Count Ambrosius had won over his unruly and heterogeneous army. Partly it was the way he took it for granted that we all knew it was our duty to obey him; partly it was the genuine enjoyment we got out of pretending to be better men than we were. Everyone admits that the world has steadily been getting more wicked since recorded history began, and we were proud to imitate our forefathers in the smallest details of our lives; the play-acting was amusing. But chiefly it was because we loved and admired Ambrosius.

He made no concessions. He was as strict with us as an old-fashioned Roman general ought to be, and on the parade ground he seldom spoke except to utter some rebuke; he exchanged no oaths and distributed no gifts, such as comrades expect from their leader; and he worked us very hard. But we all knew that he worked himself hardest of all, that he lived on his bare rations as we did, and that after drilling us all day he sat up most of the night, writing letters to his allies. His dress was so eccentric that he was always easy to identify, and that is half the battle when troops are to admire their leader; he always wore his cuirass and military cloak when on duty, whatever the weather, and a toga in the evening. You could pick him out half a mile away by his bare arms. He had two quite distinct manners; on parade he was as stern as could be, but off duty he would stroll round the camp, talking to any common soldier he met, praising our efforts and always assuming that the other man was as earnest for the liberation of Britain as he was. Since that time I have seen many barbarian chiefs, who could only command their followers by the affection that they compelled and the rewards they conferred, but no one else who could rule a disciplined army merely by appealing to the better nature of his followers. There will never be another Count Ambrosius.

We drilled devotedly, for this year we hoped to invade Kent itself, and there would be rich plunder for all. A contingent of Christian Irishmen crossed the sea to join us, and more Saxon mercenaries enlisted, so that my detachment was enlarged to forty men. The Count did not try to drill his foederati; that would have spoilt their natural method of fighting without making them reliable infantry of the line.

Constans was a changed man. He still had his comitatus

under him, and fifty more well-armed soldiers besides, for there had been promotions among the veterans of the first campaign; but he no longer treated them like equal companions, which is the whole idea of a comitatus. They had to stand at attention when he spoke to them, even off parade, and in the evening he formally inspected their food and then went off to sup alone. All this was in accordance with the ideas of Count Ambrosius, but it seemed to me rather shocking all the same, and that the freeborn comrades took it without too much grumbling was a tribute to our leader's great influence. My own Saxons were on very free-and-easy terms with me, but if I had tried to be strict with them they would just have gone over to the enemy.

These Saxons of mine had never been followers of Hengist (whom it was now strictly forbidden to call King of Kent). They or their fathers had first come to Britain more than twenty years ago, when the barbarians were still acting as loyal foederati; they had been employed as a personal bodyguard by the Count's father, a landowner near Corinium, and when the raids began he had settled them in the upper Thames valley, to watch his borders. You might think that twenty years among Christian Romans would have altered their habits and made them civilized men, but this was not the case; apart from a few casual rapes, they had not even intermarried with their neighbours, but obtained their women from Germany or Kent; and they had made no effort to learn our language. Of course, this was because they despised us as second-rate warriors, and their neighbours despised them as savages; so that both parties, though they lived in the same villages, were separated by a deep mutual contempt. I got on well enough, by tactfully treating them all as honourable German heroes; luckily my sense of smell is very weak, the first qualification for living among barbarians. Actually they were not even the best class of Saxon, for they were mostly poor and wicked men, who had been compelled to flee from their tribes because they had committed murder and could not pay the blood fine. If I ever attained independence, or ruled responsibly under the Count, they would do well enough for the rank-and-file of an army, but I would have to find more intelligent officers.

The prospect of independent rule later on was quite hopeful. If we drove the barbarians right out of Britain Count Ambrosius would have to leave officials behind him to keep the country quiet. I saw myself as one of them, for I had no ambition to follow him abroad; Emperors proclaimed in Britain always try to conquer the West, and so far only Constantine the Great has succeeded. Sooner or later the Count would be killed in battle, and then I could start ruling on my own. His nephew and destined successor, the Tribune Aurelian, was a fussy little man, and he had the job of training the recruits, which was bound to make him unpopular.

The army that set out on the 1st of June 471 was the finest that had been seen in Britain for many years, and the largest; though my father, who never could take bold decisions, did not send the rest of his forces. Numbers of men are always difficult things to calculate, and as a rule only the commander-in-chief is in a position to make a reasonably accurate guess, but the well-armed foot were divided into twelve numeri of about five hundred men each, one of which my brother commanded, and there were about as many shieldless peasant spearmen in the second line. In addition we had a thousand Irish and Saxon auxiliaries, including my little command of forty men, and about three hundred cavalry, who rode on little ponies. Weight-carrying horses are now extinct in Britain, for raiders have killed or carried off the big stallions who were stabled on rich farms, and the few mares that escaped to breed in the forests and moors have reverted to their natural pony type. It is a problem that worries all soldiers, and we were lucky to have three hundred light cavalry.

We marched down the Thames by the same route as last year, though more cautiously and slowly; for we had learnt that the Saxons had gathered a large army and were waiting for us somewhere. The Count insisted on very thorough scouting, and would not encamp until he was sure there was no enemy within a day's march; the cavalry swept the open country, but my Saxons had to search the woods for ambushes, and very nervous work it was.

We found no one at all in the Thames valley, and reached Londinium without incident. Then we once again took our old route by Ratae to Lindum; these places had not been raided in the last winter, and were beginning to revive as trading towns. This increased our already high spirits, for it showed that our campaign was already taking effect in eastern Britain.

It was now August; we had marched for two months along the enemy's borders without opposition, and we began to wonder if the campaign would again fizzle out without a battle. The Count assembled all the officers to hear him explain his future plans. Bareheaded and wearing his usual cuirass and cloak, he mounted a wooden tribunal and made a set speech in the manner of Livy, which I still remember, but whose eloquence I will spare my readers. He said that we simply must fight a decisive battle this year, for the peasantry of the southwest could not support this great army much longer; we would seek out the Saxons wherever they might be. The army would march south, but not by the way it had come; we would take the direct road, through Durobrivae to Londinium, and continue right on to Durovernum if we did not meet the enemy north of the Thames. In short, we were going to march through the heart of their territory and hem them up against the coast.

Troops always get a little slack on a long march, when there is no enemy about; but now we had a few days' extra training, and then marched south in very compact formation, ready to fight at a moment's notice. None of us had ever been along this stretch of road before, for it led through the heart of the great marshes, where the Saxons left their war-boats and changed into little skiffs before raiding up the rivers into the midlands. If we did not meet their army we might perhaps stumble on one of their treasure-hoards.

We forded two difficult rivers by the paved fords of the great disused road; near the second of these fords were the ruins of Durobrivae, a town more thoroughly destroyed than any that I have ever seen, so that you hardly noticed the nettle-grown ruins until you stumbled over them. I mention this place so that men who have learnt geography may understand whereabouts we were at that time, for the rivers are nameless. Our peasants are bad at river-names and every stream seems to be called either Avon or Ouse, in spite of the names our ancestors gave them.

After leaving these melancholy ruins we marched south for one day along the great road which skirts the edge of the marshes. Next morning, as usual, the cavalry were sent forward on our right flank, while my Saxons explored the marsh. Soon I noticed that the south wind carried a familiar stench from right ahead; it was the odour of my own men, but ten times stronger, and I knew that there was a large body of Saxons somewhere in front. This was just the sort of moment my followers would choose to change sides, so I halted them at once; I then went forward with only one companion, a young and fairly trustworthy warrior called Cutha. We crept on all fours through a beastly wet patch of reeds and lay down on our stomachs to peer out the far side; but smells are very deceptive and the enemy were not as near as I had thought. We crept and crawled a full mile farther; I knew that the Count would not trust the evidence of my nose alone. The smell grew stronger, and I could hear the hum of many voices; then we waded, bending low, through a shallow but sticky mere, and carefully parted the reeds on the far side. Five hundred yards away we saw the Saxon army.

Hengist was a cautious and painstaking leader, and had been well trained in his youth as an auxiliary with Roman troops. He had chosen a very strong position, on a neck of dry ground between two marshes; it was an obvious defile, and in the old days someone had dug an entrenchment across the narrowest part; the barbarians had strengthened this with a flimsy barricade of brushwood, for no trees grew in that marshy spot, and they were too lazy to fetch stakes from the nearest wood. I waited a few minutes, until I had impressed the whole picture on my mind, and then we both crept away as silently as we had come.

I felt very grand when I told my news to the Count; but he had on his parade-ground manner at the time, and he made no effort to thank me. As a matter of fact the news was rather disconcerting, for we had never expected that the enemy would fight behind entrenchments; it meant that the skill in manœuvre that had cost us so much time and trouble would scarcely be called upon. The army was halted at once, for it was after midday, and we were told that we would not fight until the morning.

It would be a head-on collision, favouring the fiercest rather than the best-trained troops. There had never been such a battle in the memory of any of our men; when Hengist was winning his Kingdom in Kent Vortigern had never rallied all southern Britain behind him, for the western Kings had held aloof. Neither side could afford to keep such great armies concentrated for long; Hengist had lost a whole season's plunder, and his men would begin to drift back to Germany unless they could start raiding soon; the Count had told us that our supplies were running short; our two years' campaign had reached its climax. It was a filthy wet night, but men stood about talking in the rain, and it was difficult to get the army to go to sleep.

Next morning we were given an unusually big breakfast, for whatever the outcome of the battle we would be marching all that night in pursuit or retreat, and our baggage might not come up with us for days. I remember that I was rather doubtful of victory, and ate sparingly so as to be able to run fast if it came to the worst; it is curious how the missed opportunity of a good meal lingers in the memory. Then the Count called all the officers to him, and made the usual Roman speech before battle. After expressing the sentiments appropriate to the occasion he came to his orders. I was relieved to hear that we auxiliary scouts would not be placed with the armoured men in the line of battle. He intended to make a straightforward all-out attack in dense column along the three hundred yards of firm ground in the centre, while my men and the Irish splashed about in the marshes to distract the barbarians, who are always nervous about their flanks. I should have a fine view of the battle, but the heavy going of the marsh would give me a bad start if things went wrong.

My men were on the left flank, for the Irish, as Christians, had the place of honour on the right. We began to wade through the marsh, where the mud came up to our knees. Meanwhile the main army was forming up for battle; there was just room for three numeri to stand side by side in six ranks on the neck of dry ground, so the twelve numeri were in four lines, one behind the other; behind them were the peasant spearmen in one solid and disorderly mass, and the whole array made a very impressive column. There was nothing for the cavalry to do, and they were drawn up in the background; if we suffered a reverse they might cover our retreat, unless they preferred to ride off as soon as the battle went against us. I never trust cavalry; they have done great deeds across the Channel, but horses are hysterical creatures, and they infect their riders with their own panic.

My men started rather too early, and we came within javelin-range of the Saxon entrenchments before the main attack had begun. The wind, which carried with it a thin summer drizzle, blew straight in our faces, and the enemy's darts fell among us while we could not reply. I told my men to draw back out of range and carry on shouting their war-cries; the battle did not depend on us, and it was stupid to risk casualties.

From where I stood, with the mud squelching round my thighs, I had a very good view of the whole course of the battle; I remember clearly my disappointment at the dingy appearance of the Saxon army. Our warriors of the comitatus always wore their best clothes and all their jewellery to fight in, so that if they met with bad luck they would be buried as persons of importance; but these Saxons were nearly all dressed in badly-woven dark blue cloth, which looked black in the penetrating rain, and many of their shields had not been painted for years. Shuffling about behind their brushwood barricade on top of the entrenchment, they looked like a crowd of coloni at a hanging.

But they did not fight like peasants. Our gaily-dressed

and well-drilled column marched up to the ditch; of course, the best fighting-men were in front, including all the Kings and sons of Kings; when they neared the enemy the ranks began to get unsteady, as each leader raced forward to win the honour of striking the first blow. Count Ambrosius might tell us off into numeri, but we were still a collection of jealous comitatus; it was already a disorderly crowd of emulous rivals that plunged into the ditch and began to scramble up the slippery clay bank on the other side.

Anyone who has to use even one hand to climb with is at a tremendous disadvantage against an enemy who can stand upright and keep his shield in the correct position. In that first assault our men had no chance, and I was not surprised to see them come tumbling back almost at once; in fact the clash was over so quickly that very few of them were hurt. I noticed Count Ambrosius at the rear of the crowd, for he was the only man mounted in all the Roman column of attack. It was a strange position for the leader of the army, who usually has to go in front of the first rush; but I understand it is the old Roman fashion, and it would have occurred to none of us to reflect on his courage. Now he was shouting and waving his arms, though I was too far away to hear what he said.

He managed to get them into line again, and I could see a lot of jostling and pushing, as though men were changing places. Presently the line advanced, this time at a slow walk, and when they descended into the ditch I realized that the composition of the front rank had been changed; for they all bent forward, with their hands pressed against the side of the bank and their shields on their backs, so that those behind could jump on to them and stab at the legs of the defenders; no King would turn himself into a beast of burden like that. The Saxon palisade was only an untidy heap of thorn-bushes, for barbarians are always slack in their fortification, and the Roman spears penetrated it quite easily; it must have been very awakward for the enemy, with sharp weapons digging at their knees just where their shields prevented them from looking down properly.

After a few minutes of this, the barbarians retreated from their bank and formed up behind it. Of course, our men were greatly encouraged, and the whole column pressed forward for another attack; the Saxons opposite me began to look over their shoulders, as though wondering whether to retire in line with their comrades in the centre, and I gathered my men together, in case we might have a chance to advance unopposed. I did not think they would follow me if I charged a steady line. So we all stood together and watched the progress of the battle.

For a very long time there seemed to be no advantage to either side, and this in itself was very unusual. In all the brushes with raiders and pirates that I had ever seen the first ten minutes had shown which side would win; but here both armies fought like oath-bound companions whose leader has fallen. The unarmoured peasants in the rear were now pressing forward, and the Count pushed his horse among them, shouting orders; it took him a long time to get himself understood, but at last the stupid rustics grasped what they were meant to do, and began to tear at the clay bank with their hands and spears. Our leader intended to open a way for the cavalry; my men began to cheer, for it seemed that the battle was already won.

But Hengist, that wily leader, must have realized that his men were in no condition to withstand a charge of cavalry. Suddenly the Saxon war-horns sounded a signal, and the enemy pushed our men back to the half-ruined trench, and the shield-ring was formed in its original position. The battle was back where it had started, and I was surprised, when the sun came out for a moment, to see that they had been fighting for two hours.

Everyone was being incredibly obstinate; but for Count Ambrosius on one side and Hengist on the other, we or the Saxons would have run away long ago. My own followers, who had advanced with such hearty war-cries early in the day, were now doubtful of the outcome. They stood in a clump, muttering among themselves; they were trying to make up their minds whether the time had come to change sides, and I thought I must quickly find them some more active part to play. I told them that when the fighting began again it would be a good idea to steal round the marsh, and see what sort of a guard the enemy had posted over their baggage. They received these orders with enthusiasm, and I congratulated myself on my cleverness; for if the barbarians discovered us plundering their valuables they would not welcome us into their ranks.

Soon the Romans attacked again. I beckoned to my men, and we crept through the marsh. Unfortunately it was a waste of time; Hengist had chosen a position with a really impassable flank, for once, though I know how rare such positions are in warfare; soon the mud and the water were up to our shoulders, and it was too boggy even for the desperate resort of swimming. We struggled back to our original post; I believe no one had noticed our absence, so exciting was the battle on the neck of dry ground. There the Romans fought to win the trench a second time, but Hengist had packed his men very close, and we could not drive them from the bank. Courage in battle is always a chancey thing, and any time now our side might decide they had had enough. I looked round, to pick out the best line of retreat if things grew unpleasant, and realized that something I had expected to see was missing; at first I could not make out what it was, and then I understood. The cavalry had moved off.

There was a way round Hengist's other flank. Except in the mountainous west, there are no fighting grounds in Britain where both flanks are completely secure. Now we had nothing to do except keep the battle going until the cavalry appeared, and I felt more cheerful about the outcome. I did not say anything to my men, for fear they would let it out in the taunts they were continually shouting at the enemy; these had not noticed the disappearance of the horse, for Saxons get very excited on these occasions.

The drizzle had now ceased, and though I could not see the sun I judged it to be after midday; the fighting along the trench had died down to a throwing of javelins and occasional half-hearted partial attacks. I was not playing a very heroic part; but my followers were scouts, and in any case if I led them into the thick of the fighting they might join the other side. When Hengist was beaten they would be enthusiastic in the pursuit of their fellow-countrymen, and I would be able to do something to win the Count's approbation.

At last we heard shouting from behind the Saxon left wing, and the small detachment opposite us looked over their shoulders and seemed to waver. As they ran back to their main body I jumped into the marsh and waved my followers into the hostile position. Our cavalry had gone a very long way round, and come back directly in rear of the Saxon left.

I expected that to be the end of the battle, but Saxons are very slow-minded people, and their stupidity guards them from sudden panic. It is notorious that they hardly ever flee when in close contact with the enemy; if they can get safely away from a lost battle they will withdraw swiftly, but if the position is hopeless they stand back to back, and do a great deal of damage until the last man is down. I suppose it is because they are convinced that the meanest of them is better-born than any Roman; German honour is an untrustworthy thing, but it does keep them firm in their ranks.

Our infantry were more or less fought out, and even when Hengist withdrew from the entrenchment they would not follow up with a determined attack. Most of the peasants, who were still fresh, and of course my own followers and the Irish, flung themselves at once on the baggage, and took no notice of the fight that still raged. The cavalry were not really happy, charging well-armed foot. In consequence Hengist was able to withdraw gradually to his left until he had gained the protection of the marsh. A large part of the Saxon army got away, and there was no pursuit.

Such was the Great Victory of Count Ambrosius, and oddly enough the battle never had another name. The country round about was almost unknown to the Romans, and even the rivers were nameless. As for the Saxons, all they remember of their own history is composed by their poets, and no one makes up songs about an unheroic defeat. For a few years we talked of the Great Victory; then later fighting put it out of our minds, and now I think it is wholly forgotten.

Our losses had been nearly as heavy as the enemy's, and our army was in no state for an invasion of Kent; but we had taught the barbarians a rough lesson, and central Britain should be free of plunderers for a few years. At Londinium the army was disbanded. I went home with Constans and the comitatus of the Regni; we marched boldly along the old road that runs due south through the

Forest, and saw no signs of barbarian plunderers on the way.

Now for two years there was no fighting in our part of Britain, and we all lived prosperously in my father's fortress. But I was unsettled and discontented; it seemed a useless sort of life that I was leading, as a mere replacement in case my brother died without an heir; and even that was now unlikely, for he had married the plain and sturdy daughter of a respectable landowner. There were no raiders to fight, and our Kingdom was so enclosed between the Forest and the sea that there was no point in trying to enlarge its well-marked boundaries at the expense of our Christian neighbours; in fact, such perfect peace prevailed that Constans lived at home, and Noviomagus was left ungarrisoned.

I was therefore very pleased when, in January 473, a message came that Count Ambrosius was gathering another great army from all his allies and subjects. He had never given up the idea of expelling the barbarians from Kent, but the usual tiresome war between Demetia and Venedotia had delayed him. Now he had patched up a truce, and appointed Corinium as the mustering-place; though the messenger said that our comitatus could meet him as he advanced eastwards. Constans accordingly stayed at home, but I set out for Corinium at once, to make sure that I was appointed to my old command of Saxons. It is a measure of the peace that the Count had won for us that I made the journey alone, and saw no raiders.

I found Cutha and about fifty other Saxon mercenaries waiting for me; we all settled down to the old routine of drill and early beds as though we had never left it off. But it was not quite the same army; for one thing, it was much smaller, since the western Kings did not trust one another, in spite of the truce, and kept most of their men at home;

also there were fewer cavalry and their mounts were shaggy upland ponies, for every year it becomes harder to find decent weight-carrying stallions in Britain.

Nevertheless, we were confident of victory. Last time we had driven the Saxons into a swamp and plundered their baggage; there was no fear that we would not do the same thing again. If our army was weaker than two years ago, that should be true in a greater measure of the barbarians; most of their penniless plunderers had drifted back to Germany or Gaul, and Hengist would have only the half-breeds of many tribes who tilled the soil of Kent. I remembered, from what Ursula had told me, that the best German warriors despise an agricultural life, and wander tremendous distances from their homes to live by plunder. Only the second-best would be left in Britain.

We marched easily and leisurely down the Thames, in late May, and picked up my brother and his men before we reached Londinium. The Count was delighted to find that the city was not quite deserted, and that a few of the new inhabitants were civilized men; it was his dearest dream to restore the cities of Britain, and the Great Victory seemed to be making it come true.

South of the Thames the old main road leads almost due east to Durovernum, Hengist's capital, and then eventually to the coast; but on the second day's march we came to a river flowing north, and on it the ruins of a city (rather confusingly called Durobrivae, the same name as the town halfway between Londinium and Lindum). This river was the western boundary of the territory where Hengist's followers actually farmed the land, and we all expected to fight a battle before we were allowed to cross it; but to our surprise neither the cavalry in the open country nor my men in the thickets could find any trace of the enemy, and at low tide we waded comfortably through a broad paved ford. We cheered and told one another that all the barbarians must have fled to Germany when they heard we were coming. All the same, we camped that night on a steep hill, and Count Ambrosius took great care to see that the sentries were watchful.

Next day we set out very cautiously; I think we were all a little afraid of our own daring, for Hengist had lived here so long that we thought of it as a land outside civilization, and no Roman army had ventured beyond the Empire since the days of the great and wicked Julian. The Count made one of his usual speeches before we began our march, and told us what a great historical occasion it was; he also reminded us that we must scout very thoroughly.

By now I knew my own Saxons pretty well, and it struck me that they seemed restless and upset; I wondered whether they were beginning to feel worried about making war on their fellow-countrymen, but on reflection I decided that was absurd. If they were uneasy it was only because they feared we would be beaten, and I was confident that our great Count would be victorious.

The country we advanced into was wooded and enclosed. When Germans settle down to till the soil they do not live together in villages as Christians do; each man hacks out a clearing in a different bit of forest, where he can live apart, without being bothered by public opinion. The ridges and valleys of Kent were dotted with clumps of trees, though it was not really thick forest, and everywhere we came on these little clearings, with a deserted wooden hut in the middle. It was difficult country to scout, for we never seemed to be able to see for half a mile in any direction. My particular job was to work through the belts of dense woodland, where horsemen could not ride. We saw no enemies all morning, but plenty of traces where they had been; footprints in the mud, the ashes of campfires, and flimsy bivouacs of plaited boughs. At the midday halt I reported this to the Count, but when he questioned me I agreed that I had only seen evidence of small parties; nowhere had we found the unmistakable track of a real army. He frowned and said:

'It is possible there will be no battle after all. They took this land very easily; they may abandon it just as quickly, for one place is very like another to barbarians. How are your mercenaries behaving? I rely on you to give warning of any ambush; don't trust them to report what they find, but keep a sharp look-out for yourself. Now go out and make good all the thickets within two miles of the main army.'

Count Ambrosius was always ungracious when he received a report; he thought the comrade-to-comrade attitude that other leaders adopt to win the affection of their men was bad for discipline; but his frown was most unpleasant, and we worked harder to avoid it than we would have done to win rich gifts from a more easy-going chief. I went back to my men, and chivvied them into the woods as soon as they had finished their midday meal.

We worked very hard that afternoon. The country was just open enough for the baggage to march at a good pace, yet dense little woods grew on every side; messengers continually sought me out to ask whether we knew for a fact that the next valley was clear of the enemy, and to remind us that we were holding up the progress of the whole column. I bustled my men at a trot from one covert to the next, and got out of breath and exasperated. It was quite impossible for me personally to check all the scouting, at the pace we were going, but I couldn't tell that to our general; he took it for granted that we should perform the impossible if those were his orders. We made such a noise, as we crashed through the bushes, that anyone lying in wait could easily have ambushed us, and I salved my conscience with that fact; barbarians would not have the self-control to let us go by so that they could attack the main body, and if no one sprang out it meant there was nobody there.

About an hour before sunset we heard the trumpets blowing for the halt. The Count had found a bare hill-top that would make a safe camping ground; though the valleys below, from which we would have to fetch water, were densely wooded. The evening was fine, and to the eastward I could make out a few threads of smoke, presumably marking the nearest barbarian pickets. My band was at the bottom of the hill just east of the camp, and I knew that we must climb the opposite ridge and check that the next valley was empty before we could go back to supper. We were tired, and it was a great bother, but the Count would only send us back again if we didn't; it was no good pretending we had done it if we had not, for I had already discovered that I could not tell him lies to his face. You can see from all this that Ambrosius gave me a very sound training as a junior officer.

We puffed up the hill, and I gave a cursory glance at the quiet woods below. All my men crowded to the top in a body, as though they were still as keen as ever on ferreting out a lurking enemy, and when I gave the order to retire they hesitated for a moment, and looked at me queerly. Then Cutha called out:

'Noble Coroticus, we must part on this hill-top. Hengist has followed the army all day, and he will attack as the baggage is unloaded. All the Welsh will be killed this night, but it would not be honourable for us to stab you now, because of the oaths between us. Run quickly, before we change our minds. Hurrah for Hengist, King of Kent!' At which they clashed their spears against their shields.

I began to run downhill as they opened their mouths to cheer. Oddly enough, what had chiefly impressed itself on my tired brain was the one word, Welsh. It is a term of contempt that the Saxons apply to anyone of non-German blood, and it can mean either slave or foreigner. When I heard Cutha come out with it so naturally I knew that all traces of loyalty had left his mind, and that he thought of us as his enemies; it was very lucky that his unaccountable German honour had given me a few more hours of life. Someone threw a spear after me as I pounded down the hill, but it went wide; Saxons don't usually miss at that range, so I presume it was only a hint that I had better keep moving.

I had about half a mile to go to reach the camp, and I was already exhausted after a long day's scouting; but I ran fast down the hill-side, and only halted to take breath among the bushes at the bottom. I then stopped to think out my position. It was obvious that the whole army was in a trap; Hengist must have followed us all day, and my Saxons knew it while they searched so zealously for an enemy in front; I would never have thought that such stupid people could keep a secret so well. Furthermore, they must be quite convinced that we had no chance of escape, since they had openly announced their treachery before the fight began. The question was whether it would be safer to hide where I was, or to hurry back to the camp and fight my way out later with an organized party. I am telling you frankly what I thought; you may consider me a coward, but I should like to point out that I have borne my share in many great battles, and am still alive at eighty-three, because I always got away at once when I saw that I was on the losing side; only stubborn men, who try to alter Fate, provide young and noble corpses.

By the time I got my second wind my decision was

taken. Immediate safety lay in the thicket, but I was looking to the future; I would have a great deal of explaining to do if I arrived home alone when my brother and all his comitatus had perished; people would be bound to think that I had joined with my followers in betraying the Count. In the second place, it was just conceivable that the Romans might win; in which case I would be a homeless fugitive, with every man's hand against me. The wise thing was to take my place in the ranks, and concentrate on leading some of the Regnians to safety. With my advance information that should not be too difficult.

I was barely in time to raise the alarm. A trooper heard my shouts, and rode down the hill to find out what was the matter; I jumped up behind him; but as I reached Ambrosius and the trumpets blew the call to arms, Hengist led his men out of the woods. The timing of the attack was perfect; the sun was low, and it shone level behind the attackers, so that it was difficult to make out their numbers and formation; our men were tired and hungry; worst of all, he had caught us at the very peak of the disorganization that sets in when even the most disciplined army has just finished a troublesome march. Most of the Romans had taken off their helmets and sword-belts, and were scattering to look for firewood; newly unloaded packponies were wandering all over the camp, and lying down for a roll in everybody's way; any infantryman with sore feet had already taken his boots off, and the cavalry had unsaddled their horses. Half an hour later sentries would have been posted, and the inlying picket would have been under arms, but what actually happened was that many soldiers formed up in their ranks half-naked and scarcely armed. The barbarians came on at a fast trot, howling like wolves.

I was better off than most of my companions, for at least

I was fully armed, and my mind had had time to get over the shock of surprise. My first aim was to join my brother's comitatus; I knew that they marched in the forward part of the column, and that they usually encamped towards the left of the army; so I jumped on a loose packpony and kicked him into a floundering gallop among the heaps of bedding and equipment. I spotted the standard of my brother's numerus, where I had expected to find it, and slid off the pony. Constans wore boots, and carried his shield and sword, though he had taken off his cuirass.

'My men have gone over to Hengist and left me alone,' I gasped out. 'Can I fall in with you? Look here, we must think fast. This is a carefully-planned attack, and we are properly caught. For God's sake, let's make straight for the woods. It's already too late to help the Count.' I spoke at the top of my voice, hoping that the comrades would overhear me, and take the necessary steps without waiting for orders.

But at this crisis Constans was still a regimental officer, tight in the net of discipline. Some of the men behind him moved restlessly in the ranks, but he turned on them, and yelled:

'Attention! Pick up your dressing and look to your front! Captain Coroticus will fall in on the left of the Regnians, as a supernumerary with no command. You have ten seconds to buckle your belts before I lead you to the attack.' He gave me a very nasty look as I went to my place.

A moment later we were marching towards the enemy, who by now had reached the western outskirts of the camp. The Romans did not have time to form a continuous line of battle; each numerus just went into action against the nearest party of barbarians, and already stray groups of rejoicing Saxons were pillaging the baggage. Our cavalry, who would have given us a breathing space if they had charged at once, never got formed up at all; I suppose each man rode off to safety as he caught his horse. I saw Count Ambrosius, on foot, with half a dozen of his comrades round him; he dashed into the thick of the flying spearmen, and beat them with the flat of his sword, though they went on running as fast as ever. That was the last I saw of him, though I have heard that he survived the battle. He gave us no orders, and Constans led us steadily to the brow of the hill.

There we halted. The men were exalted with that strange frenzy that makes some warriors welcome defeat, if it is complete enough and provides opportunity for a glorious death. We were about three hundred strong, all well-trained and well-armed comrades of the comitatus, of whom the hundred on the left flank were Regnians; we hastily shuffled into our normal fighting formation of three ranks, and closed in shoulder to shoulder. I was the left-hand man of the front rank, for a King's son must expose himself in battle; at least it was not so dangerous as being on the extreme right.

The Saxons came up the hill, in a dense pushing crowd of howling men. But they didn't go into us with the savage abandon that sometimes makes their attacks irresistible. I could understand what they were thinking; it is stupid and wasteful to get yourself killed when victory is already won, and there was all that good plunder lying about in the camp.

On my flank the attack was beaten off easily. But in the centre they must have been led by some young hero who wanted to make a name; a little band of them charged in desperately, and broke clean through our unsteady ranks. The numerus was cut in two, and my wing was jostled to the left. Constans was with us; he had taken a blow on the head, and seemed a little dazed; he wanted us to charge right-handed and join up with the other wing, but I thought it was high time I took over the command, while we still had a chance to save our lives. I called to the comrades to double their ranks and turn to the left, a manœuvre that we had often practised on the drill ground, and I led the little column of about eighty men straight through the remains of our camp towards the valley on the south.

There were not many Romans still fighting. Most of the peasants had fled blindly to the east; little knots of brave warriors were standing back to back and preparing for a glorious and memorable death; but I was the only man on the field who had a definite goal, and was willing to fight to get to it. I knew the land of the Regni lay to the south, beyond the great and trackless Forest.

Those Saxons who were seeking glory were already engaged, and the plunderers got out of our way when they saw that we meant business. On the edge of the flat-topped hill we closed up, and ran down it waving our swords; no one molested us. Constans was light-headed from his wound, and kept shouting that we were deserting the Count; a comrade had to pull him along, and support him as we ran. We reached the little wooded valley without trouble, and kept on southward over the next bare hill; the sun had set, but the fading light was strong enough for me to make out the endless leagues of tree-covered ridges that stretched as far as the horizon. I had always thought of the Great Forest as an enemy encompassing our land, but now I welcomed it as a friend.

Soon the night was too dark for us to pick our way, and we halted among a maze of thorn-bushes. We were all completely exhausted, for the defeat and the flight had come on top of a long day's march; Constans was the only wounded man still with us, but many of the unwounded survivors were barefoot, and none could go another mile without rest. I counted the men one by one in the darkness, and found that we totalled seventy-three, of whom thirty were Regnians. We had no cloaks, and of course we dared not light a fire, but the summer night was just warm enough for sleep. I persuaded a man who was suffering great pain from a sword-cut in the hand to take the first watch, as he could not sleep anyway, and offered to take the second half of the night myself. I had done more walking that day than anyone else, but responsibility brings its own strength. Even in that desperate situation I comforted myself with the thought that at last I had an independent command.

We moved off as soon as there was light to see a few yards. At first we thought only of getting as far as possible from that unlucky battlefield, but presently the sun rose through the dawn-mist and I set a course due south. None of us had eaten since the midday halt the previous day, and of course we carried no food, but that morning we were too thirsty to miss our breakfast. The Forest always seems damp and muddy, but it is surprising how hard it is to find drinkable water. It was several hours before we found a stream, and then of course we began to feel hungry.

At our present rate of progress it would take us at least four days to reach friendly territory, and I was not sure we could manage it without eating; a garrison shut in a fort can starve for a very long time, but on the march three days is as much as anyone can do, and one of those had already elapsed. It was too early in the season for nuts or wild berries, and though we saw deer-tracks it was no good trying to hunt without dogs or bows. I decided not to waste time looking for food, but to march due south for as long as we could stand, and make use of every minute of the midsummer daylight. I called the comrades round me and announced my decision; I told them that any man who did not wish to serve under me was free to leave the party at once, but that from those who stayed I would expect absolute obedience. No one took advantage of my offer, and they all gave a temporary oath to obey me on this journey, unless Constans recovered or they met some other senior commander. (Constans, by the way, was now delirious.) I ordered everyone to throw away his shield, and any armour he still wore, and to bring nothing but a bare sword in the right hand; this not only made us move more easily, but discouraged potential mutiny, for I kept my own little Saxon shield, which did not catch in the branches.

Well, we reached the other end, as you must have guessed, or I would not be telling this story; but I sometimes dream about that journey, and wake up hungry. We left thirty men behind, dead or dying, for I made a rule that only Constans might be carried; if we had delayed to help the others none of us would have got through. We had nothing at all but our swords and a few rags bound on our feet, and we nibbled at green leaves and twigs to keep our stomachs working; we straggled over two miles of trail, and took it in turns to go in front, hacking at the briars. I may decently boast that I was always in front, except when I helped to carry Constans; it is remarkable how the responsibility of command gives a man strength.

Why on earth didn't I leave my brother behind? That problem still puzzles me; for if he had died in the Forest no one would have been particularly surprised, and my future would have been assured. In a desperate situation one gets fixed ideas of what must be done, and the overtired mind forgets to question them; all I could think of was that it would be a great achievement to bring back as many

Romans as possible from the disastrous rout, and that Constans was an important trophy that it would be shameful to abandon.

That nightmare journey was a turning-point in my life. I had always known that I had a quick and devious brain, and my grandfather had taught me to be as good as the next man with my weapons; but until then I had always failed hopelessly when I tried to win comrades over, and I feared I might lack the personality that makes warriors obey a leader. Now I knew that if my brain was perhaps too subtle to persuade the stupid, I was yet forceful enough to compel them to carry out my commands. No one had thought of stabbing me in the back and setting up as a robber chief on his own, though it would have been a natural thing to attempt in those conditions. As I lay in the peasant's hut at the edge of the Forest where they nursed me back to health, I was certain that one day I would be the master of a powerful and obedient war-band.

By the autumn I was quite well again, but unfortunately so was Constans. I remember a family council, when my father gathered us all in his private room to make plans for the murky future. I realized, with a shock, that the house itself was going downhill; the bronze tripod had been broken, and we had no smith skilful enough to repair it; so the servants had made a fire on the tesselated pavement in the middle of the room; the smoke found its way out of a broken window, and the painted plaster on the walls was discoloured by a layer of soot. My father sat at the head of a rough plank table; there was beer in a massive silver jug, but he left his cup untasted, and we none of us liked to be the first to drink. He sighed deeply, and then spoke formally:

'I am an old man now, and the state of Britain has been growing worse ever since I can remember. For the last three years there was hope, with Count Ambrosius to lead us, and I willingly sent my men to follow him, but I suppose he is utterly done for. Let us face the new situation, in which there is no longer a Count of the Britains to lead a combined Roman army against the barbarians. The Kingdom of the Regni must stand on its own feet. But it might be worth while to make alliance with our immediate neighbours. It's unfortunate that Constans is already married, and Paul must remain celibate if he is to get his Bishopric. That only leaves you, Coroticus, and it's high time you were wed. Does anyone know of a suitable King's daughter? Valerian of Demetia had a nice little girl three years ago, but I believe she is married now.'

Nobody said anything. Neither Constans nor Paul was particularly anxious that I should make a good marriage, and I could not think of a candidate on the spur of the moment. Father always talked as though we were imbedded in a mosaic of Roman states, as we had been in his youth, although now we were a precarious peninsula jutting out among the barbarians. All the same, I had a proposal to make; but I was a bit nervous as to how they would receive it. I cleared my throat, and spoke more loudly than I intended:

'This last campaign has probably settled the map of Britain for a few years to come. We must make up our minds that Hengist will remain King of Kent for the rest of his life; but, after all, our revered ancestor, King Fraomar, was once in very much the same position, and he ended up a law-abiding Roman. Why not get in touch with Hengist, and find out if he is attracted to the civilized life? Baptism won't hurt him; ask him to become a Christian, and I will marry one of his daughters. I believe he has quantities of them, and some must be of a suitable age.'

They all screamed at me together; I was abused as a renegade and a traitor to the Empire, and Paul prayed aloud for my salvation. I hastened to withdraw the suggestion, if they thought it a betrayal of the Christian cause. Yet the idea was not absurd, for the Empire had only survived during the last two hundred years by doing exactly the same thing to dozens of barbarian chiefs, and quite often it turned out successfully; a great many otherwise sensible warriors have a queer yearning for civilization.

I wonder what would have happened if my family had fallen in with my suggestion? Hengist was an intelligent man, and he might have made a good Christian King, if his followers had remained faithful. Look how the Irish have changed in a single generation! But the idea was too subtle for my poor old father, and brother Constans was against it just because it was mine; in fact, once he began arguing his tongue ran away with him, and he made wild accusations.

'You were always more than half a German,' he shouted across the table. 'In the army you spent all your time with those stinking Saxon mercenaries; I suppose their table manners suited yours. And whose side were you really on in the last battle? It was your business to see that we were not surprised. Then, when the fighting started, and we might have held our ground if everyone had done his duty, you took advantage of my wound to lead the comitatus of the Regni in a shameful flight. Did the barbarians pay you for your services, or did you do it out of mere malignant hatred of Britain and Rome?'

His voice had risen to a shriek, and he was obviously hysterical; but he and I were the only two men at the table who had been present at that battle, and I didn't want him to start putting unpleasant thoughts into my father's foolish head. Besides, the accusation was completely untrue; if I had wanted to change sides I could have stayed with my mercenaries, instead of being chased, starving and half-naked, from end to end of the Great Forest. All this I quickly explained to my father, trying to keep my temper, though I was very angry at my brother's bitterness.

The scene ended with Constans dashing out of the room in tears. The others listened to my account of what had really happened, and I thought I had convinced them of my innocence and good intentions in the whole unfortunate affair; after all, the insuperable argument in my favour was that I had brought my brother home; even Paul saw that. Like so many of our family councils, this meeting broke up without any decision being taken.

Next day Constans was full of remorse, and told me that his head sometimes ached so fiercely that he did not know what he was saying. He was a graceful speaker, and could apologize very prettily. I was more or less compelled to treat him as a friend, outwardly at least.

The trouble is that some mud always sticks. The sorcerers are quite right; to speak a word is an important action, and once spoken it can never be recalled. Anyone who reflected for a moment must have realized that I had done my duty, and more than my duty, in that ghastly crossing of the Forest. Paul and my father were convinced, though they may have imagined that I had despaired too soon in that lost battle; but Maximus had also been present at the council, which should have been kept within the family. He saw a chance of damaging my interests, and making Constans more popular by contrast. He repeated the silly slander that I had been slack in my scouting, and that the Saxon victory was all my fault. It was the sort of elementary intrigue that appeals to a very stupid man, and makes him think that he is a clever politician.

The common people love to listen to scandal about the

great, and warriors are always ready to believe the worst about their superior officers; so that presently the comrades of the comitatus began to avoid me, and it was harder to get on good terms with the pretty girls in the town. I like to be popular, unless I can be greatly feared; and in any case no one can become a ruler unless his subjects like him, though once he is on the throne it doesn't matter so much. But what maddened me most of all was the unfairness of the whole thing. All the time I had served under the Count I had tried my hardest for the success of the Roman cause. It had been a genuine flicker of patriotism, an irrational sentiment that attacks even the wisest men, especially when they are young.

Before this scandal I had not disliked my eldest brother in the least; he was an obstacle to my advancement, and one day I should have to deal with him; meanwhile we got on well enough together, for he could be a witty and amusing companion. But now I began to hate him as a person, for I knew that it was by his encouragement that these lies were spread about my conduct in the last war. This was very unfortunate, for hatred made me act hastily.

During the winter things were fairly quiet in the land of the Regni; after the defeat of the Roman army the Saxons pursued the main body of survivors westward, and did not penetrate the hungry and unrewarding Forest to the south. The campaign had lasted into the beginning of autumn and it was too late in the season for them to get out their warboats in the Channel. But we knew that next year the raids would start, and after endless discussions in the family council we made our arrangements for defence. We had to stand alone, in spite of our wish for a strong alliance with some Christian power. Our only warlike neighbour, the King of Dumnonia, had led his comitatus north to occupy a district near the mouth of the Sabrina which had previously depended on Corinium, but which Count Ambrosius was now too weak to hold; he was not interested in his eastern border, where an extension of territory would bring him heavy fighting and poor taxes.

Our land is a natural unit, with the Forest to the north and the Channel on the south, but that does not really make it easier to defend; the frontier is too long, and there are no natural defiles; raiders can appear anywhere at very short notice. The best we could do was to hold the two strong fortresses of Noviomagus and Anderida with well-equipped garrisons of elderly men, and prepare a mobile force, mounted on ponies, to engage the plunderers in the open country. I wanted to get out the war-boat, but here I came up against the evil effects of the slanders spread by Maximus. My father had evidently made up his mind that I was not to have an independent command; I was told that commissioning the war-boat would mean a wasteful dispersion of our scanty forces, and that the Bishop would be insulted if he was not put in command of the garrison of Noviomagus, my second choice. In short, I was to be second-in-command of the comitatus, under my brother Constans.

Naturally, my father commanded the permanent garrison of Anderida, where we were stationed when there were no raiders to chase, and old Maximus also lived there and drilled the troops; so I found myself with three superior officers at home, and at least one when we took the field. The whole arrangement was a calculated insult, and it quite killed any lingering piety I might still feel towards my family.

In the spring of 474, when I was in my twenty-third year, the raids started again. The barbarians had not assembled a large army for further conquests, and I believe

Hengist stayed quietly in Kent, where he could live much more luxuriously than he had been accustomed to in Germany. But there were always small bands of hungry and desperate men who came across the sea, refitted in the barbarian Kingdom, and then wandered off to look for the nearest well-fed Romans. As they were extremely poor they did a great deal of harm; they would cut the throats of a whole family for a clay pot or a pair of shoes. I have often thought how much luckier than Britain was Gaul, for there the barbarians were willing to take tribute. Our plunderers were too uncivilized even to have organized a proper slave-market, and killed strong workmen or pretty girls as ruthlessly as infants and old people.

Still, it is astonishing what one can get used to. As the days lengthened we settled down into a routine; the coloni were thin on the ground, but the survivors furbished up the old pre-Roman forts on the hill-tops, and retired to them at the slightest alarm; when things were quiet they came down to cultivate their fields. We had arranged a system of smoke-signals, and the horsemen of the comitatus soon got on the tails of the raiders, who came on foot through the tangled brushwood of the Forest. Oddly enough, though we had a long and undefended coast we were not much troubled by pirates from the sea; when Saxons make the effort to fit out a ship, which is a complicated business for such utter savages, they usually make a considerable voyage; those we saw sailing down the Channel were generally on their way to Gaul or Dumnonia. On these occasions we always passed on smoke-signals to the west, by the terms of our treaty with King Valerian.

On the whole, we were prickly customers to raid, and yielded little profit in return for plenty of hard knocks; but there must be a great deal of fighting in this narrative, and

I will not weary you with all the skirmishes of that summer.

In the early autumn came the great crisis of my life. One afternoon towards the end of August I was sitting in the courtyard behind my father's house, basking in the sun and reading the poems of Ovid (now I come to think of it, that was the last occasion on which I read a book). Constans sat opposite me, glueing the feathers on a new batch of hunting-arrows, and I was trying to make up my mind whether I should leave my sunny corner to get away from the smell of his glue, when one of the servants put her head round the door to say that the sentry on the town-wall had seen smoke-signals in the west. We both cursed, for it was pleasant in the sunshine, but the message could not be disregarded, and we strolled over to the sentry's tower. The man reported that the signal was two uninterrupted columns side by side, which meant that it was repeated from farther west; so there was no immediate hurry, but we had better get moving before dark. The horn was blown, and Constans went to my father to decide what force we should take. It would never do to leave the eastern end of the country unguarded, because of a distant alarm from the west.

After a leisurely preparation we set out in the evening, with about sixty of the younger men of the comitatus; we were mounted on comfortable fast ponies, that would bring us fresh to the battle, but of course we all intended to fight on foot. The evening was still light enough to make the smoke-signals visible, and the track to the westward was good enough to ride on in the dark.

We rode gently all night without a pause, and in the morning saw the signal repeated from the hill above Noviomagus, which meant that the raiders must be still farther to the west, beyond the limits of the Kingdom. We reached the city about midday, and the Bishop sent to round up fresh horses while we ate our dinner. We were very sleepy after our all-night ride, but Constans decided to push on a little farther that afternoon, and get more definite information. The Bishop could tell us nothing, he had only repeated signals from farther west.

We turned slightly north, and rode gently between the Forest and the sea, which here runs northward into the land for a considerable distance. This country is nearly deserted, but a few peasants till the scattered fields, in terror of pirates but attracted by the absence of taxation. We made camp in the early afternoon, for we were too sleepy to go any farther, and built a large and smoky fire of damp wood; we used a blanket to send out separate puffs, telling any messengers from Dumnonia that there were Christian soldiers in the field.

At nightfall the expected messenger rode into camp, and the news he brought was exciting. A small party of Saxons, not more than twenty men, had surprised the newly refounded town of Sorbiodunum, raided the church and the tax office, and got clean away before the comrades in the town could assemble to attack them. Sorbiodunum was a new and rather too optimistic experiment on the part of King Valerian; it was an old Roman city that had lain desolate for at least twenty years, until the King had resettled it two years ago. That was when Count Ambrosius was still victorious, and we all hoped that the plunderers would be finally expelled from Britain. The church commemorated certain very holy martyrs from the days of the Emperor Diocletian, and the King had furnished it with magnificent golden vessels. The raiders must have received information from some discharged mercenary, for they had made straight for the treasure, and then escaped at once over the wall; unless they were suitably dealt with it would be a great blow to the whole Church of Britain, and might lead to a fresh abandonment of the city.

The raiders had two days' start, but if they had come through the Forest they would probably be on foot, and were very likely camped somewhere due north of us at the present moment. We needed rest, and it was useless to go blundering after them in the dark; but after a few hours' sleep we set out at first light, riding north in a widespread, scattered line, and searching the ground for tracks. At mid-morning, when we were already deep in the Forest, Constans was hailed by a voice from the tree-tops. It was a Dumnonian scout, a devout man who had braved the hostile ghosts of the woodland to keep the raiders under observation; he reported that he had seen the Saxons camp for the night, and had climbed a tree for safety; he pointed out the track they had left, easy to follow in the thick carpet of dead leaves.

Constans decided to follow the trail of the raiders; of course they would be expecting pursuit from the rear, and would probably leave scouts behind them; but they had cut back the bush and overhanging branches, we could follow fast, and we outnumbered them three to one. He gave orders that we should keep to the track, on foot, and each man was to make the best pace he could; but the ten slowest comrades should each lead a pony in the rear, to take up the pursuit if the barbarians made for open country. This was a risky plan, since we might be so scattered that we could be defeated in detail, but the treasure was worth a risk.

It was a long, hard chase. But I had made a much worse journey last year, and I set a pace that quickly brought me to the front; Constans kept up with me, though he was not accustomed to the Forest, as I was; I suppose it was the responsibility of leadership that, as usual, gave him the strength and determination to do better than the others.

The enemy had a good three hours' start, but they did not know that they were pursued, and they had all the trouble of cutting a path, while we followed a clear trail; we did not halt for a meal at midday, and I expect they did. Anyway, when the sun was shining through the lower branches of the trees, and we had covered a great many miles, Constans and I saw at the other end of a little glade the first of the scouts they had left to watch their track. He was just on the point of moving off to overtake his companions, but he saw us as soon as we saw him, and blew a warning on the little ram's-horn that these raiders carry; it roused our men as well as the enemy, and we all broke into a tired and stumbling trot.

Now the pursuit became really exhausting and unpleasant. My Saxon weapons were lighter and easier to carry than the Roman arms of my comrades, and I could easily have outdistanced them all; but I did not want to tackle twenty raiders single-handed, and I took care not to get too far in front. Soon we could hear the noise of the enemy as they crashed through the woods; they were no longer cutting a straight track eastward to their homes in Kent, but turning in an aimless sort of way from one open glade to another, wherever the ground was best for speedy retreat.

As we did not keep in a straight line some of the comrades at the heel of the hunt were able to cut corners and catch up with those in front; there were eight of us together in a bunch when we came up with the first barbarian. He had twisted his foot on the broken ground and his companions had left him to face certain death alone, which showed that they were most comfortingly frightened of us. He did not detain us long, but now we proceeded with more caution, for at any moment the rest of the gang might decide to stand and fight it out. The sun was setting, and if we did not catch them soon they might escape us altogether, but I suppose their nerve gave way and they wanted to get it over (I have sometimes had the same feeling myself, though I have always fought it down successfully). In another little glade we found them all standing back to back in a cluster. Even now they had not steeled themselves for one last good fight; as we formed our ranks to approach, the whole group suddenly broke up, and each man ran off by himself into the bushes. We scattered in pursuit.

I marked down the man I meant to catch. He wore a blue tunic, while most of the others were half-naked; better still, he was on the portly side, and would not give me a long chase. I soon found out that I had chosen rightly, for he was badly frightened and out of breath, and his panic made him run through the thickest patches of thorn, where I could follow him by the gaps he had broken. We had not gone a mile when I was so close that I tried a slash with my sword; it did not reach him, but he must have seen it out of the corner of his eye. These barbarians hate to be cut down from behind, for they think that the wound will show on their spirits in the next life and brand them as cowards to all eternity; he jumped to one side, and faced me with his sword out. It did not take me long to deal with him, particularly as his little round shield seemed to be too heavy for his arm, and he was very clumsy in parrying. When he was down I cut his throat with my seaxknife, and began to examine the body.

He wore a pouch attached to his waist-belt, but it contained nothing except some fragments of biscuit and half a dozen tiny silver coins; it appeared that I had not been so lucky as I had hoped. Then I examined his shield, and I had an astounding surprise; attached to the handgrip inside was a leather bag as big as my two fists, and in it a massive golden cup. This must be the famous Chalice of Sorbiodunum, the chief object of the raid. If I could keep possession of it I would be one of the richest men in Britain. I fixed it inside my shield, which I then slung on my back; it gave me rather a hump-backed appearance, but I might be able to cover that by walking bent over, as though very tired.

It was easy to follow my track back to the glade where we had separated; I walked slowly, trying frantically to make plans for the future. If I could only turn this great golden object into silver coins I would have more than enough to buy myself a following among the comrades, and I should soon be King of the Regni. But where to find a buyer with the necessary ready money? And how could I keep my prize a secret from my companions?

I had not gone far when I heard someone crashing through the bushes on my left, and I loosened my sword in its scabbard, in case it was a survivor of the Saxon band. But unfortunately it was my brother Constans. He fell in behind me on the trail, though I waited politely for the King's heir to go in front. Almost at once he spoke:

'What's that on your back, under your shield?' he called out. 'Trust Coroticus to find the richest plunder. If it's anything to eat we ought to share it with the others.'

'It isn't anything to eat, Captain. Just a bit of Saxon equipment that would be no use to a Roman soldier, which I would like to keep for myself.'

'For Heaven's sake don't call me captain when we are by ourselves. I know you only do it to annoy, and to show that you are obeying my orders against your better judgment.'

'I'm sorry, Constans,' I said quickly, delighted that I had

led his attention away from the dangerous subject. 'You are my commander, and my future King, and it is well that we should both remember it.'

My unlucky brother was not a fool, but he had a slow, tenacious mind, not easily diverted from the matter in hand. Also he was very hungry, and he knew that I often kept back food for myself. He returned to the charge:

'I still want to see what is in that package. Do you think I didn't notice those sausages you slipped into your pouch at Noviomagus? Then we all had enough to eat, so I didn't mind; but now it will cause a great deal of ill feeling in the ranks if you keep a good supper to yourself.'

'For the last time, dear brother, this package does not contain food. It is plunder that I won in single combat, and by the laws of war it is now my private property. I must obey your commands, but I would be much happier if you didn't order me to show it.'

Any fair-minded reader will see how anxious I was to spare my brother's life, but he was determined to run upon his doom; he caught hold of the shield-strap, and lifted off over my head shield and bundle together. When he opened the leather bag he gave a gasp of surprise.

'Merciful God! The Chalice of Sorbiodunum! Look here, you can't possibly keep this to yourself, and I don't think it can even remain in the Kingdom of the Regni. Every Bishop in Britain would put us to the ban for detaining church property. Father shall decide as soon as we get home, but I think we must return it where it came from.'

'Very well, my dear brother, you had better keep it now. But it is a beautiful thing, isn't it? Just let me feel its weight in my hand once again.' I put my right hand out for the package, and as his arm came forward to pass it over I slipped the little seax-knife in my left hand into his armpit;

he staggered wildly, and I stabbed him again in the big vein of the neck.

But I have often observed that the depths of a wood is not a good place to transact private business; you always think you are alone, and someone always sees you. In this case my brother was still groaning when I heard the rending of branches, and there was old Conan, with his eyes blazing and his sword out. I dashed away down the track I had come by.

I was very tired, but the rest of the comitatus would be just as exhausted, and my Saxon equipment should give me an advantage over men in cuirasses carrying large square shields. I did not fear that I would be overtaken so long as I stuck to the woodland where ponies could not follow. I kept moving until it was fully dark, then climbed a tree and slept among the branches.

III

474–476

EXILE IN KENT – MISFORTUNES OF GERTRUDE – MY MARRIAGE IN GERMANY

I awoke feeling stiff, but still good for a long journey. I ate the grubby biscuit from the dead Saxon's pouch, and presently found a stream of water. Then I sat down to make plans. The land of the Regni was barred to me, and if I went to Dumnonia I would have to give back my Chalice; evidently I must make my way north, beyond the Forest. There were plenty of Roman Kingdoms north of the Thames and in the western parts of Britain, and their Kings would welcome a good warrior. But they would soon learn why I was an exile, and conventional public opinion is strongly against fratricide; the Kings themselves would think I had set a bad example by killing the heir to a throne, though as a rule they were pretty broadminded about the past lives of their comrades. It looked as though I would never be at ease among Romans for the rest of my life.

Then I had an inspiration. Why not try the Saxons? They would never learn of anything that had happened in Roman Britain, for there was no intercourse between such deadly enemies; I spoke German perfectly, and carried German arms; they were always eager for new recruits, and probably asked no questions. The more I thought of it the more it attracted me, and suddenly I remembered a clinching argument. I was Woden-born, and knew my pedigree; I would not only be rich, but one of their noblemen as well.

My mind made up, I set off northwards as fast as my stiff legs could carry me. It was unlikely that the Regnians would keep up the hunt for long, and they would certainly never dare to follow me into Kent, but the sooner I got clear of the Forest the better. I did not know exactly where I was, but if I kept the midday sun at my back I would probably come out among the Saxon farms. Then I could pretend to be a returning raider.

On the morning of the third day I emerged from the Forest, to find myself in the wasted borderlands. This was rather a nuisance as I was very hungry; luckily I came across a stream, and making a line from the linen of my shirt and a hook from a brooch, I caught three trout, and ate a good dinner. I have made it a rule never to leave my house without the means of making fire, in case of sudden turns of fortune; I broiled the fish on a stick.

After dinner I felt very brave, and decided that my best plan was to walk boldly up to the King's house in Durovernum and tell him that I was a Roman exile come to join his war-band; though perhaps it would be wiser not to tell him the reason for my flight. That evening I came to the first cultivated fields, where the barbarians dwelt in security. I saw a little hut standing by itself; for these savages are exceedingly morose, and dislike the company of their fellows. I made plenty of noise, to show that I came in peace, and a man with a spear came out to see what I wanted. I had a few silver coins, and I offered to pay for a hot supper and a place by the fire; he gave me food willingly, but refused to let me come inside. However, the night was fine and warm.

I set off cheerfully next morning. The way led through

fields and farms that looked very strange to Roman eyes; for the Germans use a big plough with two wheels and a deep share, drawn by a great number of oxen; as this unwieldy contraption is very difficult to turn, their ploughlands are made long and narrow. They are also great axemen, and think nothing of clearing the densest bush, so that the whole appearance of any land where they have settled down to farm is quite unlike a Roman province. The land appeared to be thickly populated; but though I saw many people no one spoke to me or inquired where I was going, and this I found later was a foible of all the Saxons. They think it dignified to ignore strangers, and not even to be interested in the news; this they call minding their own business, and it makes it very easy for outlaws to wander through their land.

By evening I had come to the hill-side that overlooks Durovernum in its marshy valley. The Roman walls had not been very strong, for the citizens had relied on their water defences; of course the town had been burnt when it changed hands, but a certain amount of stonework remained, and this had been patched with plaster and timber; judging by the smoke from the hearths there seemed to be few people living in it at present, but even so the stench from its dung-heaps could be smelt on the hill-top. It did not look a pleasant city to dwell in while I rose to wealth and independence, but I had no choice in the matter; I straightened my back and walked steadily downhill to the gap in the wall that served for a gate.

A spearman was scratching himself by the entry, and he asked me who I was and what was my business. I told him politely, in my best German, that I was an independent warrior who was tired of raiding alone, and that I had come to Durovernum to join the ever-victorious war-band of the mighty Hengist.

'We don't take every robber who applies to join us,' the sentry answered in a grudging tone. 'In any case you are late for the fair, comrade. King Hengist died last night, and we haven't yet decided who is to be the next King of the Kent-folk. But you look tired and travel worn; you may come into the city, if you feel brave enough. Only remember the King's peace dies with the King, so be watchful of strangers.'

'Thank you, noble warrior,' I replied, still being very humble and polite. 'But there must be some sort of authority in the city at the present moment, or why are you on guard at the gate?'

He looked at me with more respect, and answered in a friendly tone: 'As a matter of fact, there is more law and order than you might expect. We Jutes are a civilized people, not like those Anglian savages, and really the succession to the throne is arranged. To-morrow we shall elect Oisc, the noble son of the mighty Hengist, and I am here to keep out any other candidate who might prove troublesome on election day. You don't look like a dangerous competitor, and you may come in and welcome. But if anyone murders you to-night your family would not be able to bring suit for compensation. Don't say I didn't warn you.'

I thanked him and entered the city. There was still an hour of summer daylight, and I thought I would walk round the town and choose a quiet place to spend the night. Inside the flimsy and battered wall the place was not so deserted as it had appeared from the hill-top, and nearly all the men in the streets were fully armed warriors. I saw some shabby and depressed Romans of the lowest class; of course barbarians could not hope to keep a town habitable at all without the help of civilized craftsmen, and we had heard in Anderida that Hengist had enslaved a few masons and carpenters, to patch up the ruined houses and make the sort of furniture that Germans admire; I suppose it was better than having your throat cut, but they did not seem to be leading a happy life. It would be extremely awkward if the new King decided to add me to their number, and I made up my mind to say nothing about my Roman citizenship.

I walked humbly in the gutter that ran along the middle of the street, and gaped at the houses like any newly-landed German; it was most important that I should not get involved in a quarrel before I had hidden my treasure in a safe place. But as I walked along I was challenged by a burly warrior with a most ferocious beard.

'Now then, young man,' he shouted. 'Who are you, and where do you come from? More important still, have you paid your entry-tax at the wall? I am pretty sure you haven't, from the look of you. Never mind, just hand over your purse to me, and I will fix it with the guard. Look sharp now, and don't argue,' and he put his hand to his sword.

This was very unfortunate. I turned and ran as fast as I could, and several bystanders joined in chasing me. I thought this was the end, for I must soon be cornered in a strange town; but in the distance I saw a little group of men, with one well-dressed warrior walking in front. It has always been my experience that good leaders in war dislike unnecessary killing, while a supreme ruler is usually more merciful than his underlings. On the spur of the moment I ran straight up to him, and threw myself at his feet.

My pursuers halted a few yards away, evidently in awe of this personage. They began to explain that I was a notorious bandit and outlaw, who had refused to pay the just and necessary taxation of their glorious town; but he shouted to them to keep quiet, and ordered me to give an account of myself. However, he did not listen attentively, and some of his comrades suggested that it would be amusing to watch me being killed in the street. I could see that he had not made up his mind, and I realized that my only chance was to win his favour at once. I opened the bag that hung from my shield, and held out to him the golden Chalice. At the same time I called out in a loud voice:

'This is one of the great treasures of the Welsh. I took it from their principal town, and escaped after killing many of its guardians. I thought it would make a fitting gift for the ever-victorious Hengist, and now that he is dead there is no one more worthy to receive it than yourself, his rightful successor.' I had guessed that this must be Oisc, son of the late King.

Everyone exclaimed at the cup, and though of course Oisc could have taken it and had me slain into the bargain, he preferred to give me a present in return. He unpinned a golden brooch from his cloak, and placed it on my shoulder. I joined his comrades without another word, for now we were bound by mutual gifts, and by German ideas that made us friends for life; or at least until we quarrelled.

That was how I entered the comitatus of the King of the Kent-folk, and the fact that I joined it before he was made King gave me a status superior to the hundreds of others who made obeisance to the new sun after it had safely risen.

We lived a rather nerve-racking communal life among several of the least damaged buildings of Durovernum, which they called Cantwaraburh – the town of the Kent-folk; it was probably the only city in the world whose inhabitants were German. The Kent-folk themselves were of many different races; in oratory, which these barbarians will spin by the mile, they called themselves Jutes, but when they were not being pompous Kentish was a handy collective name for all the assorted mongrels who had come to seek their fortunes in the new land. About the only thing they had in common was that they all spoke various dialects of German, so my accent was not noticed. My position as a newcomer, but one who had exchanged unusually splendid gifts with his lord, was somewhere among the middle ranks of the comitatus, and if I did well in battle I might easily become one of the leaders. There was another thing in my favour; the day after Oisc was elected King I went to the chief poet of the court, to explain to him my pedigree. I told him that my family had lived in Britain for several generations, but my story was that we had never become Romanized, and that as soon as I was old enough to go to war I had sought out the greatest German King in Britain; actually I was twenty-three, but my newly-sprouting beard (no one in Kent shaved) made me look younger, and he accepted my tale. Furthermore, he did not doubt the account I gave him of my ancestors; he was able to check the earlier names, before King Fraomar of the Buccinobantes had come to Britain. The whole thing was in a kind of metrical chant, in very antiquated German full of obsolete words, and in short not the kind of story a liar would make up. In the end he said:

'Young man, I believe you are truly Woden-born, as you say. But we must do something about your name; the comrades will never get their tongues round Coroticus, son of Eleutherus, and it doesn't sound right for a Woden-born warrior. I shall call you Cerdic Elesing, which is near enough, and might be good German.' I have been Cerdic Elesing, which means son of Elesa, ever since.

I have said that our communal life was rather nerve-racking. This was because the comrades were always quarrelling among themselves, principally to show how brave they were. The penalty for drawing a weapon at the King's court was death; so nobody ever was killed in these quarrels, but men used to wrestle and strike one another with their fists all day long. I did my best to keep out of these fights, for I have never seen the point of getting hurt merely to win glory; though once I was compelled to bite off a man's ear to make them leave me alone. In the end they accepted me as a quiet sort of chap, without ambition to make a name in the world, and if I did not make any close friends, I had no particular enemies.

I have never been a heavy drinker, not because I think it isn't fun, but because a man with bleary eyes and a shaking hand does not live very long in a comitatus; my comrades had no other amusement, so I spent a great deal of my time wandering about by myself. I found the enslaved Roman craftsmen more amusing to talk to than Germans; they had to be quick-witted, or they would have died long ago, and they were surprisingly well informed about what the King and his counsellors were planning. I had made up my mind at the beginning that it would be an impossible strain to pretend ignorance of Celtic, but I did not speak it perfectly, as I have explained, and they never took me for a native Roman. King Oisc soon found out that I knew the language, for he knew everything about the private lives of his followers, as a leader should; he sometimes used me as an interpreter. So that during the winter I gradually drifted into the same position that my grandfather had held at his father's court, in the far-off days of peace.

The King was very proud of his ramshackle city, and did his best to keep it in good repair; this brought me into closer contact with him than would have been normal in one of my rank. As a chief Oisc was rather better than middling, though he was not an outstanding leader like his father; he had done well in his raids on some islands that lie to the north of Caledonia, and I always understood that he was a very skilful sailor, though that is a thing I am not competent to judge. But he had no ambition to conquer the whole island, as his father had always meant to do one day, and I think that at the back of his mind was a hankering to rule a peaceful and prosperous state; though this was such a disgraceful ambition for a Woden-born warrior to harbour that he tried to conceal it from the comrades. If he had taken service as an auxiliary under a Roman Empire that was still a going concern, he might have ended up as another Stilicho or Fullofaudes, for all his instincts were in favour of law and civilization. But in Britain things had gone too far already; every year there was less and less civilization for him to defend. All he could do was to run his own little Kingdom according to the traditions of the best German rulers.

Unfortunately it was not a good tradition. These Germans are much too keen on assigning a rank, with appropriate rights and duties, to all their subjects. We Romans have the broad division between slave and free, and in the days when our law-courts still functioned there was also the legal distinction between honestiores and humiliores, that is roughly between rich and poor; but in a great many things all citizens were equal before the law, and certainly we didn't think of these differences every minute of our lives. In the German system there are endless grades between the first-class free man and the out-and-out slave, and everybody is conscious of them all the time. To King Oisc it seemed very wrong that his Roman subjects should be ignorant of these important matters, and he was always trying to fit them into their appropriate ranks; he used to get very angry when he discovered that the slaves took no interest in the matter at all, and he blamed me for not explaining properly. Of course, the Roman craftsmen were slaves all right, but they had no wish to improve their position. They had in practice a great deal of liberty, for none of the Germans were skilful enough to tell them how to do their jobs, and they dreaded being given arms and told to join the levy of the Kingdom. However, King Oisc chose to be angry with me because he couldn't turn rather cowardly citizens into good spearmen, and by mid-winter I had lost my influential and promising position as his interpreter.

I was thrown very much on my own resources for amusement. As I have said, the comrades bored me dreadfully, and I thought it wiser not to go about with the Roman slaves in public. In the spring I was at a loose end. It was widely known that the new King was too busy playing at being a civilized ruler to lead us out on campaign unless Kent was invaded. Without even fighting in prospect to keep me occupied (though I have never enjoyed warfare for its own sake as a son of Woden should), I cast round for some hobby to fill my leisure. The obvious thing to do was to start a love-affair, taking care to choose some girl I could not possibly marry, or I might find myself trapped.

It had struck me when I first came to live with the comrades that in matters of sex they were neglecting their opportunities. The men of a comitatus in any Kingdom are expected to live together; but they need not be celibate, and the comitatus of the Regni always had a squad of girl-friends in attendance except when they were on campaign. Considering that these Germans had conquered a substantial part of the most civilized district in Britain, and had raided a great deal more, they must have had many chances of carrying off pretty girls, but I have already explained that the Saxons have no organized slave-market, and they raid very wastefully, killing every human being they meet. On the whole, the comitatus was not interested in female Romans.

Some of the more elderly were married, and they all hoped to marry some day, so that the high descent in which they took such pride should continue to posterity; but naturally, considering the importance they attached to pedigree, their wives were all German. These were mostly a plain lot, pompous and stupid, and their husbands did not seem to have a very enjoyable time.

The position of these women was curious, and not at all what I had been accustomed to in Anderida. Once a German girl was married she was trusted utterly, and it was assumed that she would be just as shocked at the bare idea of adultery as her lawful master would be if she betrayed him; consequently these large, plain, hardworking women were allowed an astonishing amount of freedom, and could wander about alone, and talk to strange men, in a way that would have blasted the reputation of a respectable Roman matron. They were quite genuinely too proud to take lovers; it is wonderful what early education can do to the human character, particularly when it appeals to the sense of honour.

There were not a great many unmarried barbarian girls in Kent, for most of the men sent back to Germany when they wanted a wife, and the settlement was too recent for large families to have grown up; but there were a few, and they were not at all like the matrons in their behaviour. Among these queer people the maidens have a great deal of choice as to which man they will marry, or at least they can refuse the man of their parents' choosing; so naturally they spend much of their time dreaming about the wonders and delights of love. Even a pompous German father realizes that it is not safe to let them run about loose in this condition. The unmarried girls are carefully watched, lest they should form an attachment to a hopelessly unsuitable young man. I fell into that category, as a second-rank warrior of the comitatus, and the fathers of marriageable daughters were not eager to introduce me into their families.

But there was in Cantwaraburh one exception to all the rules of good German behaviour, and that was the King's own sister, the lady Gertrude. She was about twenty years old, and should have married long ago, but her father, the late King, had been absurdly fond of her, and let her have her way in everything; she had been able to reject each of the eligible young men he had suggested. King Oisc had been jealous of her all his life, and took no trouble to get her suitably married; it looked as though she would live and die a virgin. She was not at all an amorous young woman, as far as I could see, and like many of these big German girls preferred hunting with the young warriors to the normal womanly amusements. But she had this much in common with the brother who disliked her, that she yearned after the refinements of civilization; in her undisciplined barbarian way she was eager to be taught, and one day in the early summer she found out that I had something of a Roman education. She sought me out, and commanded me to tell her all about the strange peoples of the distant parts of the world, the subject in which her quick but untrained mind took most interest at that time. Neither she nor any other of the Saxons thought it odd or unseemly that she should go for long walks alone with a young man; she had been nubile for six years, and during that time she had never felt any inclination to the opposite sex, and I suppose she imagined she never would. Germans are great people for precedent, and her relatives, including the King, felt the same.

But I didn't. In Anderida I had always been able to get my way with any peasant-girl that I fancied, though of course I was helped by my position as the King's son; and I thought it rather insulting that this priggish young woman should treat me as though I were a eunuch. I was as bored as any other warrior in peace time and I thought it would be amusing to wake her up, and see if she had any of the usual human passions.

Gertrude was certainly a very strange sort of person. That is how everyone thought of her, as a person and not as a young virgin; in itself that shows how extraordinary she was. Actually she was not unattractive in a physical sense; she was much too big for Roman taste, but everything was correctly in proportion, and a good hairdresser with a box of face-paint could have made her an excellent statue of Minerva. She had yellow hair and blue eyes, of course, like all well-born German ladies, and her face was of the type that gets redder and redder from exposure to the weather, never settling down to an attractive brown; though I discovered later that her skin, where it was normally covered by her clothes, was very white and fine. Her hands also were bright red, and much too large, and her feet looked enormous in thick woollen stockings and shapeless Saxon shoes. But her tall body curved in and out in the correct places, and when my eyes grew accustomed to her scale I saw that she moved gracefully.

I remember the day when things came to a climax. It was June, and Gertrude sent a message that I was to take her out after dinner to walk in the meadows; such a message from the King's sister was of course a command, though I would have preferred to rest in the shade after the midday meal. Accordingly I went round to the entrance of the women's quarters while the sun was still high, and she joined me at once, without keeping me waiting as a Roman lady would have done; she liked to keep appointments punctually, because she thought that made her more like a man, and she made very little difference in her appearance whether she was in the women's quarters or out in the fields. I remember how she was dressed, in a sleeveless blue woollen gown and a battered hat of straw with a broad brim; below the short skirt of the gown her legs were clothed in the usual thick stockings, and on her feet were colossal leather shoes. It always struck me as odd that these Germans, though they felt the heat extremely, always thought it correct to swaddle their legs. The women were as sensitive about their knees as Roman ladies are about their breasts.

You will gather that on this occasion Gertrude's appearance was not in the least enhanced by art; but the thin blue gown, caught in at the waist by an embroidered leather belt, enabled me to follow all the movements of her healthy young body, and in any case I had not seen a decent complexion since I left home. As soon as we were in the sweet-smelling hay-meadows she turned to me her serious gaunt face, and prepared to imbibe instruction. She had not come out to be amused, and first she laid down the scope of the lesson:

'Cerdic Elesing, on our last walk you told me all that you could remember about the countries of the eastern part of the world, and the peoples who live there. Now we come to the third of the three parts into which the world is divided. Tell me about that third part, in the far south.'

'Very well, my lady. The third division of the world is called Africa, though as far as I know there is no reason for the name, no story about a lady and a God. You will understand that I have never been there, and that I am only telling you what was told to me.' (This I said because the Saxons consider it disgraceful to tell a lie when they are supposed to be teaching, though in the ordinary affairs of life they will lie like a horse-coper.) 'It lies south of the great central sea that is a highway for all civilized men, and because it lies to the south the climate is warmer than that of other lands. Don't ask me why, it is a general rule that sailors will confirm from experience. The land is very fruitful. The chief city is called Carthage, and it is one of the greatest cities in the world. There are no enemies living near, for a great desert stretches to the south, and the Ocean bounds it on the west; so it is not an important command, though enormous taxes are collected. It has very little history; the Romans conquered it five hundred years ago, after three great wars. It is not nearly such an interesting subject as the east, and that is all I learned about it in my youth.'

I was getting rather bored with these lessons in elementary geography, and most of what I had read about Africa had been concerned with the heresies that flourished there, and the rebellions that had followed them; things that I really could not explain to a pagan barbarian. But Gertrude had a naturally inquiring mind, and she wanted a picture of the world she was living in. My little exposition at the beginning of the walk was only a framework that she would fill in by asking a great many questions.

'You learnt that by heart when you were a small boy,' she said. 'Now tell me what you have heard about this great country since, and whether everything is going as smoothly for the Romans at the present time as it was then. I am not interested in the past.'

'Certainly, lady. Of course things have altered for the worse in the last twenty years; is there any part of the world where they have not? What I have just told you was true until not very long ago; now Africa has been overrun by barbarians, or rather I should say by a race of noble Germans. They are called the Vandals, and they originally came from the north of Germany, somewhere to the east of the noble Saxons, of whom the noblest are the Jutes. These Vandals now live in great splendour, and grow rich by piracy in the central sea. They have become Christians, though I believe of the wrong sort, and they oppress the native church. I have heard all this from the Roman priests in Britain, and I gather they are very worried about it.'

This was the sort of story that Gertrude liked to hear, and she pressed me for more details. When she at last understood that I had never learned the pedigrees of the Vandal Kings, so that she could not find out in what degree they were her cousins (for all noble Germans are related if you go back far enough among their ancestors, a hobby that noble Germans pursue with enthusiasm), she turned to asking more questions about the land itself. Accounts of the Roman world she found rather dull, for civilization seemed to her a boring routine, instead of the exciting and precarious adventure it really is; but the idea of a desert that no man had ever crossed fired her imagination, and she questioned me eagerly about the far south.

'What is the matter with this desert, that no man has ever crossed it? Are you sure there is no way round? Even if there is no water for travellers to drink, the same thing is true of the sea, and we cross it in all directions. I can't believe it is really too hot for human beings to live. If the people just to the north find the weather cool enough to work in the fields, a man should be able to walk gently to the south. I don't think your Roman friends are very brave explorers.'

'Perhaps not, noble lady. But I imagine the real reason why no one has made the attempt is that there seems nothing to be gained by it. In any case, the fame of the Empire as a good place to trade in, or to plunder for that matter, is very widely spread, and if nobody comes to us from the south across the desert, it must be because there is no one living there.'

'This is very interesting. I like discussing difficult journeys; it is one of the best deeds a noble German can perform to accomplish them, and I don't see why a woman should not do it as well as a man. Sit down here in the shade. Now tell me, has anyone tried going round by sea?'

She turned and stared at me with a puzzled frown on her weather-beaten forehead, as though we were seriously discussing a possible plan of campaign. We were sitting on the ground, our shoulders almost touching, yet she seemed only to be aware of me as a voice. Damn it all, this was not the way the girls of the Regni used to look into my eyes; I cast round for some way to wake her up and make the conversation more interesting.

'My dear Gertrude,' I began, which was in itself a new departure, for up to now I had never called her anything more intimate than noble lady. 'Those Romans are not a seafaring people. They think it impious to tempt Fate by sailing out upon the boundless Ocean, and have written several excellent poems to that effect. The tradition has been handed down that Africa is surrounded by the Ocean, and that you can sail round it if you try hard enough, but the Romans have had other things to think about in the last few years.'

'Then that is the way I shall win immortal fame, which is such a difficult thing for a woman to achieve,' said this earnest and ridiculous young barbarian. 'I know my brother will give me a ship if I ask him, for he is always longing to get rid of me. Will you come with me as shipmaster? I don't think you have much of a future here.'

'Of course, my dear; there is nothing I would like better than to follow you to the ends of the earth,' I answered, gazing at her with all the fervour I could assume. 'We will go on until we find a stretch of fertile ground, ringed round by the desert and the sea, and there we will build a hall where no enemies can reach us, and no King can summon us to follow him in war. We shall live as they did in the Golden Age, when our grandfather Woden travelled the earth, and rewarded those who showed him hospitality.'

She moved closer to me, until we were touching.

'Do you think we could start this journey quite soon?' this grown woman asked in the voice of a child. 'You know that I am older than most virgins; it is important to do your great deeds when you are young, so that you have plenty of time to enjoy fame before you die. We must remember to take a good poet with us, and arrange to send him back when we are settled in our new land.'

'You and I can make plans for ourselves, and that is a thing I shall look forward to doing, but I don't think we should tell anyone else just yet. Summer has begun already, and by the time we got a ship loaded it would be too late to start a voyage. Let it be a secret between the two of us; we can discuss it together during our walks, if we go into the woods alone.'

After that it was pretty easy. We went off nearly every day to some thicket where we could be unobserved, and there Gertrude would babble to me about her wonderful new enterprise; a shared secret is a wonderfully intimate bond. Please don't think that I was deeply in love with her; I have never been attracted by earnest young women, even if they are properly educated, and her total ignorance of what she was talking about made her a formidable bore. But she had an excellent body under that plain and serious face, and of course it was a great triumph, and a good score over all the men of Kent, to seduce the King's sister. Every night when I lay down to sleep in the crowded and noisy hall of the comitatus I could feel my self-esteem growing in a most comforting manner. I am enough of a German to find plenty of self-esteem necessary to my happiness.

One day in the middle of October Gertrude told me that she was expecting a child. This was very disturbing news, and I had no plan ready for the emergency. But she tried to persuade me that all would come right in the end, if we were tactful with King Oisc.

'Let us catch him in a good mood, and tell him everything. You are only a poor comrade, but you are also Woden-born; the child will be Woden-born on both sides. When we sail away to our new country, people will remember your noble descent, not your present position. We can have a solemn marriage when the winter feasts begin, and it ought to make my brother all the more eager to give us a ship, so that he can get rid of us. I will watch him to-night after supper, and when he has drunk the right amount I shall tell him the whole story.'

This would never do at all. The King did not like or trust me, and he had always been against his sister marrying anyone, for fear she should produce a family to compete with his own children for the succession to the throne. In any case, after supper was the worst time to approach him, for he was one of those unfortunate people whom drink renders more bad-tempered than they were when they sat down.

'Look here, my little darling,' I said in my most winning voice, looking into that earnest and crimson face. 'You know how angry guardians feel when the virgins in their keeping are seduced. The King will order you to be cut down before he even bothers to find out the father.

Particularly at supper-time you will not have a chance to explain the excellent reasons why it all happened. By the way, why did it happen? You always told me you knew something that had been told you by your old nurse. It isn't like you to be careless and slapdash.'

'Oh, Cerdic, my darling, I wanted to bear your child. I could have stopped it earlier on, but I deliberately didn't. Just think what a son of ours will be like; we are the two most intelligent people in Kent, so he is bound to be marvellously wise. Then you are beautiful and brave, and you always tell me that I am quite well-built, so he ought to be as handsome as Baldur. Furthermore, he will be Woden-born on both sides, and a fitting chief for any race of the noble Germans. It would be a shame and a waste to end his existence before he is born.'

'I quite see your point, my darling, though of course he may turn out to be a girl. The trouble is that the King will probably see it too; a fitting leader for any race of the noble Germans, and the men of Kent in particular, is just what he doesn't want you to produce. We shall have to keep this a secret, and arrange for a loyal and trustworthy foster-mother as soon as the child is secretly born. Can you think of any good excuse to go away and hide, before your figure becomes noticeable?'

Though I spoke as pleasantly as I knew how, inwardly I was boiling with rage. I had given a pleasant time to an extremely plain girl, who would never have had the slightest chance of a lover if I had not volunteered, and who knew perfectly well that the King did not want her ever to give birth to a son. Instead of appreciating my efforts to give her a little fun the silly fool had taken the whole thing much too seriously, as though it was an eternal passion and the main business of our lives. She was quite prepared to risk a horrible death for herself; that was her own affair, and I did not greatly care whether she was welcomed as the prospective mother of a wonder-child, or carved into a disgusting mess before all the comrades. But when the King learned that she was pregnant his second idea, after taking a suitable revenge on her, would be to find the man responsible for her plight. The news threw me into such a state of nerves that I could think of nothing but gaining time. I persuaded Gertrude to keep things quiet for the present, while I tried desperately to work out some scheme that would ensure my own safety, and if it was feasible, hers as well.

It was not easy to think of a really safe plan, and all the time this confounded baby was growing inside her. The obvious thing to do was to run away, but where was I to run to? If I went back to any Roman city the ruler would soon find out that I had been serving the barbarians, and naturally the penalty for that was death. There were other scattered settlements of Germans to the north of the estuary of the Thames, and I believe all the way up the east coast of Britain, but most of them were based on ties of kindred, and I was not their kin; they would hand me over to the vengeance of King Oisc as soon as he asked for my body. Still, unless I had a very ready tongue, it would certainly come to a flight; I began to take precautions, as secretly as I could in that crowded and inquisitive environment. I marked down a little shed outside the city where a farmer was accustomed to shut up a fairly good horse, and bit by bit I smuggled out my valuables and buried them in the earth near by. I would have liked to hide my weapons in the same place, but all the comrades kept them in the hall, and spent a lot of time cleaning them and fussing over them generally; they would soon have noticed if I had no equipment to look after.

An added trouble was that Gertrude had no reliable

women friends, who might have kept her in some retired spot on the excuse that she was ill with an infectious disease, and then farmed out the baby if she would not allow it to be destroyed. She had been so busy all her life posing as the most intelligent girl in Kent that she was thoroughly unpopular; her contemporaries would be delighted to learn that this female who knew everything, and frequently told them so, was as much the slave of her passions as any peasant woman.

It was in the middle of December that the long-expected blow at last fell. There was going to be a great feast that night, in honour of some German god whose name I forget, and to help us to get through the long dark evenings. In the afternoon Gertrude took me aside, and told me that she had made up her mind to confess everything to the King at the feast. There was nothing I could do to stop her, but at least I had several hours' warning, and could make a few preparations; I hid a little food by my secret stable, and stowed my valuables where I could pick them up quickly. The afternoons were short, and work in the fields would stop early on account of the feast, so my horse should be fairly fresh; also, on such a night I would have a good excuse to wear all my silver armlets.

I was deliberately a little late for supper, and entered the hall when the tables were already full; this gave me a chance to take a lower seat than I was entitled to, and the lowest seats were conveniently near the door. It promised to be a rowdy party later on, and many comrades had put away their weapons which normally hung on the wall, for fear they might be damaged; I said I didn't want to go out again after I had come in so late, so I put my sword, shield, and helmet underneath the bench I was sitting on. This was technically against the rules of the King's court, but nobody minded in the least; the rule had been made so that drunken men should not find their weapons handy if they wanted to fight, but they all knew that I seldom got drunk, and even then was never quarrelsome. Why did I go there at all, instead of getting a good start while everyone was feasting? Because there was, after all, a chance that King Oisc would be won over by his sister's plea, and I should look very silly if I was missing when they sought me to be married to the daughter of King Hengist.

There was the usual gala-day supper, great rounds of half-roasted beef and pork, swimming in grease, and an unlimited flow of muddy beer, unstrained and full of barley-husks. This suited me well enough, for the comrades could not chase me very fast when they were full; I myself ate very little, giving the excuse that I was suffering from toothache.

On these occasions the Saxons always eat as fast as they can, for plentiful food is not a rare treat to them, and they are anxious to get on to the serious drinking. In half an hour the wooden platters were empty; Roman slaves passed round the tables, slopping beer into any empty horn they could reach, and a poet tried to make himself heard above the noise of Germans drinking and boasting with their mouths full. It was always on these occasions that I felt myself farthest from my own people, contrasting the noise, the squalor, and the stench, with the elegant supper parties in my father's house at Anderida. After another hour the poet had shouted himself hoarse, and most of the feasters had said all they wanted to say; there was a lull in the proceedings, and the King sitting at the far end of the hall banged on the table with his gold-mounted drinking-horn.

This was a signal for any petitioners to present their complaints. It is an old custom among the Jutes that any subject can speak face to face with the King when he has eaten and drunk, and is at leisure. In old King Hengist's time this was a valued privilege, for he was just and good-tempered, and Germans thought him merciful; but not many people cared to try it with King Oisc, who was subject to blinding fits of rage, and thought it a sign of strong-mindedness never to alter a decision, even when it had been given in anger. For all his wish to found an imitation of a Roman city he was a cruel man, and he enjoyed watching executions carried out in his presence.

So to-night no one rose from his place in the hall to ask for the King's justice, and he was about to give the signal to begin drinking again when Gertrude entered through the door at the far end of the hall. Of course the Germans keep their virgins, and those whom they hope are virgins, away from these drunken and riotous feasts; and on this occasion even the married women were at home, though they sometimes come to parties. So all heads were turned to look at Gertrude, and some people muttered that it was just like her conceit to come butting in on a purely masculine function.

Everyone was staring at her, but if I made a sudden dash for the door they would spot me very quickly, and I should not have time to get to the horse I needed; also, of course, there was the outside chance that King Oisc would not be angry after all. I pretended to find a fragment of food between my teeth, and put most of my hand inside my mouth, as these barbarians frequently do; but secretly I stuck a finger deep into my throat, so that I could make myself vomit at will. Then I could leave the room without exciting remark; there was a trough along the inside of the wall where all relieved themselves, but even the comrades preferred that those who wanted to be sick should do it outside.

The hall was long, and there was a certain amount of

noise, though the King had ordered silence. I could not hear what Gertrude said, but she seemed to be trying to brazen things out. She stood there proudly, with her back straight and her burdened belly sticking out, and no doubt she told the King how lucky he was to have such a wonderful nephew on the way. Oisc did not take long to make up his mind; he gave a sudden roar of rage, and two captains who were sitting at his table sprang up and caught hold of the unfortunate woman. I did not wait to see any more; I pushed with my finger, retched over the table, and made my way, gagging, to the door. It may have looked odd to take out my sword and shield when I was only leaving for a few minutes, but my neighbours said nothing.

I never set eyes on that tiresome woman again; years later I had the curiosity to inquire what exactly had happened to her, and I was told that Oisc made her into a Bloody Eagle on the spot. This is a Saxon way of inflicting a painful death, and consists in cutting the victim's ribs loose from the backbone, and pulling them outwards and forwards, so that the body looks rather like a bird with wings outspread; it is a horribly messy thing to do, especially in a dining-hall, but actually the culprit does not suffer for very long.

Of course everybody stayed in the hall to watch the execution, and then they must have sat on arguing as to who had dared to seduce the King's sister; it would not have taken a sober man long to guess that I was responsible, but then none of them were outstandingly sober. Anyway, I had climbed the rickety city wall, and saddled my horse, before I heard the commotion of the pursuit. I galloped due north; they all knew I was a man of the Forest and that I had never left Britain, and they would expect me to strike inland.

The southern shore of the Thames estuary is a maze of

marshes and mud-flats. When I reached it I tethered my horse, and sat down to wait for daylight. I had already made up my mind to cross the sea; if I went back to the Romans I would sooner or later be charged with fratricide, and Oisc would get hold of me if I lingered among the German settlements of the east coast; but in the homeland of the Saxons I ought to be safe from the King of the Kent-folk. As soon as light showed in the east I began to walk along the beach, leading my horse, and soon came to the hut of a Saxon fisherman.

The inmates were still asleep; I suppose they also had been celebrating the feast. I tied my horse, and then burst in the door, sword in hand. The man of the house jumped in front of his children; all Saxons are prepared for death by violence every minute of their lives, and he did not give way to hysterics as a colonus would have done; I was able to argue with him and spare his life.

'Good morning,' I said pleasantly. 'I have very urgent business in Germany just now, and I rather fancy that King Oisc would not like me to leave his Kingdom. In short, I want a boat, small enough to manage single-handed. Now I can either kill you and take your boat, or you can give it to me peaceably, and I will let you have this excellent horse in exchange. Which is it to be?'

He was a calm and sensible man; very soon he was helping me to haul out a sturdy little fishing-boat, with a sail and a pair of oars. The fact that he was taking the stolen horse in exchange would ensure that he kept his mouth shut about the whole affair, and there was every chance that King Oisc would never learn that I had fled the country.

December is the wrong time of year to go sailing, and a single-handed voyage is always a strain. But in fact my journey to the home of the Saxons was not nearly as bad as the crossing of the Forest I had achieved after the defeat of Count Ambrosius. The tide carried me out of the estuary of the Thames, while I kept steerage-way with an occasional stroke of the oars; once in the open sea I hoisted the little sail and a strong westerly wind took me the way I wanted to go. On the third morning I sighted a low sandy coast. I could see the many mouths of a great river a few miles to the south, and I knew that there must be villages, and even towns, over there; but I wanted to land unobserved, so I steered northwards and ran my boat aground in a little creek among empty dunes. I drank some very nasty water from a brackish marsh, then scraped a burrow between two high dunes, and slept soundly for the whole of that day and the next night.

In the morning I set out to find a chieftain's hall to winter in. At bottom I have always been a civilized man, accustomed to dwelling among my fellows, and though I like a little privacy I am never happy for long as a solitary outlaw. I felt lonely, and wanted to chat, even with a thick-headed German.

If this was the homeland of the Saxons I was not surprised that they should brave the perils of the Ocean, and the assembled armies of all the Kings of Britain, to win other farms at the point of the sword. The tide was creeping in through many little gaps in the belt of dunes, and it looked as though the whole land was turned into swamp twice daily. The crops they could raise in their sodden fields must be scanty in the extreme, and the floors of their huts always muddy. I could see no cottages scattered separately, such as the Kent-folk use, but in the distance was a low ridge, and huddled on it a cluster of thatched roofs; a small village would suit me best as a stopping-place, where I could learn something about the political organization of the country; I trudged wearily towards it.

I slung my shield on my back to show that I came in peace, and shouted at the top of my voice as soon as I was within earshot. Presently three spearmen came down to meet me. I undid my sword-belt, laid down my weapons, and sat on the ground until they came up; they had no excuse for treating me as an enemy, and like most farmers they were men of peace. Of course their language was just the same as my old nurse Ursula's, and they were quite willing to listen to my story. I had got over the most difficult obstacle in entering a strange land; many peaceful travellers are killed because the first men they meet are suspicious warriors, who strike without waiting for an explanation.

I told them quite a good tale, with enough truth in it to seem plausible; I had obviously come from Britain, not only because of the direction of my approach, but because my jewellery could have been made in no other country than Kent. I said that I had been one of the first children born there, when Hengist was still living in peace with the Romans, and that I had served in the royal comitatus all my life; I had done very well in the raids, as they could see from my apparel, and I intended to be a professional pirate in future; I had only left King Oisc, who had the highest regard for me, because he had spent the whole of last summer at peace, and I was tired of such a pusillanimous leader. They all grunted to one another when they heard that I had crossed the Ocean by myself; it was obvious that I must have fled secretly, but I was not going to do their village any harm, and it was none of their business. In the end, after I had mentioned that I was in a position to offer them suitable gifts in return for a few days' food and lodging, they said I might stay in their village until I found a better place; but they warned me that the sea had so encroached on their fields that they were short of food, and could not take in any more permanent settlers. (This business of giving presents is rather a burden in Germany; no free German will ever sell you anything, for fear of being regarded as a covetous merchant; but they all expect a substantial gift in return for the simplest service, and it works out more expensive in the end than if they allowed you to pay your way.)

The headman put a hut at my disposal, an old woman came in each morning to cook my food, and they all did their utmost to give me a comfortable time. But I did not enjoy my rest, for now I was among the really untouched aboriginal Germans, and my Roman upbringing has unfitted me for such savagery. The comitatus of the Kent-folk were a set of noisy and uncouth ruffians, but they were after all well-born nobles according to German ideas; here I was among the lowest class of German peasant, and their bestial ignorance, filth, and grossness were quite indescribable. There were no warriors in the village, for any young man of spirit left to seek his fortune abroad when he was old enough to bear arms.

On my second day I had a long talk with the headman, a shrewd old peasant whose wisdom was so revered that he had nothing to do all day long but sit in the sun, while others looked after his swine. He told me there were a great many Kings among the confederation of the Saxons (for it is a confederation rather than a race), since any Woden-born noble had a good claim to a throne; it was easy to gather a war-band, and those who could not win a territory at home took their men abroad rather than submit to another ruler. I mentioned that I was Woden-born myself, and he grunted that any warrior with armlets like mine would be, and then at once told me I would get no recruits in his village. It is curious that I have never heard a German doubt a stranger who claimed to be Woden-born, though some of them are more impressed by the claim than others.

I then asked him who were the Kings reigning at present in the homeland of the noble Saxons; but of that he was entirely ignorant, for none of them had been in the neighbourhood to bother him lately. He had heard the name of one chieftain who lived not far away, though he believed this man had never taken the title of King; he was called Aella, and he had spent much of his youth in Britain. Now he was said to be recruiting a war-band, though as it was his first venture not many well-known heroes had come to his hall. This was very interesting. I had heard about Aella when I myself was in Kent; he had the reputation of a cunning though cautious leader, and he had been second-in-command to Hengist at the great defeat of Count Ambrosius, when Oisc was away in the north. Men said that he might have seized the throne on Hengist's death, if he had not previously gone off to Germany in a huff over some question of the division of the spoil. I made up my mind at once that here was the leader for me.

After five days I left the village, whose name, if it had one, I never got to know. I don't think my health would have endured a longer stay; lice and bugs always spoil my sleep, and though the old woman who looked after me frequently hunted through my head, I think she enjoyed the chase and would not destroy the stock entirely.

The headman gave me bread for the journey, and directions how to find the hall of the noble Aella. The country was extremely peaceful, for it was too poor to attract plunderers, and on the evening of the second day I reached my destination without incident. Aella's hall was a long narrow timber building, constructed without the use of iron nails or mortar; but the roof was of shingles instead of thatch, which distinguished it from a granary. A flimsy stockade of thorns enclosed it at a little distance, more to mark out the boundaries of Aella's peace than as a serious defence, and a spearman was stationed in the opening. He seemed quite pleased to see me, and actually smiled as he asked my business, which is not at all the German custom. I told him the truth, though not all of it, saying that I was a Woden-born warrior who had served in the comitatus of Kent, and was now seeking a new employer. He answered that the noble Aella had just sat down to supper, and that I was welcome to enter.

'But there is one rule here that you must obey,' he continued. 'That new King of the Kent-folk once tried to get my lord murdered, and now all strangers have to leave their weapons here with me. Please don't take it as an insult; the rule is the same for all, and many noble Germans have submitted to it with good grace. In any case, you will find the comrades a very quiet and decent set of men, and they will be sober at this time of the evening. If the noble Aella accepts you into his war-band, you can come straight back here for your sword.'

This was not the usual German welcome to strangers. As a rule these people are moderately hospitable; they never turn away a guest, and seldom murder him unless there is a good reason for it. But their sentries consider it right to be as surly as possible. This comitatus seemed to show a more friendly spirit.

I unbuckled my swordbelt and left my weapons with the guard; though he allowed me to keep my seaxknife, which is the badge of a free man, and without which I would not have been properly dressed. I even gave him my helmet, and entered the hall bare-headed, to show that I was willing to do more than was asked of me.

Inside, the hall was painted a cheerful red and lit by a trench of blazing fire running down the middle; in the aisles formed by the wooden roof-pillars were long boards for the comrades, and the high table was set across the far end. As I walked up beside the fire I was struck by the low buzz of talk from the company; it sounded as though everyone was chatting pleasantly to his neighbour, instead of boasting at the top of his voice as they did in Cantwaraburh. This was the first real German hall I had been into as opposed to the makeshift that Hengist had fitted up in the remains of a Roman building, and it seemed to be a more friendly place than I had expected.

Aella was a middle-aged man, very splendidly dressed with abundance of Kentish jewellery. Of course a noble who was gathering a war-band must look as rich as possible, to show prospective recruits how good he is at gathering spoil; but his brooches and collars were arranged with taste, and his whole appearance would not have disgraced a Roman supper party. He smiled at me when I reached the table, and waited for me to speak first; I told him what I had already told the sentry. When I had finished he positively beamed at me, and actually swallowed the food in his mouth before answering, a thing I have never seen done by any other German.

'Young man, you seem to be just what I am looking for,' he said. 'I am gathering a war-band for an expedition to Britain when the next sailing season comes round. I have picked a first-rate crowd of comrades; but very few of them have ever been overseas before, and we could do with a trustworthy guide. I have a prejudice against the comitatus of Kent, who cheated me shamefully in the division of the spoil; but you must have joined them recently, or I would remember your face. And I don't imagine things went very smoothly when you left, or you would not have fled alone at this time of year. However, you can tell me all about that later, if you feel like it, of course; I am not inquisitive about the past life of my comrades. Now just put your hand on this collar of mine, which is engraved with runes and intensely magical, and swear to be a faithful comrade to me and my friends, and the enemy of my enemies; then you can get your weapons and sit down to supper. I must remember to call you cousin, since Woden is your ancestor and mine.'

The whole atmosphere of this new comitatus was quite strange to me. The only Germans I had known had been the mercenaries of Count Ambrosius, poor and unsuccessful spearmen whom all other barbarians despised, and the comrades of King Oisc, whose conquests had gone to their heads, so that they prided themselves on being savage and tough. This new war-band took its tone from its leader; Aella was the son of a high-ranking officer of Roman foederati, and had been brought up to use civil manners and polite speech. Furthermore, most of the comrades were untried warriors; they had nothing to boast about, and there was no tradition that they should show their courage by fighting among themselves. Altogether they were quite pleasant companions, and I began to understand what the ancient writer Tacitus had been able to see in the Germans, which had always puzzled me in the past. They are utter savages, of course, but they can be trained into quite good imitations of civilized men, if their leaders set a good example.

I settled down among these pleasant comrades. At the back of my mind was still the hankering after complete independence that has been the guiding motive of my life, but I was beginning to be resigned to the thought that I might never achieve it. In the last two years I had been unlucky in my dealings with those near and dear to me, and an unvarnished account of my past life would not attract the best type of follower if I set up on my own. Of course, I had to kill my brother when he set about depriving me of my rightful spoil; all the same other people, hearing about it without knowing all the circumstances, might think I was to blame; fratricide has as ugly a sound in Germany as in Britain.

I was confirmed in my resolve to keep silent about this episode by the bad reception of the story of my flight from Kent. During the Yule-feast I told Aella the whole business, thinking that it would increase his confidence in me, as a deadly foe to King Oisc. To my surprise, he frowned fiercely, and said it was nothing to be proud of; he seemed to think I should have made an effort to rescue Gertrude, and died gloriously in the King's hall with my sword out. In vain I protested that I had never been in love with her, and that I certainly did not want to be tied to her for life; he answered that if that was so I should never have seduced her in the first place, and I saw that I had fallen in his estimation. After the way this story of my resourcefulness and quick wit was received I decided not to tell my leader any more about my past life.

Aella himself was rather a contradictory character; he was never tired of preaching the advantages of caution, and the stupidity of throwing away your life for the sake of a glorious reputation after death; but I think he was always so emphatic about this because his true nature was strongly tempted in the opposite direction. Certainly he had a rather un-German conception of honour. To most barbarians the word means no more than prestige, but Aella had his standards, and he would not depart from them. He had thrown up his command in Kent because he had been falsely suspected of keeping back a valuable sword, instead of adding it to the common stock. He said that the particular matter could easily have been cleared up, for he knew where the sword was hidden, but he preferred to leave a comitatus whose comrades thought him capable of such an action. He was very easy-going, and a delightful leader in peace time, but always I was aware of those unswerving moral standards underneath, and I feared his displeasure more even than that of Count Ambrosius.

He had his hankerings after civilization; in fact every German I knew at all intimately disclosed the same secret longing; but they find it too difficult to keep the rules, and they are very sensitive to ridicule. He knew that I had done some things in the past which he considered very wrong, but he was quite certain that I would improve under his leadership. Though in anyone else I would have thought this the most outrageous impudence, Aella was so serious about being a good influence over his men that I took it from him without a murmur.

He confided to me his ambition to found a civilized state, with an aristocracy of brave German warriors supported by a Roman peasantry and educated Roman officials. But the chance to do that had really passed a generation ago, and he used to lament that the West had been spoiled before he grew to manhood.

'The Vandals and both branches of the Gothic race had all the luck,' he complained to me on one occasion. 'In Italy and Africa and Spain the people submitted without fighting, or at most after losing one big battle. The land was not hopelessly smashed up by years of warfare, and the Christian priests handed over an intact civilization after the Emperor's soldiers had fled. The Germans had the good sense to adopt the very latest and most fashionable variety of the Christian religion, and now no Roman is ashamed to serve them. But the Romans in Britain are so confoundedly war-like; we have beaten them in the field time and again, but they always come back for more. The result is that by the time we have conquered a new tract of land it has been reduced to a howling wilderness. You served among the Saxon mercenaries of Count Ambrosius, and you must have had some contact with the peasantry. Do you think that if I went to an untouched part of Britain, where there has been no serious fighting so far, I could chase out the rulers in one quick campaign, and get the peasants and citizens to recognize me as their King?'

I had been forced to tell Aella all about the campaigns of Count Ambrosius and the part I had played in them; for he knew that I had not been in the comitatus of the Kent-folk while he was serving there himself. He thought none the worse of me when I explained that I had served faithfully for as long as I was paid, and had stuck by my leader until the whole army was dissolved in defeat. Now I answered him truthfully, as his inquiring mind deserved.

'I think, noble Aella, that you yourself might be able to carry out such a plan, if you could find some remote land where the Saxon name was not already hated. But you could never do it with the followers you now have. Your war-band is made up of young Saxons and Frisians who have most of them never left Germany; they are brave men of noble birth and the most impeccable honour, but do you yourself imagine that you will be able to prevent them murdering every man they come across in Roman land? You could never persuade them to spare the coloni so that next year they would have serfs to till their lands; they can't see so far ahead. And the citizens of Britain are not Italians; they have always been a fighting race, and not long ago they utterly repelled the Irish raiders. They still hope that one day they will beat the Saxons, and they will never stop fighting until you have killed them to the last man.'

Aella was forced to agree with me. The Saxons are such complete barbarians that no one could fit them into a civilized community, even as a fighting aristocracy at the top.

Quite naturally he looked on me as an expert authority on which was the best land to invade. Most small war-bands made for the marshes of the east coast, and then went up the sluggish rivers in little boats; but all those eastern river-valleys were already settled by isolated groups of Germans. He wanted if possible to land directly on Roman territory. The obvious objective was the shore of the Channel, the part of Britain that I knew best; I told him that there was a fertile stretch of country between the Forest and the sea, studded with towns and hill-forts that the Kent-folk had never been able to sack. I remember I felt some foolish qualms about handing over my own people to pillage and massacre, for even the wisest man finds sentiment occasionally interfering with self-interest; but I hid them away at the back of my mind. It was arranged that in the spring we should sail for the land of the Regni, and that I should act as guide.

As the winter drew on our comitatus increased in size, and we were joined by three more descendants of Woden. But Aella had known me longer than any of these cousins of ours, and I remained his most intimate friend. I think that one reason why he liked me was that although I was his equal in birth I was quite alone, without followers or family; while the other nobles had each his own little following. He often worried about the rather sordid reasons for my flight from Kent, and was determined that from now on I should be a credit to his war-band; he had made up his mind to get married before he went over-sea, so that he should have sons to succeed him in his Kingdom, and he thought it would be an excellent thing if I followed his example. He was always pointing out that one should take long views, and he very sensibly said that a bachelor never bothers about what will happen after he is dead.

There was a suitable girl in the neighbourhood, an orphan called Frideswitha; her mother had died when she was born, and her father had been drowned off the coast of Gaul a couple of years ago. Now she lived with a widowed aunt, and they were hard put to it to make ends meet, with no warrior in the family. The lack of relations was a great advantage in my eyes; a father-in-law with a sharp sword can be very awkward if your wife gets above herself. She was Woden-born on both sides, and it would be unseemly for her to marry anyone of lesser birth. All the arrangements were made for a double wedding at the spring festival, for I could never have afforded a feast of my own.

Aella was a stickler for the formalities, and he insisted that the girl should see me before the wedding day, to give her a chance of refusing her consent; this was a very remote contingency, since she was unlikely to get another offer, but so that all the rules should be observed I rode over to see her a week before the day. She lived in a very dilapidated old hall a few miles away, and both she and her aunt were delighted to welcome me.

I found Frideswitha very much as I had expected. If she had been a raving beauty she would have married long ago, and if she had been positively deformed Aella would never have suggested the match. She was tall and well-built, like all the descendants of Woden, but she must have been at least twenty-five years old, and her strong and resolute face was scored by a bad-tempered frown. Well, that did not matter; I would be leaving her in a few weeks, and I ought to find plenty of pretty and submissive girls in

Britain; what I wanted was an honourable mother for my children. We exchanged polite greetings, and I told her a few much-edited stories of my adventures in the past; neither of us expressed any positive repulsion, and I tendered the oath of betrothal to her aunt.

All this may sound rather cold-blooded, but I am convinced it is much the soundest way to make a marriage that will last. No man can be expected to stay physically in love with the same woman for long, and of course a woman who so guides her life by desire as to insist on marrying the man she loves will probably fall in love again before very long; then the unfortunate husband has to bring up someone else's children, or what is even worse, fight a dangerous single combat with a man who is usually younger and stronger than himself. Aella was marrying a girl of fifteen, which was rather a risky thing for a middle-aged man to do; but she was in love with the idea of being the wife of an independent King, and pride in her great position would probably keep her straight.

The spring festival, though it is not such an occasion for feasting as Yuletide, is even more important from the religious point of view; in winter the heathen celebrate a successful year after the gods have done their duty, but in the spring they have to remind the appropriate goddess, who is called Eastra, to bring them a warm summer. Saxons in general are not very devout; I think this is because their religion is bound up with the reverence of certain sacred places, groves and springs and so on; they have been gradually drifting south for more than a hundred years, from their original seat at the northern extremity of Germany, so they have left many of these sacred spots behind. But they all take trouble about the spring festival, on which the luck of the harvest depends.

I did not find it difficult to enter into the spirit of the

thing. I was brought up a practising Christian, but I have never been able to get into the proper believing frame of mind. It seems very likely that there is a God who made Heaven and Earth, and most religions have Him somewhere in the background, but I could never see why He should bother Himself about the puny and disreputable race of men; no matter whether we behave well or ill I am sure that we have no other immortality than the songs of the poets.

Some time in May a hereditary priest who lived in the neighbourhood gave notice that the feast would be held on the next day; a great many of the more prominent descendants of Woden are hereditary priests, but Aella, who could have been one, found the various ceremonial commandments a nuisance, and had long forgotten the sacred and unintelligible words of the prayers. In the morning we set out for the rather second-rate sacred grove, which had only been sanctified in the last twenty years; we stood in a close little crowd while a horse, a pig, and a condemned thief were sacrificed, and the blood sprinkled on the growing crops. One could feel that the whole crowd were rather bored with the ceremony, and only attended out of good manners; in the same spirit in which Romans listen to the speech at the laying of a foundation stone, for the sake of the feasting that will follow. It ought to be quite easy to change the religion of the Saxons, though whether they will accept the tiresome sexual restrictions which Christianity imposes is a different matter.

When the goddess had been given her due we all trooped back to Aella's hall, for the weddings and the other spring-time amusements. Aella was married first, while the comrades clashed their swords against their shields. Then it was my turn, and I walked up beside the long fire with Frideswitha, who had stretched her stern face into an unaccustomed grin; she wore a silver circlet over her kerchief, and three long necklaces of amber, and that was the whole of her dowry. I was twenty-five years old, the same age as my wife, and we made a very fine-looking couple. The priest recited a formula in a language so archaic that no one could understand it, and we both joined hands; then we were man and wife, and Woden would be seriously annoyed if she was not faithful to me.

Of course, the religious formula was only a preliminary to the real fun. All traces of the gods were cleared away, and the comrades settled down to feasting. Frideswitha and I sat with Aella and his bride at the high table, and the traditional songs were sung in our honour; some of these, and the shouted felicitations that came between the verses, were outspoken in the extreme, and as none of them liked to take too many liberties with their leader, my wife and I came in for more than our share of shy-making jokes. To my annoyance, I found myself blushing right down my back, but Frideswitha took it all in good part, and laughed at anything that was funny as well as salacious; a wedding feast is the only occasion on which a woman is the centre of attention.

At last I took my bride to the hut that had been put at my disposal for the wedding night. Frideswitha had long wanted a husband, any husband, and I had quite an enjoyable time; but the whole episode was much more than an amorous adventure, which is why I have related it at such length. By my marriage I was accepted into the family of the Aellingas, of which Aella was the head; since I had left the land of the Regni so suddenly I had been a solitary individual, with no one to guard my back, and it was a great relief to have kinsmen again. My ambition was asleep, for there seemed to be no chance of my ever becoming a King, and I was quite content to remain with them for the rest of my life.

We should have sailed in the spring, but of course nothing was ready at the appointed time; in all my long experience of armed expeditions the supplies and transport never are. It was a full two months after the wedding before we set out, and I had a longer honeymoon with my new wife than I had expected. The delay meant that I had time to learn her character as well as her body, and I was agreeably surprised.

Frideswitha was not a callow girl; she was old enough to have seen something of her own barbarian world, and she had listened to the distorted fragments of history that made up the songs in hall. She was also passionately ambitious, quite as ambitious as I was, and her advice on how to get on in the world was worth hearing. I guessed that she was serious and intelligent enough to keep a secret, and I told her about my boyhood and education as a good Roman. I did not explain exactly why I had to leave home in a hurry, just mentioning trouble with my brother, the heir to the throne; I felt that the complete story might be rather a strain on the respect that she owed to her husband. In some ways she was very like poor Gertrude, for example in her reverence for a good education. It is a common trait among the Germans; they find learning a great effort for their dull and heavy brains, and they stand in awe of those who have survived the painful operation.

She at once made the point that I was much better suited than Aella to rule over a subject population of Roman coloni. Of course the idea had occurred to me often enough, but it was quite impracticable unless I could gather a war-band of my own. I was too fond of my leader to stab him in the back, and there seemed no other way of rising to supreme command. I told her that if the expedition managed to conquer quite a number of peasants without killing them I would mention my qualifications to Aella, and ask him to put me in charge of the slaves; then, when he grew old, I might have a chance of succeeding to his territory. Aella was at least twenty years my senior, and one day he would be too old for battle.

I congratulated myself on having chosen a wife I could talk to about the things that were really at the back of my mind; so many German women think of nothing except meals, and when the next baby is coming. Of course there is a certain danger in educating a woman; the end of it may be that she thinks herself as wise as her husband, and takes an independent line in politics. But in this case I would soon be leaving Frideswitha for a considerable time, before she had persuaded herself that she was wiser than I was.

Meanwhile Aella was having a hard time fitting out the expedition. The plan was that we should sail southwest along the coast of Gaul until we were opposite the land of the Regni, cross the Channel and land by surprise at a spot that I would point out. If we were to conquer the land without turning it into a desert we would have to fight a pitched battle at once; but it would be better if we could land unopposed and fortify our camp before the defending army appeared.

The great problem in all expeditions by sea is the water-supply. A warship is narrow, and it is always crowded with as many fighting men as it will hold; if you take bedding, food, spare weapons, and all the wealth of a crew who never intend to return to Germany, that leaves little room for fresh water, and you soon have to put in at a river-mouth. Then the inhabitants know there are raiders about, and you find them waiting for you at the next landing-place. Aella wanted to go ashore only once, at the Saxon settlement on the north coast of Gaul, near the mouth of the river Sequana. Then we ought to be able to hurry across to our real objective without refilling the water-pots. But it took careful planning, with long consideration of the tide and the weather; he leaned heavily on my expert advice, though he was himself acquainted with the coast of Kent.

I found one curious difficulty in this planning. At the age of seven I had been taught to read and write, and until I left home I had been accustomed to jot down any figures I wished to refer to later; in my present position I dared not do so, for my companions would never have believed that a literate Roman was whole-heartedly on their side. I discovered that my memory was hopelessly unreliable, while Aella and the other Woden-born captains who had now joined us could remember any calculations they had made a fortnight ago. They regarded me as scatter-brained, but they still needed me as a guide, and I kept my place in the council.

IV

477–491

THE FOUNDING OF SUSSEX –
MY FATHER MEETS WITH
MISFORTUNE

I t was late in July by the time we were ready to sail, with the ships well provisioned, and all our plans settled at last. We filled three large warships, which I suppose meant that we were rather more than a hundred and fifty men all told, but I never could induce Aella to make an accurate count. The Germans hold that the gods would regard such a proceeding as in the nature of boasting of one's invincible power, and that they would at once take steps to see that the numbers were diminished; it is the same belief that makes gamblers reluctant to count their winnings while they are at play, but it does not make the task of the commander any easier.

We could have taken more men, for Aella was popular, but he only had the three ships, and he could not afford to buy more; as it was, he had been compelled to make a gift of his hereditary lands in Germany to a boat-builder. He was a rich man, for he had done well in earlier raids, but the maddening German system of present-giving caused him to waste a great deal of his wealth; as a famous leader he had to set an example of generosity. Even his comrades, including myself, had parted with many of their armlets; we would have to make a success of this expedition, or remain poor for the rest of our lives.

The weather was fair, with a northeasterly breeze. We relied on our sails, and coasted without incident past the mouths of the Rhine; it is a notorious spawning ground of pirates, and we saw a number of their vessels, but they would not molest three warships filled with fighting men. There were three Woden-born warriors in the fleet, besides Aella and myself, and each had been given the direction of a ship, under the supreme command of our leader; he, of course, travelled on the biggest, and I went with him as guide and spare officer. It may seem odd, but it is the fact, that I felt no compunction about leading this attack on my native land. Constans had tried to take my fairly-earned plunder, and I had been compelled to stab him; I had finished with Rome, and Christianity, and all the ways of civilized men; I was a Woden-born noble of the family of Aellinga, and a wolf to every peaceful sheep of Britain.

We reached the Saxon settlement in Gaul without using oars. All the pirate ships of the Channel water there, and we filled our pots without asking leave, or giving presents to anyone; the Saxon settlers round about were a poor lot, faint-hearted spearmen who had found raiding too danger-ous, and they watched our well-armed swordbearers from a distance. As fifth-in-command I was too grand to take part in manual labour, and I kept a general eye on things in a dignified manner; thank Heaven for that, since taking in water for a fleet is about the most back-breaking task that seamen ever do.

Then we hung about off the Gallic coast for three days, waiting for a calm, and a wisp of fog with it if we were lucky; I knew exactly where I wanted to land in Britain, but if you depend on sails the best pilot can overshoot the mark, especially in those fast-running Channel tides.

Of course our chief problem was one of numbers. We had three ships, say between a hundred and fifty and a hundred and eighty men; with this army we intended to conquer a Kingdom that supported a permanent comitatus of five hundred men, and could also put into the field, in an emergency, about four thousand able-bodied peasants. The solution I had proposed was that we should land in the far west of the Kingdom, and strike inland at once for the shelter of the Forest; there we would lie quiet for a few days, allowing the Regnians to think we had gone north to the raiding grounds of the midlands. Meanwhile we would send messengers to the Kent-folk, where Aella was remembered as a popular leader; many of the comrades would probably desert the unwarlike Oisc to enlist in our band. So we had to land exactly at the right spot, where there would be few armed inhabitants to dispute the landing, an easy passage up the cliffs, and a good track leading to the Forest.

The third night was perfect. There was not a breath of wind, and the mist made it impossible to see for more than half a mile in any direction. We rowed gently during the short darkness of July, and landed at dawn at a little beach below a chine in the cliffs. We took a solemn oath to conquer or die, without ever returning to Germany, and left the ships drawn up on the shore. The Saxons frequently take this oath, which has a special formula well known to all of them, but I cannot say that it has a great deal of influence on their conduct; a beaten Saxon army is just as anxious to escape as a Roman one.

The landing-place lay about six miles from Noviomagus, on the open coast to the southeast. We took our gear out of the ships, and were heavy laden as we struggled up the rough path to the top of the cliff; but there was nobody in that neighbourhood except a few families of coloni, who had the good sense to flee at once. An hour after the ships had touched the ground we were ready to set off; I led the way inland, over steep grassy slopes that were exhausting to climb, but open and dry.

It might have been a nuisance if the garrison of Noviomagus had come out to fight a battle while we were laden with our baggage and still stiff from the voyage; but I calculated that the fugitives would be in too much of a hurry to count our numbers, and that the commander of the town would think first of closing the gates and manning his wall. All the Romans were well used to giving safe passage to German raiders, so long as the enemy did not linger to plunder; he would be glad to hear from his scouts that we were marching swiftly inland.

Before it was completely dark we reached the outskirts of the Forest. It had been a very tiring day, endless slogging uphill over slippery, grassy slopes, and no food since the breakfast we had eaten before dawn. But in my experience nine-tenths of raiding is very hard work, and one could earn a living with less toil by growing corn peacefully at home.

We had brought enough bread to last three days, and every man was furnished with a short bow and hunting-arrows; the Forest is full of wild deer, and they are at their fattest in the late summer. The only trouble was that we had not dared to bring hounds, for they would certainly have given away our hiding-place, and these Germans, who dwell in swamps and open heaths, are not very clever at finding game in dense woodland. We would be hungry while we waited for the reinforcements from Kent; well, that was one of the charms of a raiding life, and we would just have to grin and bear it. We slept in the open, without fires, and in the morning I led half a dozen men to a little farm, where I remembered that my father's horses were put out to grass. We caught the whole family working near the homestead and killed them, so that no one got away to raise the alarm. I forbade the men to set fire to the huts, and they obeyed; for they were youngsters on their first campaign, and still rather awed that it was so easy to kill human beings. One peasant recognized me, and cried shame on me for a traitor before we cut him down; but my men understood not a word of Celtic, and thought he was only shouting defiance.

This episode worried me a little, for I did not want Aella to know that I was waging war on my father; no German would understand the excellent reason I had for such a drastic step. It would be wiser if in the future I kept in the background when men were being slain in cold blood, or it would seem curious that the victims always insulted me in particular; in battle anything a Regnian shouted would be taken for no more than a war-cry.

We found three fat grass-fed ponies on the farm, which was what we were looking for; three messengers were despatched at once to the comitatus of the Kent-folk, to say that all who were tired of the peaceful Oisc would find good plunder waiting for them in the band of their old leader, Aella. Then we settled down to exist on very scanty meals until they arrived.

For about three weeks we lived somehow in the Forest, ekeing out our bread and then falling back on deer and berries. It was a miserable opening to a campaign, and it made us weak for the battle we soon must face, but nobody actually died of hunger; I have always associated Forest-life with an empty stomach, ever since I led that ghastly retreat after the defeat of Count Ambrosius. But the volunteers arrived, two hundred strong, on the evening of the twenty-first day since we had landed, and they had the forethought to bring food with them.

Now we could abandon all concealment, and the sooner the comitatus of the Regni found us the sooner we would conquer their land. Three hundred and fifty Saxons should be more than a match for the force they could bring against us, for they had to leave garrisons in the two cities of the Kingdom, and probably a few detachments on the coast as well. On a fine August morning in the year 477 we marched southeastward to the open country, aiming at a point midway between the two cities. We set fire to everything that would burn as we swept across the countryside. It was important that we should fight while we had a good meal inside us, for no one had any idea where the next one was coming from.

It was about six hours after we had started when the left-hand detachment, under a leader called Cymen, sighted the enemy; they had occupied the remains of one of the old hill-forts that are dotted about the country in my native land more frequently than in any other part of Britain. We checked and drew into one body when we saw the position they had taken; Saxons are very easily baffled by any sort of fortification. But we could not march by the enemy and tempt him to come down to us, since from their lofty station they could see exactly what we were doing; and we should give them an opportunity to attack us in detail when we scattered to plunder. By good fortune I happened to know that hill-fort very well, and I was able to tell Aella that it was not so formidable as it appeared; the ramparts were grass-grown, and the decay of centuries had weathered the outer face to a gentle slope; an active man could get up anywhere without using his hands. There was also a broad entrance on the far side, where at least five men could charge in abreast. Aella decided to take the risk of an immediate attack, for the sake of the moral effect on our own men if we were successful. We marched swiftly towards the hill-fort, brandishing our swords.

This meant close hand-to-hand fighting at once, in

which our savage and well-armed men would have an advantage over the more civilized enemy. It is always a mistake to expose Germans to skirmishing in open ground; they are bad shots themselves, and sometimes their ridiculous honour makes them reluctant to dodge the darts of the enemy. Aella was naturally going to place the veterans from Kent at the head of the column, since they were his best troops; but I dared to give my advice, though I was only fifth-in-command. I pointed out that this would be a very hazardous attack and that the Kent-folk had been beaten off many times in the past when they tried to storm Roman entrenchments; they would advance knowing the dangers of the enterprise, and warriors who half expect a defeat are well on the way to earning it. Would it not be better, I said, to send first the untried recruits, many of whom had never seen a battle; if we did not exhort them too much they would think the attack must be a simple affair. He took my advice and, since it was my idea, I was expected to lead the forlorn hope.

I have always taken great care to preserve my life in battle; I have been a warrior for nearly sixty years, and I have very few serious wounds to show for it; but there are a few rare occasions when the leader simply has to show courage, if the operation is to have a chance of success. I believe that you are born with a certain limited stock of bravery inside you, and that if you don't squander it foolishly it will be there when you desperately need it. I set my teeth and led the raw recruits straight at the gap.

We got in all right, but it was one of the most desperate fights I have ever seen. The other borders of the Regni must have been at peace, for all the best warriors of the comitatus stood waiting for me. I don't think I was recognized, for in close battle a sensible man watches his opponent's swordarm, not his face, whatever the fencing-masters may say; and the general outline of my appearance was shaggy and barbarian. In a stand-up fight, when there are only a few hundred men on each side, Saxons ought always to beat Romans; they are accustomed to eat more, and are altogether bigger and stronger, man for man; it is only when the armies are large enough for drill and tactics to count that the well-educated Roman leaders have the advantage. The rear of our column put down their heads and pushed, and I had to perform prodigies of valour to keep a space clear in front of me. Finally, after what seemed like hours, Wlenca, the third of our Woden-born captains, led his detachment over the grassy bank to take the enemy in flank. There was no doubt that the Romans were getting the worst of it, and the normal ending to such a simple fight would have been for the weakest of them to slip quietly away, while the heroes closed up their ranks and fought to the last. But old Maximus must have been in command (for I would have noticed if my father had been there), and he was much too wily to fight to the bitter end in a battle that was already lost. Just when it was time for the heroes to win immortal glory, all the Romans began to retreat together. They disengaged so neatly, and formed up in well-ordered ranks so quickly, that we were left panting and exhausted on the hill-top while they withdrew. I knew that their horses would be hidden somewhere near, and that pursuit would be fruitless. Aella agreed, and called on the whole army to reform where it stood; we held the place of slaughter at the end of the fight, which is all the poets ever think about, but our success was a very technical one.

The battle had really settled nothing. We were no nearer a successful siege of one of their towns, where all the valuable plunder would be stored, although we had the run of the open country; we could have recruited more men from Kent, but Aella did not want to swamp his original followers with newcomers who might wish to set up another leader, and King Oisc might come down on our rear if we began to take away all his army.

In the end we decided to stay where we were. There was a good stream of clear water at the foot of the hill on which the fort stood, and we could scarp the ramparts again and reinforce them with a palisade of stakes from the Forest. Then we could begin to take the harvest away from the coloni as fast as they reaped it, while the fighting-men of the Regni manned the walls of their cities. It was a new experiment in tactics; previously the Saxons had either raided destructively over a wide area, and then dashed off home with their plunder, or settled down in a little corner, wiped out the native inhabitants, and ploughed the land. We would make the Romans work for us, without the hard fighting of a formal conquest.

The plan worked very well during that autumn and winter. The comitatus of the Regni made one effort to dislodge us, but it came to nothing; we had captured enough horses to have a good screen of scouts all round the hill-fort, so we had warning of their coming. Some of the young warriors wished to give battle in the fort, arguing that since we had turned the Romans out with approximately equal numbers we ought to be able to hold the ramparts against anything they could do; but I persuaded Aella to take refuge in the Forest. I have always dreaded the outcome of a siege of barbarians by Roman troops; civilized men can usually arrange for a regular food supply, and they keep their camp clean and so avoid disease; while barbarians insist on eating enormous meals whenever they feel hungry (which is all the time), you cannot get them to bury their rubbish, and you lose half your army by dysentery and hunger. As you will learn later in this book, the only serious defeat I ever suffered was after I had allowed myself to be shut up in a hill-fort, although on that occasion it was the only refuge within reach.

We burnt our huts and took our plunder to the Forest; the Regnians were anxious about keeping their forces so far inland when there were pirates hovering off the coast, and soon made up their minds that they had driven us away; they went back to Anderida, and when our scouts told us they had gone we returned to our hill-fort again. After that they left us in peace for the winter.

We gathered plenty of food from that harvest, but Aella's plan that we should get the coloni to grow corn for us was not a success; it depended on leaving them enough of their own food to keep them alive until next year, and even more on not killing them wantonly for amusement. The young warriors on their first campaign might have been amenable, for cruelty comes with practice; but the veterans from Kent were convinced they knew all about how to settle a conquered land, they had learned to enjoy slaughter, and they soon got the recruits to follow their example. I quite agree that there is great pleasure to be got out of destroying a village, and on the appropriate occasions I have enjoyed it myself, but a little restraint then would have meant an easier life for all of us in the future. We kept our Yule in a deserted wilderness.

After the feast Aella called a council, to decide on our long-term plans for the next few years. Cymen and Cissa, two of the captains, made the obvious suggestion that we should move on in the spring, find untouched country, and harry that bare until it was exhausted. But we would never found a state by laying waste a different countryside every year, and Aella wanted to die a real King, of a Kingdom with ploughed fields and defined boundaries. Wlenca also wished to settle down; he did not aspire to an independent Kingdom, but hoped for a large estate and the position of a leading nobleman under King Aella and his successors. That made us three to two in favour of staying where we were, and eventually Cymen and Cissa agreed to submit to the majority.

I had thought of a plan, and I persuaded the rest of the council to give it a trial. It was based on the fact that the Kingdom of the Regni rested on the walls of two strong cities more than fifty miles apart; when I was dwelling peacefully in Anderida I had often reflected on the awkward shape of the Kingdom, whose available forces were nearly always concentrated at one extremity of the arable and tax-paying land. With a little encouragement the Regni might decide to give up the less important of the two cities, which was undoubtedly Noviomagus; Anderida was the stronger fortress, and the favourite home of the King. I proposed that we beset Noviomagus closely, without actually committing ourselves to a siege of its Roman walls. If the garrison marched out to offer battle we would retire, and assault the town in their absence; otherwise we would leave them alone, but we would make sure that they usually went short of food, that the warriors got no hunting, and that the Bishop was unable to visit most of the parishes in his diocese. I remembered how the citizens of Calleva had abandoned their city with its walls intact, merely because they could not endure to live in the midst of incessant raids. If we kept up the pressure the citizens of Noviomagus might come to the same conclusion.

I explained all this to Aella and his captains, with a good deal more eloquence and logic than barbarians are accustomed to hear. In the end they agreed to give my plan a trial. It was slow and not very exciting, but it promised the secure Kingdom that most of them wanted, if only they could persuade the lesser warriors to stay for several years in the one stretch of wasted country. That would be the most difficult part of the scheme, and probably the tough Kentish veterans would soon drift away to more exciting employment; but the young recruits from Germany were fairly biddable, and we ought to be able to raise more men from the overcrowded mound-villages of Frisia.

That winter passed in peace and what the Germans consider to be comfort. We had turned the hill-fort into a permanent encampment, and collected a large flock of sheep which grazed under guard in the valley below. The great advantage of keeping sheep, rather than cattle, is that they are slow movers; they cannot be galloped away by a raiding party of horsemen. We were not far from the outlying groves of the Forest, and I was impressed by the use the Saxons made of it; their axes are better than anything the coloni are equipped with, and every man knows how to fell a tree and split it into planks as well as he knows how to use his weapons. The palisade was high and thick and sharp, and the huts were built almost entirely of stout squared logs, where a Roman would have used nothing more ambitious than turf. Nevertheless, though the huts that they built were stouter than the shacks of the coloni, they were also far more draughty; I would have liked to make a turf-hut for myself, but no one had ever taught me, a King's son, how to go about it, and I could never keep a captured peasant alive long enough to show me.

That was one of the principal troubles in the camp. The leaders would point out to the young warriors how much more comfortable everyone would be if we had plenty of servants to carry water and clear away the rubbish; the young men would agree most willingly, and bring back a good collection of able-bodied peasants from the next raid; but the warriors naturally wore their weapons all the time, they were quick-tempered and harsh, and they demanded willing service from the communal slaves. After a few days in the camp a prisoner would look surly, or fail to understand some complicated instructions in a language that was quite unknown to him. Then the nearest German would split his head with an axe, and we would find ourselves short-handed again.

So we never seemed to have enough slaves in camp to keep the place reasonably clean. That did not matter much in winter, for offal does not stink in cold weather, and smoke from the numerous fires kept the flies and other insects at bay; but next summer we would have an outbreak of disease if we didn't do something about it, and Aella decided that the best remedy was to fetch some respectable women over from Germany. As soon as spring came it was easy to send a messenger across the channel in a small boat. We hoped that Aella's wife would be able to raise enough money to fit out a small warship, with a crew of reinforcements and a cargo of wives. It meant that I would see Frideswitha sooner than I had intended, but I found it rather a bore living alone and doing my own chores. In certain circumstances any woman to keep house for you is better than none.

When the campaigning season opened we began to put into effect our plan, which we hoped would one day lead to the evacuation of Noviomagus. A few more warriors had come in from Kent, where Oisc seemed to be more ambitious to make a success of his rich farms than to win fame as a mighty war-leader; but others had drifted away, when they realized that our plan would entail a very slow and toilsome series of campaigns; our numbers were no greater than at our first battle.

The army was divided into three detachments, which relieved each other in rotation. One rested in camp, looked after the flocks, and did a little ploughing in the deserted fields. Another raided in untouched territory, more especially for silver and jewels; but they went out only to the north and west, so that the men of Anderida in the east should think themselves free from German raids. The third was entrusted with the task of making Noviomagus a miserable place to live in; they had all the ponies we had managed to get hold of, that they might retreat quickly if the garrison came out to offer battle, and their mounted scouts hung about, day and night, just out of range of an arrow from the walls. If any party of less than fifty men left the shelter of the town we attacked them at once, and when the citizens came out in a body to plough their fields we kept them standing to arms all day. I was permanently attached to this part of the army, as an expert on Roman agriculture and how to hinder it; I also had the very difficult job of seeing that the men before the walls were fed and supplied with their fair share of plunder. It was a wearing occupation, for Germans are very slack about keeping appointments, and most of them are quite unable to reckon numbers accurately; but they are not so sly and quick to see their own advantage as Romans, and I managed somehow to get enough food. The other leaders pitied me for having drawn such a dull task, while they each had a turn at the delights of raiding; but I was satisfied. Every man in the army came under my orders sooner or later; I thought that if anything unexpected happened to Aella, I would have a good chance of succeeding to the supreme command, since the whole army was accustomed to obeying me.

In the early summer the comitatus of the Regni came out once again, to see if they could chase us right out of their Kingdom. We concentrated at our old camp, but the Romans had levied a thousand peasant spearmen, and it was ridiculous for us to think of meeting such numbers in the open field; at the last moment we retreated to the Forest, leaving a very neat little ambush hidden in a dip of the chalk.

Presently pirates began sweeping the eastern marshes and carrying off the sheep, and a band of the Kent-folk raided right up to the walls of Anderida. The Kingdom was all boundary, hemmed in as it was between the Forest and the sea, and the profits from its chalky soil would not support enough warriors to defend such a frontier. As soon as the comitatus had dispersed we came back and destroyed very thoroughly the cornfields they had planted. Then we cut stakes for a new palisade, and re-fortified our old camp; it was a little too far from Noviomagus to be quite convenient, but I told Aella that nothing would get more on their nerves than to find us back at the very same spot.

The Romans must have guessed by now that we were led by an intelligent and educated man. I suppose I was one of those suspected, but most Regnians had a very exaggerated idea of the dangers of the Forest, and many of them believed that I had died of exposure during my flight. Occasionally a mounted man would ride up to our camp in the dark, and shout abuse in Celtic at the renegade who was doing them such harm, but I was the only man on our side who understood what he was saying.

By the late summer things had settled down to a stalemate, which must eventually lead to a victory for the Saxons. The citizens of Noviomagus were unable to reap their fields; we, on the other hand, managed very well on the plunder of the open country, and our men had begun to prepare new land at the edge of the Forest, where German axes easily cleared the trees. This new land was the most fertile in the country, far more promising than the bare chalk that Roman peasants preferred because it needed no labour to clear, and if we only kept our men steadily at work we would be assured of plentiful supplies in the future.

One thing that would encourage the lesser warriors to stick to their farming was a wife and family. It fitted in very nicely with our plans that at this time the ship arrived from Germany. There were more than fifty women and girls on board, including Aella's wife and my own Frideswitha. To my great surprise and delight she brought our infant son, to whom she had already given the noble name of Cynric. He was a fine sturdy boy, who displayed remarkable intelligence. I enjoyed playing with him in camp, and no longer volunteered for more than my fair share of duty with the outposts.

Frideswitha was no fool, and she understood exactly what we were driving at in our constant harassing of Noviomagus. She even thought up some new ideas to make the Romans abandon their city; for example, ten men were told off to blow horns and simulate an attack on the walls every night, and when the garrison got used to the din and began to disregard it we made a real attack, and damaged one of the gates. We also fouled their water-supply with dead bodies, though that had less effect on their health than we had hoped; I suppose because they had been accustomed to drinking foul water all their lives. During that autumn Frideswitha was at her best; Aella's wife was so young that nobody consulted her about anything, although in theory she held the highest position among the women; the mother of my son was the recognized leader in all female affairs.

In the spring of 479 the Dumnonians at last sent help. A force of about three hundred well-armed warriors of the comitatus marched in from the west, and reinforcements

also came from Anderida. The combined army made a
serious effort to chase us right away. They did not halt
when they came to the edge of the Forest, as they had done
in the previous year; our scouts kept an eye on them, and
we always marched in time to avoid battle with superior
numbers, but we were driven right into the open country
to the north. The Romans kept on our heels, and we had to
march so fast that there was no time to forage; of course the
children would die first if we had to face serious hardship.
I particularly wanted to keep Cynric alive, not only
because he was my son, but because he was really a most
remarkable infant. In this predicament I remembered my
first campaign, and the journey to the upper Thames with
which it had begun. I guided the whole army northwards
to Calleva; the walls were still standing, and the puny band
of robbers who sheltered there, joined forces with us. We
palisaded the gaps where gates had stood, and our pursuers
halted, refusing to attack such a strong fortification. The
country round about was uninhabited, and there was not
much food to be gathered from the woodland. I suppose
the Dumnonians felt they had been away from home long
enough, and the Regnians must have been getting anxious
about the coast. Before any of us had actually died of
hunger they retreated.

At first Aella was rather inclined to stay where he was.
He wanted a Roman town to dwell in, where he could play
at being a civilized man; and here was a town, with
defensible walls and no war-like neighbours. I was against
the idea; I pointed out that the Romans had left the place
desolate because it had no natural boundaries and was
exposed to incessant raids; that although the soil was
fertile it would need great labour to clear it; and that so far
inland we would be out of touch with Germany. I think
my advice was right, though I had an ulterior motive in

giving it. I wanted to stay on the open chalk; all the advantage of my local knowledge, that gave me prominence as a leader, would be lost if we embedded ourselves in a forest; and I really did fear a decay of the little culture that we struggled to teach our children. At the present day Calleva still lies desolate, and Celtic bands, with no trace of Roman civilization, lurk in the tangled woodlands to the north.

The lesser warriors agreed with me, and the brutish and badly armed robbers who had joined us said that Calleva was a hungry place in winter. The day after the enemy had left we beat the woods for many miles, to kill game for our homeward journey; next day we marched south. We were getting quite expert with our hunting arrows by now, though the deer in the Great Forest are shy.

I must have crossed the Great Forest more often than any other living man, and I know all the dodges for finding an easy way and picking up something to eat as you go along. But I have always hated the journey, and there is really no way of doing it without considerable hardship. On this occasion we were hampered by women and children, but we also had ponies to carry our gear, and the sick could ride except where the branches were too low. By the end of June we were back in our old camp, and our scouts were once more shouting rude remarks to the sentries on the wall of Noviomagus.

We had sown enough corn to see us through until next harvest, so long as we could supplement our bread with stolen cattle. In any case, we were raiders, living on other people's food, and I have always found that it is much easier to starve on stolen property than on the proceeds of your own labour; just as warriors will cheerfully dig a trench after a long day's march, when the same men would take it as an insult if you ordered them to dig a drain. The citizens had none of the exciting consolations of active service; they were merely trying to earn an honest living in extremely discouraging conditions; and they must be getting very tired of it.

All the same, they hung on through that winter. The Romans of Britain are noted for their stubbornness, which is why most of them are dead now, instead of earning a living as slaves.

When the spring of 480 came round we had been outside Noviomagus for nearly three years; there was a good deal of murmuring among our men, and I feared that we would have to give up just when we ought to be in sight of success. It was the presence of the women that saved the situation; they had been living in the camp, and regarding it as their only home, for a year and a half, and it is really surprising the amount of heavy and useless rubbish a woman can collect in that time. They knew that if we made a fresh start in some different countryside they would have to begin all over again, building fresh huts and finding another washing-place by a new stream; they backed me up when I pleaded with the army to give my plan another trial, and see if this year would not finally rid us of those obstinate Romans.

The men of Anderida took the field once more. Again we retreated from our camp, but this time they only pursued us to the edge of the Forest; and when they began to return home we followed them boldly, at a distance of only two miles. Then they gave way to despair. The whole army of the Regni marched to the city of Noviomagus, and stayed for a few days. Our scouts watched with growing excitement as they saw smoke rising from many parts of the town, and much burying of the dead in the cemetery outside the walls. At last, at the time of year when the days are longest and travellers are in least danger from ambush, the whole able-bodied population of Noviomagus came out. They had endured a blockade of three years, and during the last winter conditions must have been very bad, for there were no old people and very few small children in the column. I was proud of my British blood as I watched these obstinate creatures struggling along with all their possessions on their backs, to the very delusive safety of Anderida.

Soon we were streaming down into the abandoned city; of course the Romans had burnt everything that would burn, and taken special care to break gaps in the walls. Even so the remains of the stone houses, and the piped water-supply that picks and shovels could not destroy, made the place a paradise to our women. Aella divided up the available space very fairly, and Frideswitha was given a nice square house with a courtyard, and the remains of mosaic on the floor of the principal room. It was too late to sow corn that year, but we had plenty of grazing and unlimited hay. Next year we ought to live very well.

Best of all, the town had a harbour. A beginning had been made, and now the Kingdom would grow.

The next ten years were the longest period of peace that my stormy life has known. I was in my thirtieth year when we took over the deserted city of Noviomagus, and I did not fight another serious campaign until just after my fortieth birthday. The little Kingdom of Anderida to the east of us accepted the defeat that reduced its territory by more than half, and the comitatus of the Regni made no effort to reconquer their old homeland. This meant that there was a wide belt of ravaged villages on the chalk hills where the Romans had grown most of their corn, and it was not worth while to plant seed that would certainly be trampled by warriors before harvest; but we found a solution for this problem by clearing the valleys to the north; we used the chalk as grazing for sheep, which could be driven into the hill-forts when raiders were about. It made a complete break with the old system of cultivation; but then the previous population had been completely wiped out in the course of the three years' campaign.

In the spring of 481, when Aella proclaimed that there would not be another campaign that year, there was discontent in the war-band. For the last two summers he had been the only important Saxon leader who was waging aggressive war against the Romans, and warriors had come to serve him from all the German settlements of the east coast; they were a mixed lot of professional plunderers, calling themselves Angles as well as Saxons, so that poets began to praise him as Bretwalda, meaning war-leader of all the barbarians in Britain. They were not men who had the patience to grow rich slowly by farming good land, and most of them left us for the Anglian settlements in the northeast. The places of those who left were more than filled by crowds of low-class peasants from the mounds of Frisia, who came flocking to take up new farms that stayed above sea-level all the year round. Few of them had any better weapon than a spear, and they could not boast about their noble descent; but they knew all about growing corn in a damp climate, and they made very satisfactory subjects. From now on we would not be so formidable in battle, but then we had no powerful foes on our frontiers; the Regnians were cowed, to the north a desert stretched from the Forest to the Thames, and the Dumnonians to the west had troubles of their own. If we kept quiet, and did not provoke our neighbours, there was no reason why anyone should invade us.

Rather to my disappointment the three Woden-born captains decided to stay with us and live as peaceful landowners. Aella had not taken the title of King, for he only ruled half of quite a small Kingdom, and that meant that his leadership need not necessarily descend to his son. They were considerably younger than he was, and I suppose they all had hopes of the succession. The trouble was that I had made similar plans for myself; I quite genuinely liked Aella, and was content to be his follower as long as he lived, but a married man with a son must look to the future.

The Woden-born watched each other like hawks, and there was danger of a premature civil war breaking out before the command was vacant. Aella saw what was in our minds, and decided, for the sake of peace, to give us each a little district to defend from casual raiders. Cymen was sent down to the coast, where the settlement of Cymens-ora is still called after him, though some ignorant people think it is where he first landed; Wlenca farmed in the north between the chalk and the Forest, where the Wlencingas still dwell; Cissa was given charge of the city of Novio-magus, whose name was changed to Cissas-ceaster. Aella himself travelled from village to village, settling disputes among his men and eating the rents in kind they owed to their leader. He kept me as his companion on these travels, for he found the smattering of Roman law that I had been taught as a child useful in giving his dooms. The position was rather irksome; nothing is more annoying than to give sound advice without any guarantee that it will actually be followed; and I could never forget that I was dependent on his bounty, since I had no land of my own. In fact, my place was very like that of those Roman officials in Gaul who have thrown in their lot with the barbarians.

Frideswitha was not contented either. She had her full share of the devouring ambition that is the mark of all the children of Woden, and it maddened her to see three other leaders intriguing for the succession while her own husband had such a poor chance in the struggle. She used to tell me, far too frequently, that I was being done out of my rights; and that I ought to pick a quarrel with Cissa, the weakest of the captains, and kill him in single combat. I think I could have done so, but it would have entailed a tiresome blood feud. In any case, Aella would be angry with me, and I might have lost the fairly prominent position I now enjoyed.

But I should have to do something for my Cynric, who was really an outstanding child, and deserved a Kingdom. He was the only child I had, and Frideswitha had gone through a difficult time at his birth; the old women told me that she would henceforth be barren. I could have taken a second wife, or got rid of my present one by a convenient accident; but no woman of good blood would take the status of a concubine while my chief wife was alive, and on the whole I quite liked Frideswitha. She no longer shared my bed, since it would have been a waste of time, but I gave her all the honour due to a Woden-born lady; the pretty slave-girls were kept well in the background.

The astonishing thing was that our new little state managed to survive without serious fighting for more than ten years. Of course, there was a certain amount of trouble with the pirates of the Channel. But we were not the sort of people who were profitable to wandering pirates; we had plenty of corn and pork, but very little gold and silver. The Dumnonians were a better quarry, and the Gauls better still. On the land side we had peace, apart from a few young men of Anderida who wanted to show that they were not afraid of Germans; these occasionally crept over the open chalk to burn a farm and run away before we could catch them. In all those years our war-band never marched out in a body to meet a foe of equal strength.

In the meantime Cynric was growing up. In the year 490

he was twelve years old, and I was thirty-nine. He was a very brilliant and charming boy, and already showed great promise with his weapons; but his future was obscure. Frideswitha became worse-tempered with middle age, as happens to so many women, and she was always badgering me to do something for our son. The real trouble was that we had settled down into a routine. Aella was growing old, quite glad that there was no fighting for him to do; he had even suggested once or twice that we should send envoys to Anderida, to come to an agreement with the Romans there. None of his subordinates was in favour of such a course, for they liked to feel there were enemies to be raided on every frontier; and history shows that these truces between Germans and Romans soon break down. I was consulted, as the expert on the ways of civilized men, and I was able to stop anything being done; I pointed out all the obstacles in our way, and the unpopularity of the scheme even with our peaceful low-class farmers. I certainly did not want any intercourse between Cissasceaster and Anderida, for I knew that Roman envoys or traders would soon spot me as the runaway son of old King Eleutherus; Aella would despise me if he learned that I was a traitor to my kin.

Frideswitha was puzzled by the vehemence with which I rejected all talk of negotiation with our neighbours, especially as I had the reputation of being in favour of as much civilization as our farmers could cope with; she was a very intelligent woman, and saw that it did not fit in with the rest of my character. In the end I decided to tell her the whole story; I paid her the compliment of assuming that she could keep a secret, particularly if it was in her own interest to do so, and warned her that I would cut her throat at once if the business became generally known. I could see that she was shocked; any woman would be a little upset to learn that her husband is a fratricide, quite prepared to be a parricide if he gets the chance.

'My dear husband,' she said, when I had finished my explanation. 'It has all turned out for the best, and you have a greater position now than you would ever have held as the King's brother in Anderida. But you were very rash and ill-advised to come back as guide to a hostile army. We won't discuss the slaying of your brother; I know that such things happen among warriors who constantly go armed, though the murderers sometimes find that they have incurred a hereditary curse on themselves and their descendants. Have you felt the Gods of the Family bothering you? No, I should have noticed if you thought yourself under a curse. Very well, we will put this unfortunate affair at the back of our minds, and never refer to it again. As you seem to have dodged the curse of the Avengers of Fratricide I suppose you can safely make war on your father without interference from Heaven. The best solution is to destroy Anderida, and everyone in it, before the whole story becomes known to Aella. You must get him to see that our only chance of living here undisturbed is to wipe out that city.'

Frideswitha was quite right; I should have seen to it long ago that Anderida and my surviving relatives were put out of the way as quickly as possible. The reluctance I felt was very curious. I have always prided myself on being the completely rational man; yet here I was, delaying such an obvious step because of some nursery tale, which I had already found to be greatly exaggerated, about the curse of blood-guiltiness that might fall on my darling son. It is very hard to be completely rational and strong-minded, if you have been brought up by a Saxon nurse.

My chance came in the spring of 491. Aella was more than sixty years old, and soon he would be unable to go on campaign; but his son was only twelve, the same age as my dear Cynric, and though he already carried arms he was too young to lead the war-band. During the previous winter I had been impressing on Aella that he ought to round off his land while his age still allowed him to take the field, and that the easiest way to do it was to make an end of the fragment of the Regni. One side or the other were bound to start raiding as soon as the young lambs were big enough to march with the rest of the plunder, and then it should be easy to fasten a quarrel on the Romans.

One slight nuisance was that the gossip of the Channel pirates had exaggerated the strength of Anderida, so that our men thought it impregnable. I suppose that it was once a very strong place, and it had beaten off many a pirate attack; but its strongest side naturally faced the sea, and it was not so well prepared for an assault from the land. I also reflected that in my boyhood I had never seen repairs done to any part of the walls, and I was pretty sure that in the last seventeen years not one dressed stone had been laid upon another anywhere in Britain. I knew a way of climbing in without disturbing the guard, which had come in useful for my boyish love-affairs, and I might be able to lead a small party of good men on a successful escalade.

Our Woden-born captains were in favour of the scheme; they also had sons growing up, and they wanted to see them rich men and great landowners before their own fighting days were finished. But the peasant ploughmen from the valleys had no particular wish to better their condition, for they had already as much land as they could cultivate. That was rather an obstacle, since an unwilling army, always thinking of the work that ought to be done at home, very easily finds itself beaten. The obvious remedy was to recruit a number of the professional warriors who lived by plunder on the outskirts of Kent, though that would mean that the Romans would get word that we were coming.

We decided that this was a risk that must be taken. Our council was composed entirely of Woden-born nobles, and they had a very poor opinion of peasant spearmen; though I found in later years that even the lowest class of Saxon will fight, if he has his heart in the work.

We would not be ready to start before the early autumn, which gave me plenty of time to examine the fortifications we must overcome. The long nights of winter would really have been better, but nothing had been definitely decided until the spring, and I had been reluctant to show myself where I might be recognized. In any case, I have sometimes found that you can have a good look at a place that is not expecting you if you take advantage of the early summer dawns, when daylight comes while men are still asleep; in winter the lower classes are usually stirring before it is light.

I borrowed a fast pony from Aella; a sure-footed beast guaranteed not to neigh even if there were mares about, and clever at getting up and down the steep hills of the chalk country. I rode gently to the last farmhouse that was safely in our hands, and spent the afternoon sleeping. It was the middle of May, and the nights should be long enough for me to do a twenty-mile ride and still arrive outside the walls before dawn.

The sky was unclouded when I set out after sunset, and the stars gave enough light to ride along the crest of the hills. All this open, dry land had been constantly harried by Romans and Germans, but the grass is very good, and our peasants had little fortified sheepfolds dotted over our share of the open country. At least a dozen spearmen lived in each one, and the flock was safe from anything except a raid in force. I expected that the Romans would live in much the same fashion once I was across the border, and that after dark they would all be inside their thick thorn hedges; we had purposely made no serious raids that spring, and it was unlikely they would post sentries in the open, among the evil spirits of the night. I cantered briskly along, without trying to hide the sound of my approach; they would not leave their valuable sheep to investigate a solitary horseman.

The high chalk-land stops short some miles before Anderida, which lies on a low knoll among the marshes of the coast. I picked my way carefully down the last slope, and went cautiously on the low ground; shepherds keep to a fairly strict time-table, but here were fishermen and wildfowlers, who are often about at all hours of the night. It was hard to see among the mists of the marsh, but I noticed that conditions had changed since I was a boy; there was much more cultivation, and an attempt had been made to drain the land with deep straight ditches. The shift of population was interesting; obviously the light, open land that the coloni had preferred to cultivate twenty years ago had now become too dangerous, exposed as it was to raids; they had been compelled to grow their food in the marshes, with a great expenditure of labour to prepare the ground. That must have caused great reversals of fortune among the landowners; the little Kingdom of Anderida would be suffering from a discontented aristocracy and a disturbing crowd of the newly enriched; perhaps the social strains would be reflected in their resistance to invasion.

I left my pony in a hollow, where a drainage ditch had been dug wide for the winter floods, and the receding water had left a little beach. He was trained to raiding, and would stand quietly at his picket.

Of course, my ride in enemy country had taken longer than I had planned; in my experience such things always do. The sky was reddening when I made out the black shape of Anderida against the shimmer of the sea, and I lay down in the nearest ditch until it would be light enough for me to discern the sentry. Presently I picked up the gleam of his metal helmet; he was staring out to sea as I had expected. The land gate had recently been repaired with fresh white timber, and it remained closed after the sun was fully risen; I was surprised to see so little activity at the chief entrance to the city (for no traders would nowadays come to the water gate). Presently the sleepy sentry was relieved by another; but I could see no officer going his rounds with the new guard, as Count Ambrosius had told us was the correct thing to do, and still no one bothered to open the land gate. At last the mystery was explained; from the sagging roof of the parish church came the sound of many voices singing. I tried to remember what festival of the Christians fell about this period of the summer; then suddenly I recognized the hymn they were all singing at the top of their voices, and a thousand recollections of my boyhood came flooding back; they were celebrating the Coming of the Holy Ghost in the Feast of Pentecost.

Sounds are more evocative of the past than anything you can see. I was once more a little boy, yawning through the long service, and fidgeting in the clothes that a King's son must wear for great occasions. I wondered how they were all getting on in that mutilated and threatened fragment of the great Empire of civilization, and whether any of them were foolish enough to hope that their children's children would still be singing Christian songs in that old, purposeless, unrepaired building a hundred years from now. I had a strange impulse to enter the city, to join the tattered remnants of the Roman army that lurked behind the moss-grown wall, and to give my life in their inevitable defeat. Then I recalled that they would at once put me to death, as the murderer of my brother. I was here to spy for their destruction, not only to enlarge the realm of my friend and patron, Aella, but because the information about my past that they might give would lead to the loss of the honourable position that I held among the barbarians. I hardened my heart and began to look more closely at the wall, where the low early-morning sun showed up every weakness in the alternate bands of brick and stone. I only mention the incident as an example of the curious pull of Christian civilization, which can be felt even by the most savage barbarians.

This was my best opportunity to get close to the wall, for no one would leave the gate while the service was in progress, and the sentry was as usual staring out to sea; in the afternoon there would be no work done, even by the slaves, and the citizens would come outside to picnic and enjoy themselves. I scampered from one bit of cover to another while the sentry's back was turned, and soon found myself up against an angle where a semicircular bastion jutted from the curtain. The masonry was rough and irregular, a mass of unshaped flints embedded in great quantities of rough mortar. Roman mortar is made to endure for centuries, and this wall was not more than a hundred years old; but the stones that the great Theodosius had used as filling for his concrete had been gathered at random in the neighbourhood, and some of them had weathered away in the frosts and gales of a century. There were plenty of footholds for an active man, and I was still active at forty; soon I was lying full length on the ramparts.

So far so good, but I wanted a secure hiding-place where I could remain until nightfall. I saw a heap of firewood in the backyard of a large house that encroached on the pomoerium between the fortifications and the dwellings; by all the rules of city management this space should have been kept clear, so that the garrison could quickly reach any part of the defences, but I suppose the owner of the house had enough influence to disregard the laws; that has been the great weakness of all Roman rule for as long as I can remember. Anyway, there it was, and I found it a very convenient hiding-place; I burrowed in among the corded bundles of brushwood, and pulled others over me until I was safely hidden.

Nobody came poking round wood-piles on such an important holiday, and I was left undisturbed until nightfall. When it was quite dark I went boldly up the nearest stair to the ramparts, and climbed easily down the angle of the wall by the way I had entered the city. I had learnt all I needed to know: the Regnians kept a careless watch, and active men could climb quietly within the walls without raising an alarm.

I rode home rather slowly, partly because I was still depressed at the thought of the destruction I should bring on Anderida, and partly because I was very tired and sleepy. Daylight found me still among the sheepfolds of the Roman coloni, and they sent their dogs snarling at my horse's heels while signal fires were lighted on the hills; but the shepherds themselves all went on foot, and they had no ambition to meddle with a well-armed Saxon who was not driving off their sheep. I rested at one of our own fortified farms, and rode into Cissas-ceaster on a very stiff and hungry pony the following afternoon.

The report I had to give was as good as could be expected. If the Romans had time to call in the shepherds from the outlying farms, and the guards who must be stationed at the edge of the Forest, any war-band that Aella could gather would be considerably outnumbered; but of course his men would be trained swordsmen, while many of the Romans would only be coloni armed with spears and clubs. What it all boiled down to was that we could easily break into the city if we could approach it unobserved; but that would be a very difficult task to accomplish, since for the last fifteen miles we should be marching through Christian territory. In theory one could surprise them from the sea, but I had seen enough to realize that in that direction they kept a very good look-out. Wlenca, who was by far the most stupid of the descendants of Woden that I have met (most of them are intelligent as well as strong), suggested that we should send a party in disguise, pretending to be travelling merchants. I had to point out that there had been no travelling merchants in our part of Britain since the Aellingas had landed. The obvious way out of the difficulty was to rely on cold-blooded treachery; Aella had been thinking of sending an embassy to delimit the frontier, and they might carry hidden arms, or rely on their seaxknives like Hengist's men long ago. But when I put forward this plan it was badly received; they all spoke of the oaths the envoys would have to take before they were admitted to the city, and the very bad luck that generally pursued oath-breakers; Aella said that one day he might want to make a genuine peace with some other Romans, and that a reputation for dishonesty hampered a ruler in all his subsequent negotiations. They were too shy to make speeches about the sacred honour of a Saxon, but I saw that at the back of their minds was a superstitious fear of treachery.

Since an attempted surprise from the sea would be discovered by the sentry, always on the look-out for pirates; since we could never carry out an approach in disguise, and since they had these ridiculous scruples about naked treachery, there was only one way left of getting to that wall before the garrison knew we were coming; we should have to get there faster than the news could travel. Nobody fights his best after a fifteen-mile forced march, but we could scrape together enough horses to mount the best men of the war-band, and the rest must be employed on a diversion to draw out the garrison. The drawback was that the Regni would at any rate know there was a war on, though they would not be expecting an attack on their city. But it was the only scheme that had a chance of success. The whole council unanimously agreed that I was the best man to draw up the plans, and I retired to what had once been the study in a ruined house; there I could make notes, and even draw a sketch-map, without my comrades finding out how well educated I was.

I decided to begin the war at midsummer, as soon as the volunteers from Kent arrived; and to divide the army into three groups. Our low-class peasant spearmen, about a thousand strong, would march directly east and harry the Roman shepherds of the chalk uplands; the Roman peasants would gather to repel them, and they would probably be joined by reinforcements from the comitatus. When enough time had elapsed for the enemy to concentrate in full force on their western frontier the well-armed warriors from Kent would threaten another invasion from the north; there would only be two or three hundred of these, but they were all good swordsmen; the Romans would have to send some of their best comrades to counter the threat. Then, when the city was empty of its best defenders, I myself would lead a little band of noble and well-armed Germans straight for Anderida, across the chalk and the marshes; there would not be more than sixty of us, but we ought to be able to escalade the wall in face of the weakened garrison. We should attack at dusk, and the rest of our forces must march all night to join us in the morning. The whole plan depended absolutely on the other detachments arriving at the appointed time; it was a very ambitious scheme to attempt with barbarian troops, who never remember the date and dislike forced marches. But success was certain if only the time-table was kept, and it had the great advantage of giving me a prominent place in the campaign; Aella would realize that he owed Anderida entirely to my courage and skill, and must reward me suitably. I explained all this to Frideswitha, so that she should press the claims of Cynric to my reward if anything happened to me; and though she was appalled by the complication of a campaign in three columns, a thing no barbarian would ever undertake, she finally agreed that I was a more skilful warrior than she had supposed.

The council readily agreed to my plan, although it took a lot of explaining before they understood it. The chief difficulty would be fixing the date. The Saxons use a calendar for religious purposes, and have borrowed the Roman names for most of the months; but the warriors seldom bother to keep track of it, and they are always extremely inaccurate. Aella commanded the peasant spearmen, who adored him, and Cissa was to lead the volunteers from Kent, who thought Aella was too pacific; they were both intelligent men, who could probably count up to twenty without making a mistake, but for greater safety I gave each of them a peeled stick with nine notches; every evening they were to enlarge one notch, and the night they finished the last was the time when they should set out for Anderida.

On midsummer day we lit the usual bonfires and sacrificed an ox; it should have been a horse, but all the horses we could get hold of were needed to mount my storming party. Then Aella led his spearmen eastwards, and Cissa took his party of Kentish volunteers into the

Forest; they had all crossed it at least once to get to us at all, so I hoped they would not lose their way before they appeared on the northern frontier of the Regni. I stayed behind for a week, and made my followers practise riding in close formation after dark; no German noble is afraid of anything on four legs, but horsemanship is not their strongest point; they did not fall very often, and did not mind if they did, but they were inclined to scatter over a very wide area as soon as we began to gallop.

On the eighth day we moved gently up to the border, and camped in a sheepfold. A messenger from Aella told me that the Roman shepherds were hanging round his force, avoiding battle but making sure that he could not scatter his men to plunder; that was just what I had expected, and it fitted in very well with my plans. On the ninth morning we began to ride slowly eastward; now that the Romans were collected into an army they would not have many scouts in the open country, and any who saw us would think we were reinforcements for Aella. We came up with his army at midday, and he told us that a small force of the enemy, including all their mounted men, had been seen to move off to the northeast that very morning. Evidently Cissa had made his presence known on the northern frontier, and he was in the right place at the right time.

Now was the opportunity for my men to ride unobserved to the city. Those chalk uplands look very open, and it is true that from the hill-tops you can see other hills many miles away; but they are cut by very steep valleys, with rounded slopes, so that a man riding along the bottom is out of sight of a sentry on the hill-top. I could see the defending army massed on the skyline a mile away; they had taken shelter within the ramparts of an old hill-fort, and they were watching Aella's men on the lower hill opposite. There was one of these steep ravines behind us, and I made my men stroll down in twos and threes, leading their horses as though they were taking them to water. Once we were all assembled at the bottom I led them at a steady trot along the winding valley floor.

The horses were tired enough to go quietly, and as they had been exercised together for more than a week they had no urge to carry their heavy-fisted riders away from the column. About an hour before sunset we reached the edge of the chalk uplands, and saw Anderida lying in its marsh six miles away. Now came the most hazardous part of the journey; we were in the midst of the enemy, and if they heard in time of our presence we would be overwhelmed by superior numbers. I put the tired horses into a gallop, and trusted that we would outride the news of our coming.

That marsh was always damp, even in midsummer, and we did not raise a betraying cloud of dust. Then as the sun set I had an unexpected piece of luck. A thick mist began to rise; these mists off the marshes are quite unpredictable, and I had not dared to count on one coming to my assistance; but I knew that it would last until the remaining light of the afterglow had faded into complete darkness. Presently we halted, and I ordered my men to dismount and turn their horses loose. I was afraid I might have trouble in getting myself obeyed, for Wlenca and Cymen were with the party, and horses are valuable and scarce; but all of Aella's regular followers were sensible law-abiding men; though there was grumbling at such a wasteful proceeding no one openly defied me.

When we were all on foot I led them quietly along a stream that I knew flowed close by the wall I was seeking. All round us in the darkness I heard voices shouting that Saxon raiders were about, and someone in the city blew a trumpet to get the garrison under arms; but they would not expect a direct assault on the walls they considered impregnable, and were more likely to send out a strong party of well-armed comrades to look for the raiders in the open. Just as the outline of the wall loomed up through the grey fog we heard an outburst of shouting and trumpet-calls some way behind us; the Romans must have stumbled on our horses, and now they would try to follow up our tracks. Well, they had won good plunder, but we hoped to get something even more valuable in exchange.

We crept closer to the wall. The mist lay low; though we were hidden, the top of the rampart showed clear against a starry sky. There was a trumpeter on the landward side of the wall, blowing his hardest to exchange signals with the reconnaissance party; he was making such a din that no one heard our approach.

My band was composed of trusted veterans, and some of them were rather stiff in the joints for climbing sheer walls; but I had foreseen this, as I seemed to have foreseen everything on this very lucky venture, and I had specially picked out one brave and steady young man, whose hobby was climbing trees to steal eggs; he went up first, very quietly, and let down a knotted rope to help the old gentlemen. The Romans on the wall did not observe us until we had half a dozen men in position, and the rope was full of others climbing up; then the trumpeter sounded an alarm, and the rest dashed towards us. It was just the sort of fight I had hoped for; a series of desperate single combats at close quarters, where Roman drill and discipline would go for nothing, and all depended on the strength and ferocity of the individual combatants.

At first we pressed them back, clearing about fifty yards of the wall. Then numbers told, and we were forced to defend what we had won. This was all exactly as I had planned the assault. We held a bridgehead inside their defences, and all we had to do was to hang on until the rest of our army joined us at dawn. The fighting platform behind the battlements was about six feet wide, built of solid masonry; so there was no question of breaking it down to right and left of us, as we could have done if it had been the usual gallery resting on wooden beams. But some of the stone merlons that crowned the wall were old and decayed, and piles of brushwood for signal fires had been left lying about in a most unmilitary fashion; we managed to make little barricades on both sides, and set ourselves to hold them until dawn. Of course, these flimsy heaps of brushwood and broken stone were not a serious obstacle, but the moral effect of holding a fixed line is very great.

This was the first deadly fight in which I had commanded really first-class Saxon warriors; all my men were wealthy nobles, equipped with the best of arms in the Saxon fashion, and they were veterans. I was quite amazed at the ferocity with which they fought. I had expected them to stand firm and guard their heads carefully, like Roman soldiers; instead, they were always leaping over the barricade and dashing for their enemies, and their war-cries filled the night with ghastly noise. Even an elderly grey-haired German can fight like a tiger when he is aroused, and in fact if you don't let them attack all the time they will run away.

The best men in the comitatus of Anderida had marched out to the north to counter the threat from Cissa, and the young boys had formed the patrol that discovered our horses. As a result we were opposed only by second-line troops, and an elderly Roman is no match for an elderly Saxon. I wondered if I would see my father, but I never noticed him on the wall; he must have been over seventy by now, and I expect he found the steps too steep to climb.

The Romans seemed to have no leader, or else they had several, which is even worse; at least, instead of drawing off until they had assembled all their force, and then making one great attack to sweep us from the vital point we had gained in their defences, they attacked in driblets as each man armed himself and ran to the fighting.

I kept myself well in the background. My part had been to lead the storming party to a place where they could climb the wall unobserved, and I had carried it out with complete success; but I naturally expected that if I took chances while leading an attack on my father the gods would see to it that I lost my life. It is on just such occasions that good warriors are killed by women throwing roof-tiles, or find the stones turning under their feet when a little boy comes at them with a knife. So I stayed by the rope, and kept a look-out that no Romans should climb up behind us. My men did not mind; they were enjoying themselves, and they knew that I had been trained in a Roman army; if they noticed it at all, they put it down to Roman caution.

The sky was unclouded, but there was no moon, and I could hear what was going on better than I could see it. After little more than an hour the fighting died down; presumably the Romans were satisfied that they had us hemmed in one segment of the wall, and were waiting for daylight to destroy us with arrows from a safe distance. They never dreamt that barbarians would have the patience and the skill in organization to work out a combined attack by three separate forces; they thought we had merely set out on a raid that had gone farther than intended. Germans are notoriously easy to beat if you can pin them down to be shot at, and they were quite right to wait for better light to finish us off. They built little barricades themselves to stop us from spreading farther along the wall, and lined the open spaces inside the city (the pompoerium) with slaves and peasants armed with spears. By this time the patrol that had found our horses must have returned to the city, and they would have plenty of cavalry to pursue us if we tried to retreat in daylight.

We were all very hungry and tired, though as we had filled our water-bags just before we began to climb the wall we did not suffer from thirst. We lost about fifteen men killed, a quarter of our strength; but we had only one seriously wounded man with us, for in that sort of fighting anyone who was knocked down was usually finished off at once. The wounded man was Cymen himself; he had caught a spear with his left hand, and the point had ploughed a deep and jagged cut from his wrist nearly to his shoulder; his arm was already beginning to swell and throb, and he would die in a few days when the poisoning really set in; but he did not seem to mind, and spoke only of how lucky he was to get his death-wound in a famous fight, instead of dying in bed. Saxons never show fear when they know they must die, though they take reasonable precautions to stay alive as long as possible.

We crouched behind our barricades, and the Romans shouted rude remarks at us from theirs. I was glad that none of them had recognized me, and that Aella would never know I had waged war on my own father. At last the summer night drew to a close. As dawn broke the enemy began the arrow-shower that I had expected. We were a sitting target and could make no reply, for Saxons only use the bow for hunting, and they are atrociously bad shots even then. Our barricades helped us a certain amount; we picked up all the large Roman shields that we could find where the fighting had raged, and my men were amazingly agile at dodging those arrows they saw coming; but that is very tiring work, and they would not be able to keep it up for long. If the rest of our army was late they might find us already driven from the wall.

But everything went right at the taking of Anderida. As the sun came up over the sea I looked back and saw the two detachments of Cissa and Aella hurrying through the marsh towards us. The Romans noticed them, too, and they mustered their men for an all-out attack before we were joined by our reinforcements. But we held them for the necessary half-hour, and then Aella had driven off the force that tried to bar his way outside the town, and was leading his men up the knotted rope.

After we had joined on the ramparts the fight could only have one end. Some Romans from the other defending forces on the border had followed our men to the city, and the townsmen still outnumbered us slightly; but we were all trained warriors, and they had many unarmoured spearmen in their ranks. When the ramparts were won Aella led us down among the gimcrack houses of the town. No Roman asked for quarter, and certainly no German thought of giving it when his sword was wet; even the women and small children did what they could with roof-tiles and kitchen knives; it was all very messy and unpleasant, and I found that I could not fight with any enthusiasm. Of course, it was all my father's fault; if he had made me his heir, instead of Constans, I am sure the Kingdom of the Regni would still be a flourishing state.

I took my place in the second rank of the fighters, and devoted all my attention to finishing off any wounded man who might otherwise have recognized me and called out my name. The Romans knew that all was lost, and were more anxious to find a quick death than to attempt to drive us back. Quite soon they had abandoned most of the city and taken refuge in the stone-walled church; there they barred the doors, and began to cut the throats of the women while we prepared to burn our way in. I was one of the first to enter when the door collapsed; I had to make sure that all the elderly citizens, who remembered me, were killed as quickly as possible. My father was not there, and in fact I never learned in what obscure alley or cellar he met his death. But I saw my brother Paul, standing on the steps of the High Altar at the far end. I made straight for him, and gave him a merciful thrust through the heart; as he fell I cut his throat with my seaxknife, to prevent any tiresome dying declaration, but I don't think he realized who I was. The thatched roof had caught alight from the burning door, and presently collapsed on the piled corpses.

That is how we took the city of Anderida; a very remarkable achievement for barbarians unskilled in siege-work, and entirely owing to my cunning and knowledge of the ground. It is the only Roman town in Britain that has fallen by bloody assault; Cantwaraburh was taken over with its slaves and lower classes, and most of the other ruined cities were evacuated for fear of the raiders, like Calleva and Noviomagus. I believe the Sack of Anderida is the subject of a famous poem among the Aellingas; although my name is left out of the official account, for reasons that I shall now relate.

In the evening we held a feast among the ruins. A little wine had been found in the debris of the church, and there was a great quantity of beer. When the drinking began the comrades hailed Aella as King of the South Saxons, a title which was his due now that he had conquered the whole Kingdom of Eleutherus. Then a poet began an ode in praise of the cunning Woden-born leader who had brought them inside the walls; this was me, and I listened with great pleasure. But Aella banged with the hilt of his sword for silence, and called for me to come and stand before him. I thought he was going to announce that I was his heir, or the guardian of his young son, which would come to the same thing in the end; but he frowned as he looked on me, and spoke thus:

'Cerdic Elesing, you won this city for me, and I am duly grateful. You may take as reward all that you can carry of the spoil. But when you have chosen you must depart at once. Leave Anderida in three hours, and my Kingdom in three days; then you will be outlaw, and any man may slay you for your wealth. I found dying in the street a captain of the Romans, and because he had fought bravely I offered him the mercy of a quick death. But as I leaned over to cut his throat he spoke, in the camp-Latin I learned when I was a child on the Rhine; he told me who you are, and why you had left home. He said that you are the second son of the Roman King of this place, and that you fled from your father because you had murdered your brother, the heir. Now you have destroyed your father's city, with all your kin inside it, and it is quite possible that you have killed some of them with your own hands. Answer me yes or no; is this story true?'

'Well, King Aella,' I answered. 'Everything he said was true, but there were various extenuating circumstances. I killed my brother in fair fight, when both of us were armed, because he tried to take from me my rightful spoil. Afterwards my father sought my life, and surely I was justified in making war on a German by descent who fought for the Romans. I did not tell you all this, since it is an involved story that needs a lot of explaining; perhaps I should have done so. At least you will agree that while I have been in your comitatus I have served you as a loyal comrade. I know the ways of the Romans, and if you allow me to remain in your company I will lead you to even better plunder.'

I really wanted to stay with the Aellingas, or the South Saxons as they would be called in future. They were very pleasant companions, for Germans, and I could be happy with them if they ever lived in peace. But Aella had made up his mind, and I could tell, from the muttered growls all round me, that his followers agreed with him.

'Then you admit the truth of the accusation,' he said grimly. 'You have served me well and faithfully, as you claim; that is why I am allowing you to depart in safety with your plunder. But we are noble Germans here, and we prefer not to share our feast with a scoundrel who has brought about the death of his father and his kin, besides committing murder on his elder brother. We none of us wish to be standing near you when the thunderbolt falls. Go now, at once. Remember that in three days you will be outlaw; and with the wealth you have from this city there will be many warriors eager to slay you. Give him a sack, so that he can carry the reward of his treachery.'

There was nothing that I could say in reply to this sanctimonious speech. In fairness to Aella I must admit that he allowed me to take all the gold and silver I could carry, and he stood over me himself, with his sword out, so that none of the comrades should stab me while I was filling the sack. I thought to myself that if there really was a curse from Heaven on all parricides it was operating at that moment. I was being driven out of a successful war-band at the very time when they would all begin to live like wealthy nobles, with the fertile fields of Anderida to support them. And, of course, I was losing the rather nebulous chance of the throne that I had hoped for in the future.

I was very tired and sleepy, and so was my horse. I rode a few miles out of the town, and spent the night under the wall of a burnt hut in the marsh. I woke at dawn, and considered what to do next; I was a free man, and rich, and I could take service with any war-band I chose, except the South Saxons. But in fact my choice was rather narrow; if I went west to the Christian rulers of the surviving Roman states, sooner or later the history of my youth would follow me; Kent was at peace, and anyway Oisc would still be seeking for my head; all the middle part of Britain, from the Sea of Vectis up to and beyond the sources of the Thames, was a welter of little bands of raiders and squatters, both Roman and German; their savage encampments were no place for a civilized man. My best course was to return to Germany. The next question was whether I should take Frideswitha also, or whether it would be better to vanish without trace. It would be enjoyable to live as a wealthy bachelor, even among the sunburnt and grubby women of Germany, and Frideswitha was quite capable of looking after herself. But there was one snag, my son Cynric. I could not bear to leave my only child for ever, particularly a child of such promise; if I could not have him without his mother, then I would put up with her also.

When I reached the ruined house where she lived in Cissas-ceaster there was only one left of my three days of safety, and I had little time to explain the unfortunate end of my victorious enterprise. Luckily Frideswitha was at her best when things were disastrous, and she did not indulge in useless lamentations. There was a little fishing-boat in the harbour, that could take three passengers to the mouth of the Rhine, and she sent Cynric down to bargain with the master while she packed our cooking-pots and best clothes. But when the boy was out of the way she told me exactly what was in her mind.

'I knew very little about your past life when I married you, but I took you for life, as a daughter of Woden should. Aella's war-band is made up of very decent folk, and it is a pity you are not good enough for them. We shall start afresh in Germany. But now that I have heard the full story I have a natural fear that I am next on the list to be murdered. Cynric is probably safe, for you seem to adore the spoilt brat. Now I warn you that I always carry my seaxknife, as a free Saxon should; if ever you give me cause to fear for my life I shall slip it into your guts without thinking twice; but behave yourself reasonably to me and I shall do my duty as your lady and the mother of your son. What are your plans when we reach Frisia? With my brains and your lack of scruple, we ought to end up with a Kingdom of our own.'

On these uncomfortable but fundamentally quite sensible terms we prepared for our flight to Germany.

V

491–515

THE FOUNDING OF WESSEX –
MY WIFE MEETS WITH
MISFORTUNE

We made a safe voyage across the Channel, and then coasted up the German shore until we reached the mound-villages of the Frisians. There we landed, and journeyed inland to the more fertile and less crowded country where Aella had been living when I first came to his hall. I had a sack-load of gold and silver, and everyone was pleased to see us, though I gave out quite frankly that we had left Britain because I had been turned out of the war-band of the South Saxons. Of course, I did not say why I had been turned out, that would have been altogether too frank; I think most people assumed that Aella had considered me a dangerous rival, and a menace to his young son. Frideswitha was sensible, and she wanted me to be a great man for the sake of Cynric's future. In public her attitude to me was one of respect and admiration, whatever she thought of me in private, and since men and women mix together a good deal among the Germans she helped to sway public opinion to my side, as the harmless victim of a suspicious ruler.

The Saxons of the Continent are much poorer than their fellows who have plundered the rich provinces of Britain, and my sack of treasure made me the wealthiest man in the countryside. During that first autumn and winter of the year 491 we moved from hall to hall; but I found the lavish gifts that were expected of one in my position a serious drain on the sack, and next year I looked round for a permanent home of my own. As I have already told you, it is almost impossible to buy anything in Germany, for fear of insulting the possessor. In any case no one would dream of selling land, which is a hereditary possession that belongs to the family as a whole. But as all the German tribes are constantly on the move, land does in fact change hands, and not only through the death in battle of the original occupier; the system of mutual gifts provides a way out. I found a comfortable hall, with a good stretch of land attached; it was occupied by a lady whose husband had done well on the northeast coast of Britain, and had sent for his family to join him. In the course of a complicated transaction she made me a present of all future harvests until she or her descendents returned to Germany, and I gave her a well-founded ship to take her to the new settlement by the Wall. In a Roman province one would have said that I bought a lease, but here any such suggestion would have been an unforgivable insult. There is a great deal to be said for the straightforward Roman system of land sales by auction.

I lived peacefully in my hall for the next three years. There were plenty of homeless peasants who were eager to do the actual work in exchange for a share of the crop; and I gathered a few young warriors round me, not enough to form a serious war-band, but sufficient to deter my neighbours from raiding. Frideswitha managed the household, and we were on friendly terms when we met; but we tended to go our separate ways, though she was too honourable to take a lover. Meanwhile Cynric was growing up, and learning the management of arms; he was a very promising youth, a splendid fencer with the scramaseax, an intelligent leader who could carry the lie of the country in his head, and a cheerful and witty companion. Such a young man had a right, when he grew up, to some better inheritance than a squalid little German hall.

In theory I owed military service in the war-band of a local King, but in practice we were at peace; I joined the muster every spring to demonstrate my loyalty, and then we were all dismissed to our homes. So far my independence was complete, and independence was what I had been looking for all my life.

But Frideswitha pointed out that my position was not really secure, and that I might not be able to transmit it to Cynric. One evening in the third winter, when we were drinking together, I said something about how contented I was with my present lot, and she at once took me up.

'Remember that this hall is not an allod,' she said. 'The Wulfingas may be driven out of Britain one day, and then they could demand it back from your descendants. You are not even a true-born Saxon; according to your own story your ancestor was a King of the Alemanni. That means that you can never acquire a good title to land in Saxony, and your sons after many generations will never be true freeholders.'

'Very well, my dear,' I answered. 'I am sure you are quite right as you always are. I can hold this little farm against all comers except a real army, but one day I shall be too old to fight, and we have Cynric to consider. I suppose you mean we should travel to one of the Roman provinces, where land is bought and sold, and you can leave it to your descendants.'

She saw I was mocking her hankering after Roman civilization; but she took it in good part, for though we were no longer lovers we were old companions. All she answered was:

'Which part of Britain would be best to raid? Will you enlist under some established chief, or do you think you could raise your own war-band?'

'As you frequently remind me, I am under a curse from any gods who may be looking after the morals of Britain; although in view of the state of that island I think those gods must be taking a holiday. Seriously, my dear, there are not very many parts of Britain where I would find a welcome. King Aella has been superstitious enough to outlaw me after I had helped him to conquer his valuable Kingdom, and King Oisc of Kent would kill me at sight. We could go to the far north and join our landlords, the Wulfingas; but it seems silly to go right up there, where I should be a stranger, when I know the country south of Thames. We might land on a deserted part of the Channel coast, and hurry inland to the debatable land north of Londinium; but the settlers in the midlands are a brutish lot, and it would be a very savage country for young Cynric. If he did not end up as a bestial robber it would only be because he had sunk into a peasant ploughman.'

'That would never do at all. You have had a good education, and we want Cynric to be more civilized than the average Saxon from Germany. We shall sail to some part of the country that you know, or at least have marched through in your youth. What is the land like immediately to the west of the South Saxons?'

'I have been there, when I went to join Count Ambrosius for my first campaign. I suppose the next Kingdom to the west is the Roman state of Dumnonia, a poor land, and able to deal firmly with raiders. But there used to be a wide belt of devastation in between, inland from the Sea of Vectis. The Irish pillaged it before the Germans began to cross the sea, and it is one of the most desolate parts of Britain. You would find it just as savage as the midlands.'

'But if it is on the coast it would be easy to bring in Saxons with their wives and families complete. It is only when you men go off to live in the woods without women that the decent customs of home are forgotten. If you went there with a good war-band, and enforced the laws you chose to make, would there be room in that land to found a strong Kingdom?'

'That is a very sound suggestion, my dear. It should be very easy to land anywhere on the Sea of Vectis; but the trouble would come afterwards, when we try to found a Kingdom. Who would till the soil? We both hope our grandchildren will be civilized men, eating bread and drinking beer, and for that you must have a lower class to work on the land. I am not sure that our best plan would not be to go south and find some Roman land where the farms are still a going concern, and the coloni alive to till them.'

My doubts were very real, for I thought that Hengist had long ago skimmed the cream from Britain, and I wished to see the great cities of the south. But Frideswitha was certain that it would be ridiculous to waste my local knowledge by going to an unknown country when there was still room in Britain for more German Kingdoms; she eventually persuaded me that our best landing-place would be somewhere on the Sea of Vectis. She pointed out that the difficulty of having no labourers to till the soil could be overcome so long as we kept control of a good harbour; we could conquer the land with a war-band of nobles, and send for farmers to join us later. I was not so sure that the farmers would come when we sent for them, since there was plenty of vacant land anywhere between the Rhine and the Ocean, now that Franks, Visigoths and Suevi were all making hay in Gaul; but she answered that farmers would not want to take up vacant land that might at any moment be plundered by any one of six raiding armies, and that we ought to be able to promise them peace.

My son Cynric was sixteen years old, and it was only fair that he should have a voice in these discussions. He was rather shaken when he learned the whole truth about his parentage, for up to now he had thought himself a pure Saxon. When I had explained that his grandfather Elesa was really King Eleutherus of the Regni, and that he was a mixture of Aleman, Roman, and Saxon, he quite understood that it was necessary for him to start a new life in a new country, before someone challenged his right to take part in the assembly. I did not tell him who was responsible for the death of his grandfather; I did not want him to grow up feeling that he was under a curse from the Gods of the Family, and I hoped that the whole story would eventually be forgotten. At first he was reluctant to go oversea, when Gaul and Italy seemed to offer such rich prizes to a brave warrior; but he saw the disadvantage of having no tribe of his own behind him, and the necessity of founding a new Kingdom in an empty land. Once his mind was made up he threw himself into the business with enthusiasm, enlisting many of his young contemporaries without making extravagant and embarrassing promises. Such prudence does not come naturally to young men, but my son seemed to have inherited the good points of both his parents, and not their bad; in after life he never intrigued against authority like his mother, or made a snatch at the throne as I should have done in his place.

The whole expedition was a gamble; and when I gamble, which is not very often, I like the stakes to be high. I remembered how it had been touch and go in the first years of Aella's invasion, because we were not strong enough to fight a pitched battle as soon as we landed, and I made up my mind to take a really large force at the outset.

That meant using all my wealth as presents to comrades and boat-builders, and I would land in Britain with no possessions at all; but that made the gamble all the more exciting. During the rest of that winter and the spring of 495 I was busy on the endless round of present-giving, flattery and drinking bouts without which you can never get Germans to do anything. Of course, Frideswitha and Cynric knew no other way of doing business, and they went about it with infinite patience, but I often sighed for the straightforward contracts of Roman law.

At last I got together a good war-band of first-class warriors; many of them were exiles from various tribes, or of no tribe at all, like myself; but there were enough Saxons among them to enable me to call the new Kingdom by a Saxon name. I found that I had enlisted men to fill five ships, which meant we could give battle to any force that met us at our landing-place.

We were ready to start after the sacrifices at midsummer; I really think that sacrifices the worshippers cannot eat afterwards are a stupid waste of valuable possessions, but Frideswitha was a stickler for the right forms and ceremonies, and we certainly needed all the good luck that the gods could give us. She threw into the fire a ring worth several oxen, and I hope she got value for it in the next world, which she soon entered.

I had to take her with me, for I was now too poor to keep a wife in Germany while I was fighting oversea; we travelled together in the biggest ship of the fleet, but most of my followers were young bachelors, and we brought no other women except a single slave to wait on her. Cynric sailed on the smallest ship, in his first independent command. I suppose we were a little more than three hundred strong, though no one would let me count exactly, for fear of ill luck.

We met with fair weather, but the breeze soon died away, and we had to row to the Saxon settlements in Gaul. We reached their coast one day about sunset, and lay off the shore all night, with the men at the oars to hold us in the tides and currents. It was that night that I overheard a private conversation, which made a great difference to my domestic life.

My ship was the usual narrow rowing-boat, and of course it had no deck anywhere; but the bow and stern were a little higher out of the water than the waist, and there was a platform aft for the man to stand on who wrestled with the heavy steering oar; underneath this was the only covered place in the boat, and Frideswitha and I were lying there together. In the middle of the night I awoke as she rose and went out; but I lay perfectly still, and went on breathing deeply; when I wake suddenly I am on my guard. I saw my wife crawl from under the low platform, and thought she was going to relieve herself; but instead of walking to the side she climbed very quietly on to the roof above me. This was queer, unless she was going to give orders to the steersman, which she had no right to do; he was an old fellow called Boda, who had once fought in the same war-band as her father; just the man who would make an unauthorized change of course, if a great lady asked him. Slowly I pushed my head through the curtain that closed our little hutch at the stern; no one could see me, and I could hear all that was said to the steersman.

'So you see that he is under the curse of all the Gods of the Family, and especially those who manage the affairs of Britain,' Frideswitha was saying with great earnestness. 'The raid has no chance of success under an accursed leader, and we shall be defeated and slain in the first battle. I would not mind for myself, I am his wife and have sworn to share his good and evil fortune; but there is my son to consider. I come to you because I know that you will serve me faithfully.'

'Don't you worry, my lady,' answered the double-dealing old ruffian. 'I served your father thirty years ago, and now I take orders from you, not from that parricide. At the crisis of the first battle I shall get behind him, and give him a whack with my shield on his swordarm; when he is disarmed some Roman will do the rest, and there will be no wound from a Saxon weapon to make men suspect treachery. Then your noble son will succeed to the command, and the gods will be on our side.'

'Yes, Boda. That is a good plan. Get him killed without raising suspicion of foul play, and I will see that Cynric appoints you chief captain. Now turn away while I sit on the rail, as though I had come up here to relieve myself.'

I pulled my head in and lay down. I now knew that I had two deadly enemies aboard my own ship; the first question to answer was whether there were more of them. On the whole, I thought not; it seemed from what I had overheard that my wife had just opened the subject for the first time, and to the man on board whom she most trusted. Once I had dealt with the two traitors any other discontented comrade would be awed by the bad luck that had befallen them and would conclude that the gods were on my side after all.

For I had quite made up my mind that it would be unwise to take action openly. If I just put my sword into my wife without giving any explanation I should start a blood feud with her kin, and perhaps Cynric would turn against me also; I could not bring her to a formal trial without making public the whole story of my father's death, and if I just packed her off home to Germany she would still intrigue against me. I must arrange for an accident to Frideswitha as soon as possible. Boda could wait; he was not the man to start a plot, though he would carry out anything that strong-willed woman planned for him.

So that afternoon my decision was made. But time was pressing, for it was not more than two days' sail to the Sea of Vectis, and we would probably have to fight as soon as we landed. Luckily the calm continued that night, and we remained off the Gallic coast. It would be foolish to arrive in Britain with the warriors exhausted by long rowing, and we wanted to cover the last few miles, after we had been seen by the defenders, as quickly as possible.

Soon after dawn a strong easterly breeze sprang up, which would take us to our destination with full sails and no tiresome labour. The ship bowled along at a good rate, with her four consorts in line abreast. When we were in mid-Channel the coast of Britain began to show clearly, and naturally the crew clustered in the bows with their eyes fixed on the outline of their new home. I went to the little stern-platform, and took over the steering oar myself, for we were getting into waters where I had gone fishing as a boy. I called Frideswitha, and began to point out to her the eastern entrance to the Sea of Vectis. A Roman fishing-boat had recognized us and panicked; the fishermen were trying to get away with oars and sail, and our men were watching to see if we could overtake them. I put my back against the steering oar, so that I had both hands free, and nudged my wife in the ribs to make her turn towards me. As her head came round I hit her with all my force on the point of the jaw, and then gave her a jab in the stomach with the other hand that sent her tumbling into the sea. I shouted to the crew, and abandoned the steering oar to run to the mast; the men were all in the bows, and I got to the mast-head first, which was the trickiest part of my plan. I did not want some officious and keen-eyed ass to keep her in sight while the ship came up into the wind.

It all worked out perfectly. The tide was running strongly up Channel, and the body was swept away as the unsteered ship hung in the wind. At first the crew all rushed to the side, and several vital moments passed before anyone thought of taking over the steering oar; many were landsmen making their first voyage, and such people always think that because a ship can move fast in one direction it can be made to go wherever you want as easily as a horse. At last old Boda came to his senses and took over the helm; but from the mast-head I conned us wide of the floating body, and once we were downwind of her they had to get out the oars before we could continue the search. Presently I saw her sink for the last time, though a woman's clothes keep her afloat much longer than you might expect. We gave up the search, and continued our voyage to Britain.

It was a very merciful death to give to a woman who had plotted the murder of her husband, and perhaps in strict justice I should have thought out something more elaborate and painful. But I had always been rather fond of Frideswitha; not, of course, as a man is fond of a pretty girl, she was too old for that and she had never been beautiful; but as someone with an adult mind, with whom I could discuss my plans. I am glad she had no time to see death approaching, and drowned without a cry.

We had lost more than an hour of the favouring tide, and our fleet was widely scattered. By the time we had picked up our formation there was not much daylight left, and I gave orders that we should anchor for the night off the coast of Vectis. I wanted to have a talk with Boda before we landed; he must have guessed that the death of Frideswitha was more than an accident, and he would keep his sword handy and his back up against something solid while I was about; but he was a sensible man, and I might be able to come to an arrangement with him. I was prepared to offer him a good bribe to go away and keep his mouth shut, but he spared me that expense. As soon as it was dark he must have slipped over the side and swum ashore; next morning he was missing, and I have never heard of him since; I suppose the Jutish raiders who use the island as a base knocked him on the head for his weapons. The whole affair was nicely tidied up, and since then no one has tried to put Cynric on my throne, nor has he rebelled of his own accord.

In the morning we penetrated the inland sea, our sails set to a favourable wind, but with oars ready to keep us clear of the numerous shoals. We had to steer a winding course, which meant that we were observed from the mainland for some hours before we landed, and the local inhabitants had plenty of time to gather their forces to oppose us. This was a disadvantage, for no one fights his best after a tiring and cramping voyage, and the enemy would bury their valuables before we could start plundering. But I did not greatly fear any levy that could be raised on the shores of the Sea of Vectis.

Ever since I can remember that land has been without a ruler. To the west lies the powerful Kingdom of the Dumnonians, and on the east was once the Kingdom of the Regni; it is always a sensible plan to have a desert on your boundary, and neither my father nor the Dumnonian King had given much help when pirates landed to ransack again the ruins of the once flourishing city of Portus. That city had suffered a nasty civil war soon after the Emperor's authority was withdrawn from Britain, and its trade had vanished when the sea became unsafe for merchants. Presently it had been deserted, like so many other cities of

Britain. By the time I was a young man, twenty-five years before I landed with my army of Saxons, the whole district had lost its Roman civilization; there was no central authority, gathering taxes and paying a comitatus, between Regnum and Dumnonia. That is not to say that the country was entirely empty. Anyone who took the trouble to clear away the trees would find rich soil underneath, and there were plenty of Romans who preferred to live in a land without law; they would be exceptionally tough warriors, but there ought not to be very many of them, and they would probably not unite under one leader. We expected that we could face them in open battle.

Soon after midday we rowed up a little creek in the shore of the mainland that I am proud to say is still called Cerdics-ora, meaning Cerdic's landing-place. The five ships were close together and we were able to drive the bows into soft mud and run ashore dryshod. A few Romans had collected to oppose our landing, but we were three hundred strong, much more numerous than the average party of raiders, and we must have outnumbered them considerably; we soon drove them from the battlefield, without ourselves suffering much loss. It was Cynric's first battle, and the dear boy exposed himself freely; but I had seen to it that he had a good bodyguard of experienced veterans, and no harm came to him. In one way it is a good thing to win a reputation for courage in early youth, for it is very hard to lose afterwards, and gathers good men to the war-band; but I had a serious talk with him that evening, and explained that there was no point in my founding a Kingdom if I had no heir to succeed me. He promised to take more care of himself in future.

Now we were established on the coast, and the perennial question of what to do with our ships had to be settled. Of course, we had made up our minds to live permanently in

Britain, and we did not need them to take us back to Germany; on the other hand, ships are valuable possessions, and I could not bear to watch them burn. Finally I sent away all five, with very small crews; four were to be exchanged for good presents, after the German manner of selling, and the largest was to come back carrying the crews of the other four, and a few recruits as well. We would have to wait in a fortified camp until it returned; but that would be in about six weeks, and the neighbourhood would supply us for that time.

We lived peacefully in our camp for two months. There was no local ruler who could bring a regular comitatus into the field against us, and the Dumnonians were on the defensive now that they had no organized Roman state to the east of them. My present territory was at one end of the wide belt of devastated country that stretched through the middle of Britain, I believe right up to the Kingdom of Elmetia somewhere near Eboracum; there was no ruler who felt it his duty to turn me out at all costs.

All the same, I was not satisfied with our present hunting ground; for the land immediately north of the Sea of Vectis is so thickly wooded and so little cultivated that it is a hunting ground and nothing more. A gang of hunters with wooden clubs, who had forgotten their laws and lived bestially in small family groups, was no sort of inheritance to leave to Cynric.

Also we were too near the coast. I am told that the Empire still lingers on at the eastern end of the Middle Sea, but it will be many generations before a powerful fleet brings law and order to the pirates of the Channel. I have seen from my boyhood what a terrible drain it is on the resources of a Kingdom always to keep a look-out for raiders from the sea; I did not want Cynric to spend his life sitting on the beach waiting for news of pirates, and incessantly driving his cattle to shelter. I must go inland, to a hilly country where beacon-fires would give good warning of the approach of enemies, and where there was open grass for farmers to plough.

But I had to persuade my followers of this, for if I gave them orders that they did not like they could march off and join the South Saxons on our eastern border. In any case we would have to winter at Cerdics-ora, since it was too late to plant corn. We did not have a very good time, but we managed somehow with deer from the woods and fish from the streams. I kept my men together as much as possible, so that they would feel they were one community, and in the evenings we held long discussions about our future plans, in which I tried to guide them to fall in with my ideas. Cynric was a great help to me; he was always cheerful and active, even when food was scarce, and the younger men would follow him anywhere. He will make a splendid ruler for the organized Kingdom I have founded after so many years of gruelling warfare.

There was another point on which I tried to influence my men to comply with my wishes. The real wild Germans of Germany, who have had no contact with Rome, are in the habit of burying with their dead most of the valuable possessions of the corpse; it is a pious idea, and a strange contrast to their usual appalling avarice. But in our present situation we really could not afford to bury good swords and golden arm-rings in the earth. We needed all the treasure we could muster, and I set myself to alter the religious prejudices of my men.

This was not as difficult as you might expect, for the Germans are not a religious people; they are sensible enough to be nervous about the future, and they take what precautions they can; but they themselves do not believe that their sacrifices have much effect, for the gods are fundamentally hostile to mankind. Furthermore, they have an uncomfortable feeling that other people know more about the supernatural than they do, and any outlandish wizard impresses them enormously. I had been careful not to bring with me any holy men, and of course we could not set up sanctuaries in this new land until someone had dreamt the appropriate dream; we got on very comfortably that winter without any religion at all, and were none the worse for it. I had hopes that when we moved north in the spring they would bury the dead with nothing more than their best clothes; especially as we had no women with us, who are always the conservatives. There was not a single woman in the camp, which was rather unusual; Frides-witha's servant had been drowned as an offering to the ghost of her mistress, and I ordered that no Roman women should be caught alive. I did not want Cynric to get into any entanglement before he was safely married to a Woden-born girl with a good dowry.

Our numbers were slightly greater than when we had landed, for we had lost few men in battle, and there had been no serious sickness; while the ship had arrived with reinforcements. That ship was a great bother; I could not bear to part with it, but I did not want to split the army by leaving it guarded. When we were ready to march in the spring I put on board a small crew, and sent it back to Germany to bring more men. For miles to the north the land was empty and uncultivated, and I could promise good farms to all who joined me. These farmers are not the best type of recruit for serious fighting, being mostly poor and badly armed; but if I picked my way carefully I ought to be able to reach open country without rousing any Roman King against us.

During winter hunting parties had scouted the neigh-bourhood thoroughly, and I knew the lie of the land. The

abandoned ruins of Venta and Calleva lay attractively just
to the east of our line of march, but I regretfully decided
that it would be unwise to take them over just yet. Nobody
lived in them, but the South Saxons might regard them as
within their sphere of influence, and I did not want to start
a war with the settlers on our eastern border. I could not
diverge to the west without bringing the fierce Dumnonians on my track, but there were several alternative
routes, since most of the rivers in that land flow
southward. Some hunters had found a good track leading
overland to the westernmost of these rivers, which was
called the Avon (like half the streams in Britain). From the
look of the winter floods I guessed it must rise in chalky
country, and as the chalk will not bear forest there must be
a stretch of open land between us and the Thames valley.
This was the gateway to Britain that I chose.

In the beginning of May in the year 496 we set off to
found our Kingdom. We were about three hundred and
twenty strong, all fighting-men without a single woman or
child. Aella had founded South Saxony with less; but that
had been on the coast, in sight of the pirate ships that
could reinforce him or take him back to Germany. I could
not conceal from myself that an attack on the inland
country was a more risky undertaking.

We advanced for two days, and had covered about
thirty miles when we emerged on to the uplands. These
were rugged hills, much steeper than the smooth crests of
the land by the Channel, and as always with chalk it was
hard to find drinking water; the grass was rougher than I
had expected, and there did not seem to be many sheep
about.

The inhabitants were the greatest surprise of all. I
thought I knew southern Britain, and the kind of people
who lived in it; if I had been asked to describe them I

would have said that they were the ordinary type of citizen, growing more and more barbarous as order decayed, and beginning to copy the Saxon method of fighting; at the very bottom of the scale were a class of coloni who spoke Celtic in their homes, though of course their masters ordered them about in Latin and their tools and methods of cultivation were Roman. But this rugged plain was covered with little hill-top villages where Celts ploughed with the implements that their ancestors used before Caesar came to Britain; they spoke no language but Celtic, and seemed to pay rent to no landowner. The only possible explanation was that no one had ever interfered with such a poor district.

Quite recently someone must have taken an interest in the land, for on its northern border was a great entrench-ment that did not look to be a hundred years old. My men were worried for fear the builders of such a mighty work might come and chase them into the sea; but I guessed that it had been built by the Dumnonians when Saxon mercenaries first came to the upper Thames, and aban-doned soon after, when they realized that those savages were not dangerous. My followers called it the Ditch of Woden, which to them was a satisfactory explanation of any remarkable object that they could not have made for themselves; it was a complete waste of labour, in any case, and had no influence at all on the course of future campaigns.

I did my best to get into touch with the miserable Celts who lurked on the hill-tops, but without success; they always fled when I sent an envoy to negotiate with them. The trouble is that nowadays no one trusts a Saxon even when he wants to make peace, and of course I was quite unable to persuade my men to spare the life of anyone they caught while he was running away. In that respect Saxons are like greyhounds, and just as impossible to stop once the pursuit has begun. So I learned nothing of the history of that part of the country; probably the brutish Celtic peasants could have told me very little.

That first year we lived well, for the crops had been sown before our invasion began, and we had nothing to do but harvest them as they ripened. But the future was doubtful. We were right in the middle of Britain, and there were organized Roman states on our western border; any day they might send a confederate army to drive us out. That meant that it was unsafe to scatter to different ploughlands. Once again the dream of every barbarian invasion had failed to materialize; it would have been very nice to have ruled as a warrior aristocracy over a population of hard-working peasants, like the Goths in the south, but my men were too savage to refrain from killing the goose that might have laid golden eggs. Luckily we had captured more sheep and cattle than we could eat at once, so we had a little stock of breeding animals to begin the next year. But it was not the kind of life that satisfied my instinct for civilization; nomad shepherds can keep a sort of culture, particularly in military affairs, but isolation in family groups leads to the decay of traditional learning.

I talked over the problem with Cynric. We decided that at all costs we must keep in touch with the coast, and encourage a stream of lower-class immigrants from Germany. We still had the one ship, and sent it on several voyages that summer to bring back working settlers; these began to clear the valleys by the Sea of Vectis.

But the life that I planned was not what the warriors wanted. The whole Empire was a prize for adventurous swords, and in other places more valuable plunder was to be gained than mutton and woollen cloaks. Many nobles left me in the autumn of 497, when they found that I intended to remain in the empty land that I had conquered. I was able to fill their places with other recruits, to whom good food was a greater booty than gold; but these were not so well born or so well armed, or above all so capable of absorbing civilization. I was worried about what would happen if we were attacked by a really good Roman comitatus.

The only thing to do was to keep very quiet where I was, and trust that the increase in the numbers of my following would outweigh the decline in its quality. A professional Saxon raider was a match for three Romans; even peasant spearmen ought to be able to hold their own against equal numbers. These people brought their women with them, for they needed labour on the land; that was a stabilizing influence, since the women made them wash occasionally, and eat meals at stated times, and sleep under a roof. Men alone are always trying to prove how tough they are, and how like brute beasts they can live; without women they would soon run naked and forget how to speak.

I did not marry again. I had brought bad luck to both Gertrude and Frideswitha, and it seemed I did not possess the art of ruling women. I was now forty-six years of age, and quite content to sleep alone most nights. It is unusual for a chieftain to be unmarried, and most of them want as many descendants as possible, but I had put all my eggs into one basket. I thought only of Cynric, who should have an undisputed succession, without kinsmen to intrigue against him. He was still attached to the memory of his unfortunate mother, and that was another reason for my celibacy; a stepmother often clouds the relationship between father and son.

So I settled down as the ruler of a peasant folk; it was a small and backward country, and I did not make myself a laughing-stock by taking the title of King. But every year more settlers came, brought in my own ship and owing obedience to me, and more woods by the Sea of Vectis were cleared for the plough. I myself, with my dear son, lived in the open country to the north, and we herded our sheep from one hill-fort to another; the peasants of the coastland kept us supplied with bread and beer. We fought many little skirmishes with the miserable Celtic squatters, but we had no set battles with rival armies, and we ate abundantly, even in the spring. It was not the sort of life I had planned when I left Germany; then I had dreamed of ruling a subject population of civilized men, the ambition of every German raider; now I was nothing more than the war chief of a very barbarous band of nomads. But at least I had won the complete independence that had been my object since I was a child; the orders I could give my men were circumscribed by a thousand customary rights and obligations, but nobody could give me any orders at all.

Every spring I led out small parties of scouts; we were careful not to attack any place that was guarded by well-armed men, but of course we destroyed any village that could not defend itself. In this way we won definite borders for our infant state, and our neighbours grew accustomed to having us there. To the south our country stretched to the sea, to the west there were the Roman states that were best left alone, and to the east, after many miles of empty forest and ruined farms, one would come to the outposts of the men of Kent. On the north we had no defined border; Londinium was now a deserted ruin, and there were no Roman cities south of the Thames, though warlike bands of Romans dwelt on the high hills north of it. In the valley itself the sons of the Saxon mercenaries I had led under Count Ambrosius still lived in peace in their riverside clearings. They now paid tribute to no ruler, and had settled down to a very savage and poverty-stricken life of fishing and hunting; when their weapons broke they had no metal to make new ones, and they had interbred with the lowest class of coloni, so that they had degenerated from even the low level of culture that they had managed to retain when I first knew them. They were a useful object-lesson of what happens to men who try to live an independent life without women of their own kind, or a competent ruler. But it fascinated me to think that they had come to their present home by the rivers that flow out on the east coast, and that we had met them coming from the south. The German invasions, after fifty years of steady infiltration, had mastered all the southeast of Britain, and there was not a walled city or a properly-run villa anywhere east of the territory of Corinium.

I was not afraid of the Romans of the west; they had got used by degrees to owning only half of the island, and they were too busy murdering one another for the thrones of the remaining cities to undertake a war of conquest.

For three years we lived in peace, the quietest period of my middle life. The land I ruled fell into two definite portions; in the north was the open chalk, a broken country of steep slopes and sudden valleys, where armies could move freely in any direction; in the south were the rivers, running through thick forest to the sheltered sea; they were swampy and liable to sudden flood, but small boats could bring new settlers with good German spears. In the north my little war-band of very inferior comrades moved peacefully from one hill-fort to the next, as our sheep ate the grazing; and in the valleys of the south the corn-lands increased year by year where new farmers cleared the woods.

The year 500 passed in that peaceful manner. To me it was a landmark, as such a nice round number, but no

Saxons counted the years, and I believe the Romans, hopelessly out of touch with the civilized world, now dated by the regnal years of their ephemeral Kings. I was in my fiftieth year, and Cynric was past his twenty-second birthday; though he was quite content with his position as my heir, and waited patiently for me to die a natural death. I might have ended my days as a petty war chief of the open chalk; but various dangers came upon me one after the other, and the action I was forced to take raised me to my present exalted position.

My first trouble came not from the Romans, but from the side of Germany, and it was one I had long foreseen. In the full summer of the year 501 I was sitting quietly in a little hut of turf in the hill-fort where my band was halted. There was a light drizzle, and I was eating my supper under shelter, for I had already begun to suffer from the rheumatic pains that are the natural penalty of campaigning in the climate of Britain. My men were making the usual disgusting mess of their supper in the rain outside, and I was glad of the excuse to eat neatly and silently, with no companion except my son. German table-manners have always been the greatest trial I have had to endure while living among these barbarians, and they still offend me after fifty years. But I could not often indulge in the luxury of private meals; the Saxons know in their hearts that they are rather disgusting people, and they are always on the look-out for fancied insults. My rheumatism had given me the chance of a little treat, and I was enjoying myself talking sense to Cynric instead of bellowing war-songs with my dear comrades-in-arms.

Then a messenger pushed his way, crouching, through the low door of the hut, and sat down beside me. Of course, there was no room to stand up, but a civilized man would at least have asked for permission before plumping himself down. He was only a farmer from the south coast, of the lowest class of Saxon who was counted as really free, but I had to shake him by the hand, and offer him food from my bowl, before I could ask him why he had left his squalid clearing to interrupt my rest. I have always managed to be a good comrade to the shaggiest barbarian, but even after all these years it is a strain, especially with very smelly peasants at meal-times.

As a matter of fact he had important news, and he had done right to come and tell me. Two strange warships had come to land at Cerdics-ora by the Sea of Vectis, and the crews were helping themselves to the produce of the farms near the coast without paying for what they took; so far they had not killed anyone.

My dear Cynric was for blowing the war-horn at once, and summoning the whole countryside to drive them to their ships; since they had come in only two we must outnumber them, and we ought to be able to make their stay uncomfortable, though pirates fight much better than farmers. But I persuaded him to sit quiet and talk it over, for that evening at least; I never start a war until I am pushed into it, and those two ships might be the forerunners of a fleet. My heart sank as I thought that from now on we would face that perpetual watch against sea-borne raiders that had been the most unpleasant feature of my youth in Anderida; I suppose that men who settle down to grow corn in any part of the world are at once the target of every ruffian who would rather fight than dig, but it was a wearisome prospect. I held a council, to see if we could deal with the matter without fighting.

My war-band at this time consisted of no more than fifty warriors who had never stiffened their muscles by doing useful work of any kind, though of course I could raise a large army of clumsy peasants; most of the ambitious and blood-thirsty men who had come with me from Germany had moved on in search of better plunder. Those who remained were happy to be at peace for as long as possible, and nobody enjoys waging war on pirates, who fight very fiercely and possess no riches, otherwise they would not have gone to sea. The chief thing in our favour was that we were hardly worth plundering either; the raiders could not have intended to come ashore in a German land, where all the craftsmen had long ago been killed, and the scanty gold and silver traded for weapons and ploughs. They would either sail farther west, or if they were seeking new corn-lands they could take axes and go into the forest, where there was room for all.

So my captains decided, and from their point of view they were sensible; but it might make my position very shaky if an independent leader shared my territory. We arranged that I should try to get into peaceful discussion with the new arrivals; I sat up late with Cynric, planning how I could keep the leadership of my own men, and if possible become the war chief of the pirates also. It depended on the personality of their present leader. He might be a man who kept his oath, and in that case I could make him my subordinate and ally, as though he was a barbarian chief seeking employment from a Roman ruler; but that was how all the trouble had started between Vortigern and Hengist, long ago, and I knew that sworn promises seldom checked a leader of pirates if he saw a chance of bettering his position. I could not make any firm plans until I had met him and sized him up.

In the morning the whole war-band started south; I went ahead with the ten best-dressed men as an escort, and we marched openly along the track, without attempting to scout for an ambush. But half a mile behind came the rest of the warriors, with a crowd of armed peasants; they marched with their swords loose in the scabbard, ready to come to our rescue as soon as they heard the alarm. Cynric led them, and I knew he would do his best to save us if we were received with treachery. Most rulers would never have dared to put their safety into the hands of the heir to all that they possessed; but Cynric was the prop of my old age.

We spent a night in camp on the road, for the journey was longer than a comfortable day's march, and I had decided against riding the wretched little ponies that we sometimes used. We would look more impressive if we walked steadily in close order than if we straggled along the trail on those cow-hocked, razor-backed nags, that always stopped to nibble the grass of the wayside when you wanted them to keep together. Even the kindliest critic could not say that Saxons are good horsemen, and a dozen of them riding together are a horrid sight.

On the second day we marched along the track, singing to keep our paces in unison, with a green and leafy branch borne in front of the little procession. So many wars have started by accident, because two bodies of armed men had to approach closely to discuss terms, and some nervous ass drew his sword, out of sheer fright. On the other hand, it would be putting an appalling strain on the honour of a pirate commander if I walked up to his camp by myself, without escort. His sentries would see the army marching half a mile behind; but they would only conclude that they had to deal with a sensible and experienced war-band, that wanted peace but could defend itself at a pinch. For the same reason we pretended not to notice the fresh footprints of their scouts when we passed them on the track, and kept our eyes turned away from the bushes; I gave strict orders that no one was to see a stranger until we had reached the main camp, and begun to parley.

Our peasants, who had fled from the pirates, were also hiding in the woods. They did not show themselves to my small escort, but came out of their refuge to join the supporting force, and Cynric had the sense to send forward a messenger with their news. It appeared that the pirates were not seeking war; they had given everyone time to run away before they pillaged a farm, they had not killed the sick who had to be left behind, and after helping themselves to what they wanted they had left the huts unburned. This information cheered me up; the newcomers would not be so careful to avoid starting a blood-feud unless they intended to have peaceful dealings with us in future.

It was quite late in the afternoon that at last we arrived at the pirates' camp. The track led to a little creek where the woods had been cleared. Just outside we found a small body of pirates; they had evidently been told by their scouts how many men I had with me, for their guard was of exactly the same strength, and their leader stood in front, waving a green branch. I gave a sigh of relief; we had managed to get into touch without fighting; now surely my Roman education would give me the advantage, when it came to negotiating with an ignorant barbarian.

Our respective escorts remained about fifty yards apart, and I met their leader alone. We began, of course, by giving our names, and the names of our ancestors right back to Woden. He was called Port, and he had with him his two sons, Baeda and Maegla, and two shiploads of lesser warriors, all Saxons. Germans never lie about their descent, and I accepted this quite easily, but the reason he gave for coming to my small and ravaged land was really very extraordinary. He said that he had had the misfortune to kill a peculiarly sacred bear, and that the witch who was the servant and guardian of the animal had told him that to avert the unpleasant consequence of his sacrilege he must sail to a land already called by his own name, where the local priest would have power to cleanse him of his guilt. He had inquired diligently from travellers in his part of Germany, and at last had heard there was an old Roman city on the shore of the Sea of Vectis called Portus. Then he gathered a war-band, including both his sons, and here he was.

I say that this story struck me as extraordinary, although it is a fair example of barbarian witchcraft. That is because he was the first German I had met who put himself to inconvenience for religious motives; the Germans have a great quantity of religious beliefs, and a whole crowd of competing gods and goddesses; but no great poet has ever brought order into their Pantheon, as Homer did for civilized men, and they worship whichever Divine Power they find most handy. The normal German thing to do, if you have the misfortune to kill the sacred bear of Freya, is to switch over at once and worship Thor instead. Germans have an enviable capacity for proving to themselves that whatever they did was really right, or at least that it was the fault of someone else; Port was the first who had ever to my knowledge suffered from remorse.

Of course, I pretended to credit everything that he said; if I had not, the fighting would have begun at once. I pointed out politely that I had a prior claim to anything of value that might remain in the deserted city of Portus; but the whole land was underpopulated, and he was welcome to dwell there, if he would come to my war-band and be my faithful companion. I ought soon to be able to learn whether he was really a priest-ridden ass, or whether some deep scheme lay at the back of this astonishing tale.

He was delighted to be given his spiritual home without having to fight for it, and we embraced before the two escorts. Then we all went into his camp, and feasted on cattle stolen from my farms; but in future we arranged that he should pay, or at least owe, for the food his men needed until they had harvested their first crop. After supper, Port spoke again of the need to get himself cleansed from the blood-guilt of the sacred bear. His earnest request for the services of the local priest put me in a difficult position. For the last six years I and all my followers had got on very well without any holy men at all; now here was my new ally inquiring earnestly for a priest, who would have to perform a fairly complicated ritual.

I filled the gap myself. I did not want to detail a comrade to act as a temporary priest, for it might have put ideas into his head; a ruler must always beware of those who pretend to know the will of the gods, and take it upon themselves to proclaim what the laity should do. We have no bears in the south of Britain, otherwise the obvious thing would have been to order Port to sacrifice pretty heavily to the first bear he met; but I made up a most colourful and impressive ritual. I made him fast for a whole day, and sacrifice his jewelled sword-belt by hanging it in a tree where I could retrieve it later; he also provided a Roman, though they were scarce in the neighbourhood, who was burnt in a large fire at midnight; I then recited as much as I could remember of the Penitential Psalms; as a climax to the whole proceeding I baptized him. The joke is that the baptism was probably valid, for I am a baptized Christian myself; if there is any truth in what I was taught as a child, Port must have been very surprised when he died shortly afterwards.

When the religious nonsense was finished we made a satisfactory treaty. Port and his measly little war-band were allowed to dwell in Portus and the country round about, and he remained in authority over them, an authority he might transmit to his heirs; of course, subject to my supreme command in time of war. This brought in the danger of separatist tendencies in my new state, a thing that I had always tried to avoid up to now; I think my comrades were surprised that I conceded it so easily. There was a reason. I had taken Port's measure. I knew he was a fool, and I was confident that I could eliminate him before he became a nuisance.

We had one more day of feasting and drinking, and then I marched back to the open sheep-runs of the north. I had decided to wait for at least a year, to lull any suspicions that the Portingas might harbour, and then I should not be at all surprised if a sad accident befell that intrusive religious nincompoop. There was no hurry at all, for my men would never desert me to follow him; the danger would come in the next generation, if he left a capable son.

We remained at peace, living comfortably on our flocks and the corn from the southern valleys. We even began to plough the sheltered ravines of the open country, wherever there was water; the Roman peasants had clung to the infertile hill-tops, which were bare by nature, but our heavy ox-drawn ploughs did better on deep soil, and we had good axes to cut down the trees. Huts were built near the new fields, and they were warmer and more comfortable than the hill-forts, which were presently left to the shepherds. I have noticed the same thing in other lands permanently occupied by Saxons; after a few years the whole pattern of settlement is changed, until you would have to dig to find traces of the Roman inhabitants.

Port and his little self-governing settlement in my territory still rankled. I did not want to pick a quarrel and wipe out the whole war-band; if Port and his two sons died suddenly his followers would be useful reinforcements for my own army. What made the whole enterprise difficult was that I dared not take an accomplice into my confidence. Cynric must continue to believe that I was an honourable chief, otherwise he might start plotting to succeed me. Also the plan must arrange for the deaths of Baeda and Maegla at the same time as their father; the two young men had no religious scruples and were governed by nothing but self-interest; to allow one of them to inherit his father's power would merely be exchanging King Log for King Stork. I racked my brains in vain; the stock arrangement on these occasions is a hunting accident, but the objection to that was that I wanted to kill three people, and it would be altogether too much of a coincidence if I shot all three of them in mistake for a deer.

I suppose my mind had grown flabby during the years of peace we had enjoyed, for it took me a long time to remember that I possessed one great advantage; I was the only German in Britain who could read and write, and no one among my following suspected that I had acquired so much effeminate and useless learning. I could safely arrange by letter the deaths that were necessary for the peaceful succession of my son.

Once I had thought of this solution it was easy to work out the details. Only Romans could read the letters I must write, so I would have to get into touch with a band of Roman outlaws, capable of killing three well-armed Saxon nobles; and I would have to arrange matters so that they got some advantage from the murder, or thought they were going to, which would do just as well. I listened carefully to the reports of our scouts on the Roman outlaws who hung around the outskirts of our settlements. They were mostly dispossessed peasants, who knew that the Dumnonians had no farms to offer them, and who enjoyed the idle life of the woods. The trouble was that probably none of them could read either; but years of outlawry had made them into hardened campaigners, and I thought it likely that exiled Roman noblemen would presently start to form them into a comitatus.

I pretended that the occasional raids of these outlaws were more of a nuisance than they were in actual fact, and appealed to our farmers for information about their depredations. I heard rumours of a Roman leader who sounded like the very man I wanted. In the western woods quite a large band had been formed; it was led by a relative of the King of Demetia, who had left home in a hurry. He was known to my men as Natan-leod, a quite impossible name; but Germans often make the most horrible mess of foreign words, since the strange noises of their ugly language have no parallel in Latin.

I gave out that I was seriously alarmed at the danger represented by this band of half-armed peasants, and offered a reward to anyone who could bring in one of their men alive. Some of our best warriors went out to hunt them, and caught a prisoner. He was an intelligent man, and I talked to him in private; I told him frankly that I wished to get in touch with his chief, and that I would arrange his escape so that he could deliver a letter. He said that the real name of Natan-leod was Venatianus Leoninus, and that he had been a noted warrior of the Demetians until he had been mixed up in an unsuccessful rebellion; a man of that standing would certainly be able to read, so that was one difficulty solved. But there still remained another: what reward could I offer to Leoninus to make him my ally? I could do nothing openly, of course, for my men would not have obeyed me if I told them that a Roman chief must be left in peace, as my friend. I did not dare to lose a battle so that he might win, for men would leave me if I got the reputation of an unsuccessful leader. Besides, though one often hears gossip that the result of a battle was arranged in advance, and that one commander lost on purpose, actually such an affair is very difficult to work out.

Eventually I wrote a long letter. I explained frankly my reasons for wanting to get rid of the Portingas as a separate community, and offered to leave a small flock of sheep in a certain spot, as evidence of my good faith. When Leoninus had taken the sheep he was to leave a letter where I could find it, and then we would make a plan to ensure the deaths I wished for. I knew that sheep would be an acceptable gift to the outlaws, for they were always short of clothing, especially wool.

The prisoner escaped the night before we were to sacrifice him, and after the flock had been taken I found the letter. The rest of the plot was quite easy to fix up, although in the end I had to hand over the reward that I had promised. I possessed very little treasure, but the outlaws were easily satisfied; they were short of weapons and everything made of iron, for they could not trade with the Roman Kingdoms, who made war on them just as we did. Accordingly, I offered a consignment of sword-blades and scrap-iron if Leoninus would carry out the little commission in which I needed his help.

My plans were worked out by harvest-time. Leoninus made a small but very impudent raid on the flocks that grazed outside the hill-fort where I was staying. I summoned Port and his two sons to a conference to decide on measures against these raids, but I told him that we would not take the field until the end of autumn, and that he could leave his followers to get in their crops. I asked him to let me know by what route he was coming, so that I could send an escort; I then passed on this information to Leoninus, and arranged for the escort to go the wrong way. Port, Baeda, and Maegla were killed after a brave defence.

Venatianus took away his promised payment in excellent steel, and the Portingas, leaderless, agreed to merge their identity in the common mass of my followers.

Meanwhile we all lived in peace and prosperity, the grazing of the north admirably supplemented by the corn of the south. Each summer several boatloads of new immigrants arrived direct from Germany, until the southern valleys were lined from end to end with fertile farms. Dear Cynric several times suggested that it would be fitting for me to take the title of King, now that I ruled so many men and such rich land; but I was against it. I pointed out that though the number of able-bodied men who came to my annual law-moots was large, they were nearly all stiff and clumsy spearmen. My war-band, who did no work and were supported by the rents of the farmers, was actually smaller than it had been when I first landed. I also said that I thought it silly to announce myself as a King, for no particular reason except that we were growing rich; let us wait until the next war broke out, and I could be properly hoisted on a shield amid the slain.

I was perfectly content to go on with things as they were. I was now too old, in my middle fifties, to enjoy warfare for its own sake; I was at last completely independent, and my nearest equal was far away in the land of the South Saxons. For the rest of my life I had no ambition except to safeguard what I had won.

Cynric was in his twenties, the age when all Woden-born young men delight in war; it was really very good of him to put up so quietly with the peaceful ways of his father, but I have already said that he was a remarkable son. Of course he now led my little war-band when they had to go out after raiders, and he did most of the work that is involved in the defence of a land surrounded by enemies; but he remained faithful to me. I don't know what

I have done to deserve such an obedient son, but I long ago made up my mind that there is no justice in the way the world is run, and I sincerely hope there will be none in the next world.

Considering the disturbed state of Britain as a whole, our little corner was remarkably peaceful. The South Saxons had relapsed into a quiet and vegetable existence in their narrow strip of land between the Forest and the sea; their King, Aella, had once been the most prominent German war chief in Britain, but now he was very old. They had wiped out the Roman population, and in fact even their purely German culture was in decline, as happens so easily when new settlers live a rough life in a conquered land; they get used to camping out and living hand to mouth, they do not bother to bring good German craftsmen, and very soon their farms and their weapons are more barbarous than anything they would have put up with at home. Even the elementary civilization of Old Saxony was only kept in being by constant effort; in the new land they were letting it go downhill. It was a warning that I took to heart, for I was determined that my own followers should finally end up as civilized men.

The Cantwara, on the other hand, were doing well; though they also were at peace. But then their conquest had been a gradual process, occasionally interrupted by truce with the Romans, and in consequence large numbers of the original population had been enslaved instead of killed; these included many of the best metal-workers, so that now Kent was a famous centre for jewellery and drinking bowls. I believe King Oisc was still alive, and he seemed to have laid the foundations of an enduring civilized state. His men were proud of their prosperity, and now called themselves Jutes, after their ruling family; I suppose they were ashamed of their mongrel origin.

Those were the only German neighbours that I had to reckon with in politics, though I heard rumours of a new Kingdom of the East Saxons that had been set up north of the estuary of the Thames. What was happening beyond them was something that I never knew accurately, although I believe there was a continuous belt of German settlements on the east coast as far as the Great Wall; unfortunately the occasional wandering poets who sang of battles in the north used German place-names that meant nothing to me.

One thing was clear: the Saxon invasion of Britain had come to a standstill. The Roman Kings had given up hope of expelling us, and were far too jealous of one another to combine for the task. Luckily, there seemed to be no surviving representatives of the dispossessed rulers, except for the descendants of Vortigern in the far west. I suppose it is natural for Kings to be slain in battle when their land is conquered, as my father had been, and in any case these dynasties were less than a hundred years old; so there were no pretenders lurking in the woods for a chance to turn us out. My only important Roman neighbour was the King of Dumnonia, and I had never done him any harm; of course, my followers would never allow me to conclude a formal truce with him, for they looked on all Romans as deadly enemies; but in practice we respected our mutual boundary.

I devoted my attention to the never-ending task of keeping up our level of civilization. I was determined not to end as the headman of a group of complete savages, and I took the interest in their culture that is more natural for a stranger than for one born to it. I encouraged wandering poets; I even named some old pre-Roman grave-mounds after the best known of the great men of old, so that their stories might still be sung; Woden and Thor were not forgotten, and of course the farmers kept up the ritual of Baldur and Freya, for fear that otherwise their seed corn might not know how to grow. But I was most careful to discourage costly sacrifices of precious objects that we could not replace, although if men were going to slaughter an ox for food I saw no harm in their dedicating it to a god. I also made it clear that each farmer and landowner was responsible for worship on his own land, and that he must conduct the services himself. No secular ruler would wish to introduce a professional priesthood into a land where luckily it is unknown.

I did not bother so much about material comfort. That comes easily enough when the time is ripe for it, if only men's minds remain civilized. On the exposed northern frontier where I usually lived we had to move from place to place, as our sheep ate up the grass, and it was easy to build some sort of shack in the nearest of the numerous hill-forts. I like plenty of food, and a warm fire, but I am indifferent to the appearance of my house, and I had long ago given up hope of having a decent bath; in fact I very much doubt if there was a real bath anywhere even in the Roman parts of Britain. To accustom my men to the idea that cities were quite good places to dwell in, I held an annual meeting to decide important lawsuits in the ruins of deserted Venta. Nobody lived there, for most Germans think that deserted cities are haunted by the ghosts of war-like Roman soldiers. I was planning for a future I would never live to see.

I was quite independent, and the fact that I had no title greater than war-chief did not worry me in the slightest; Cynric, or his son, would sooner or later become a King, unless the Romans made a bigger effort to dislodge us than they had up to now. The dear boy was married, to a healthy and tractable daughter of Woden who had been imported from Germany for the purpose, and she bore him a child every year. I gave her a separate establishment in the south, on the excuse that it was the safest part of the country for young children, and I saw very little of her; the real reason was that Cynric was too fond of his family, and I hated to take second place in his affections. Of course, he spent most of his time with the war-band.

There was only one cloud on the horizon. That tiresome Venatianus Leoninus had done me a considerable service, and had been well rewarded for his pains. Unfortunately, he had persuaded himself that it was entirely his own courage and skill that had caused the death of the chiefs of the Portingas; fools with short memories often reason like that. His band had increased now, he had good weapons at his disposal, and I had been careful not to interfere with his activities in the south, where he raided impartially both my Germans and the Dumnonians. I thought he might come in useful one day, since it is always handy to have an unscrupulous ally whom one can disavow at need. But he did not understand that he only existed because of my unwillingness to crush him, and he went on gathering recruits until he could only feed his men by incessant raids on my best land. I tried sending him a letter by the usual secret route, but he did not deign to answer it, and his pillaging continued.

In the year 508 he finally stirred me to action by his own foolishness and pride. He was doing very well as a chief of outlaws, and I am sure he had never been more prosperous in his life. But he had the audacity to proclaim himself King of the Durotriges, an archaic title that he took from the tribe that lived thereabouts before the Romans came to Britain. By doing this he annoyed the King of the Dumnonians and the other rulers of the Romans, and deprived himself of any hope of winning their alliance in what he called his holy struggle against the invading Germans; as soon as I heard of it, by the roundabout gossip of the countryside, I knew that I must crush him.

When the harvest had been gathered I called up the whole levy from the farmlands, to join the small band of professional warriors about my person. I was fifty-seven, and it was more than twelve years since I had led an army in person, but I would have lost all authority if I had appointed anyone else as commander-in-chief. Apart from the rheumatism that afflicts anyone who has lived fifty years in the climate of Britain I was quite fit enough to order a line of battle, and I did not intend to charge at the head of my men.

The peasants came willingly to the muster, for they were very tired of feeding Natan-leod and all his followers as well as paying tribute to me. I was amazed at our numbers when I reviewed the troops on an open plain; there must have been more than three thousand men, which is a remarkable increase for an army that came to Britain in five ships only thirteen years ago; of course, since then new settlers had been arriving every summer. By contrast, my true war-band of professional warriors was barely a hundred strong. That made the army weaker than its total numbers would seem to imply, but it was natural enough after the long peace of the last decade.

Our first task was to locate the enemy, who lived in the dense woodland to the west of our river valleys. In the winter it was their habit to take refuge on an island in some impassable swamp, but in the summer, when the swamps dried up, they roamed the forest. I thought that since Leoninus had proclaimed himself King he would find it beneath his dignity to live like a Scythian nomad, and that he would set up a permanent palace. That should make it easier to bring him to battle; I had no fear of the outcome of a fight, but I knew that his bandits could probably march through familiar country faster than my men, and I dreaded chasing him for months on end, through the damp and haunted forest. If he had been foolish enough to found a permanent capital, there would be a place he would have to defend.

It is a heart-breaking business trying to make Saxons take prisoners alive, even when their own convenience and the safe outcome of the campaign depend on their doing so. The robbers were still raiding our farms, all the more easily now so many of the defenders had been gathered into my army; my men continually skirmished with them, and often drove them away before they could do any damage, but they would insist on killing everyone left on the field, and I could not get the reliable information about the lair of the robbers that is easy to obtain if you torture a wounded prisoner properly. I had reluctantly made up my mind to wander through the trackless woods until we stumbled on them by chance, and had given the order to set out next day, when I had a great stroke of luck.

We Romans of Britain were citizens of the Empire until not so very long ago, and in those days we acknowledged no superior except the Emperor and his civil servants, who might easily be our own relatives. When we set up all these Kingdoms, only two generations back, there was no tradition of loyalty to a hereditary superior, and many people disliked the thought that one particular family had got hold of all the power and prerogative of an Emperor. In consequence the Kingdoms never ran very smoothly, and when a local chief decided to make himself King there was always an outburst of discontent among his followers. The Germans, on the other hand, have had hereditary Kings from time immemorial, their followers obey them from long habit, and rebellions, apart from disputes about the succession among the members of the royal family, are very rare. Now Leoninus, or Natan-leod, had just proclaimed himself King, and naturally his chief captains, who had hoped to succeed him, were angry. One of them, who must have learned that I could read, shot an arrow into our camp by night, with a letter attached.

Next day we marched southward. I had not dared to tell anyone, even Cynric, that I now had true information of the capital of the outlaws; I pretended that we were merely marching in what I considered a likely direction. As I have said already, I had no fear of the result of a pitched battle. My army was composed of peasant spearmen, and the lower class of Saxon are tough, stolid fighters, who don't mind seeing their comrades killed beside them; their only drawback as soldiers is that they are slow and clumsy, from following the plough through thick clay for days on end. My men would be fighting for future peace and prosperity; the outlaws were rootless wanderers, and they would prefer flight to a stubborn defence.

We pushed through the thick woodland, and soon came on traces of the enemy; their scouts moved through the undergrowth much faster than we could, and there were always a few of them hanging about in front, screaming abuse and loosing an occasional arrow. I rather hoped Leoninus would try an ambush, for my men were well closed up and that would bring us to close quarters; but he avoided battle, although we lost a few men from long-range arrows.

I did not make straight for the enemy's camp, but wandered for a few days in the neighbourhood; I did not want my men to think that Woden was leading me in person, for an undeserved reputation for divine assistance can be a nuisance in later life. But after enough false starts to make it seem plausible we eventually stumbled on our objective. I had feared that Leoninus might withdraw towards Dumnonia; my awkward army could not follow him into a hostile land, and in that case the whole expedition would have to be repeated next year. But luckily he had raided to the westward so often that the Roman Kingdoms would not give him shelter, and he had no choice, when his refuge was discovered, but to give battle or disperse his men in flight.

He chose to stand a siege, counting I suppose on the notorious inconstancy of a barbarian army; it is well known that Saxons do not as a rule have the patience, or the organized food supply, to remain for more than a few days in front of a fortified place. But this barbarian army was led by a Roman, and I had made arrangements for ox-carts to follow with biscuit and bacon. The outlaws' stronghold was a little island of firm ground in the middle of a swamp, and a good timber breast-work had been built all round it. But at the end of a dry summer the swamp was not impassable, and after spending two days in making a causeway of logs I led my men straight at the wall.

I let Cynric win glory by being first inside the enemy camp; at the age of fifty-seven a commander is justified in showing his troops where to attack, and then waiting behind with the reserve. As a matter of fact, the battle was not nearly as fierce as I had expected. The robbers were not patriots defending their homes, like the Romans of the west who die with all their wounds in front; they were lazy thieves who had chosen the easiest life open to them in a war-torn land. As soon as our axe-men had hewn a breach in the palisade, they began to melt away to the rear. Leoninus fought gallantly until he was killed, as befitted a King, and he had a few comrades whose honour compelled them to die beside their master; once they were down, the resistance of the outlaws collapsed. They broke and fled in all directions, but a great many got stuck in the marsh; for in choosing the driest path of approach I had hit on the principal entrance to their fort, and my men blocked the way of escape. It was not until they began to scatter that I realized how numerous the enemy had been for they had been packed in close order behind their palisade; I think at the beginning they actually outnumbered us, and my followers claimed afterwards that they had slain five thousand men. Of course, this was a great exaggeration, as the tale of enemy losses always is, and many of the people killed were unarmed servants and camp followers. All the same, from the point of view of numbers engaged, this was one of the greatest victories of the Saxons during their settlement in Britain, and the poets composed many famous songs about it; yet it won us no new territory.

After that great victory we were no longer molested by the type of robber who descends on a farm or village and plunders it by force, although naturally there were still raiders who drove off unguarded cattle and avoided battle by the speed of their flight. Cynric had won enough glory to make him content with a few more years of peace; the songs celebrated chiefly his courage, though my inspired leadership on the march was also mentioned. Best of all, my followers were now convinced of their own fighting capacity, and the next time they went into battle they would expect to win, even against superior numbers. It was suggested that I might now assume the title of King, but I pointed out that we had merely cleared the land of domestic robbers, and that such a step should wait until I, or Cynric, had enlarged our borders.

VI

515–519

MY ONLY FAILURE – ARTORIUS AND MOUNT BADON – THE GREAT VICTORY OF CERDICS-FORD

Five years later I decided that I must lead an invasion. I had won prestige by my famous victory over Natan-leod, which was rather surprising; for it had not been a very desperate affair, though it had evidently caught the fancy of the poets. But I still did not call myself King, though I had two German Kings for my neighbours. I was growing older every day, and I could not then foresee how many more years of life I should be granted; before I died I wanted to have a throne to hand on to Cynric. My dearest ambition as a young man was to win complete independence, and I then thought all titles of honour were the playthings of foolish minds. But ambition is never really satisfied; the plans I had made for a purely selfish existence were not capacious enough now that I had to think of the happiness of my descendants.

The time seemed ripe for a forward move against the Romans of the south; the three civilized states of Dumnonia, Corinium, and Demetia were at loggerheads among themselves, and there was no outstanding warrior among their Kings. A wide belt of no-man's-land ran through the midlands, which could be settled by anyone brave enough to dwell there without the protection of an army and a law-court; so that I could have extended my dominions gradually, a little every year, without provoking a serious war. But that would not satisfy me; I wanted to win a famous battle, and overthrow a well-known dynasty; then I could call myself King of whatever land I conquered, and my family would reign after me with all the prestige of successful annexation. When I first suggested something of the sort, in the winter of 514, Cynric was eager to try his luck at once, like a true child of Woden. But I knew that a successful campaign must be planned, and nothing should be done in haste.

Of course, the professional warriors of my war-band feasted with me at Yule; but there were very few of them, considering the extent of the lands I ruled. I don't suppose we sat down more than a hundred strong in the hill-fort I had chosen, and we realized that our numbers were not equal to the task. That meant we should have to send out messengers to all the wandering Germans in Britain, and possibly overseas as well. I was faced with the same difficulty that had menaced me when the Portingas arrived; some chieftain might come with a war-band that completely overshadowed my little troop, or a warrior might do so well in the campaign that others were eager to follow him. In spite of the oaths they are always taking, no German thinks it wrong to leave the chief to whom he has sworn allegiance if he can better himself by following another, and I was already too old to take a prominent place in the front rank of a pitched battle.

I explained all this to Cynric. I told him that his chance of succeeding me peacefully depended on how well he did in this war, that all our forces must always be under his command, even if he saw an obvious advantage in sending off a separate detachment, and that if any rival was making a name he must see to it that the man was killed in battle.

It was no use inviting the Kings who lived to the

eastward. If a real King came with all his force I should have to take second place before the campaign had even begun, and that would be the end of my hopes for a throne. On the other hand, the masterless men who lived brutishly on the Roman borders were not the best material for a conquering army. Most of them had been turned out of the regular war-bands precisely because they were too turbulent to live under the rule of a King, even a German King. In the end we decided against sending a popular poet into the lawless lands to recruit these ruffians; but it would be equally dangerous to send openly to the Kings' halls, asking the comrades to change their leader. What we really wanted was a strong rumour that there were good pickings to be had by those warriors who came to Venta next autumn, when the mighty Cerdic Elesing was about to take the field; it would have to be quite unobtrusive and unofficial. I wished that I still had about me some of my old Roman companions; it was the sort of delicate underhand business that a Roman politician would have enjoyed, but I had to work through heavy-handed Saxons, whose only idea of finesse was to tell the most obvious and easily-detected lies. We puzzled over the matter, and finally my dear Cynric volunteered to go on the dangerous journey himself. There was, of course, a risk that he would never come back; but being the heir to a ruler is a dangerous trade, as my brother Constans had long ago found out.

It is a common German custom for the heir to a great man to fill in the time while his father is growing old by visiting neighbouring countries and comparing foreign manners and customs; it may possibly enlarge his under-standing, and at least it puts him where he cannot cause a fatal accident to the parent whose death he is waiting for. Cynric was too honourable to do me any harm, but we could use the custom to send him on tour of the more organized courts of German Britain, where he would make a point of dropping hints to all the warriors he met. The dear boy was after all my son, and he must have inherited his father's cunning.

Then I made a public speech summoning all the peasants who were bound to serve in my army, to be at the meeting-place in Venta immediately after the harvest. In normal circumstances it would be ridiculous to give such long notice, for the Romans were bound to hear of it, and we threw away all chance of taking them by surprise; but this campaign was not to be a raid to capture unguarded booty, but a full-scale attempt at conquest; I should be all the more pleased if I found a large Roman army where I could defeat it in one great battle. I also hoped that an early announcement would help to spread the news among those Germans who were tired of peace, and bring some of my neighbours to Venta without further invitation.

I have already explained that though our land was rich in corn and sheep, it was not a good place for gathering portable treasure. Before Cynric could set off to visit his Woden-born cousins in the Kingdoms of the east, I had to empty the cellar in a ruined Roman villa where I kept my secret hoard for emergencies. As all the well-born warriors, both Roman and German, carry a great deal of their property into battle in the form of jewellery, every little clash between bands of raiders yields a good dividend to the side who hold the place of slaughter and can strip the dead; so that during all these years there had been a steady trickle of valuable objects into the hoard. It was a wrench to empty my emergency reserve, for if anything went seriously wrong during the summer I would have to flee ill-provided, and start again as a poor hired swordsman at the age of sixty-four. Yet in a sense the very magnitude of the gamble gave me a thrill; I had not taken a chance of that kind since I entered the Sea of Vectis with five ships twenty years ago. I had finally made up my mind that the only way to be happy was to trust Cynric absolutely; he might go off and raise a band of pirates with the gold I had given him, and there was nothing I would be able to do about it; but if he wanted to he could have done it ten years ago. This perfect trust between possessor and heir is a very rare thing in this degenerate world, and I suppose it accounts for a good deal of my success. But it is wrong to say that I was merely very lucky to have a trustworthy son; I have had plenty of tiresome relatives in the past, and if I had not trusted Cynric I would have dealt with him as I had dealt with Constans and Frideswitha.

So Cynric went off to celebrate the spring festival at the court of the South Saxons. Of course, when he gave presents to his hosts they would offer him gifts in return, and as they were Kings they would probably enhance their dignity by giving him something more valuable than they received; a covetous man could make quite a good thing out of visiting vainglorious and boastful Kings, if he started with a capital of really good presents. But though Cynric would be richly rewarded before he left each court, he ought to come back empty-handed if his mission was a success: he would have to give presents to the comrades, and all he would get in return would be a promise of swords in the autumn.

To keep up my courage, I sometimes reminded myself that it is not every man of sixty-four, with an assured position in the world, who would risk all he possessed in a great throw of double or quits. All the same, I was very relieved when at the beginning of September the first recruits began to drift in; Cynric had not failed me.

These first recruits were mostly homeless warriors who

wandered over the length of Britain, fighting each year under a different King. They were accustomed to a very high standard of living, and they liked to wear gold on their weapons and round their necks, but most of them were genuinely more eager for glory than wealth, and would follow a skilled leader even if he were poor. They must not be confused with the savage dwellers in the Marches, who raided for their daily food and never went near any King who kept some sort of order in his hall. These were actually a very good class of men, and true to their given word, though they never gave it for long. Of course, they knew what was happening all over Britain, and I tried to learn whether any other leader was waging war on the Romans; it would be awakward if a great war had broken out in the north just when I was trying to enlist every unemployed warrior. They told me that all the Kingdoms were at peace, and that even the savage borderers were trying to settle down in an organized Kingdom of Marchmen, although they were still fighting among themselves to see who would be King of it. But they also told me why the north was at peace, and when I heard the reason I felt a little worried.

It seemed that the Romans of the north had found a new leader, and that he had given the Germans of those parts such a drubbing that they were now on the defensive. That meant I ought to get plenty of good recruits for my expedition, but I did not like the tale of Romans beating Germans in a set battle. It seemed somehow against nature, although Heaven knows it used to happen often enough a hundred years ago.

I questioned every new arrival who claimed to have come from the north. I wanted particularly to learn what territory was ruled by this new champion of the Romans, and whether his family was likely to have an alliance with the Roman states of the south. For as long as I can remember the Romans of Britain have not been such good fighters, man for man, as the Germans; of course, they still hold more than half of the island; but that is because they have stone walls, and their superior civilization enables them to plan their campaigns more coherently. But they had no business seeking out a German army in the open, and defeating it.

None of my informants had actually taken part in these battles, for they told me that there had been more than one; in fact the overwhelming majority of those Germans who had met the new leader were dead; but he was now the talk of all north Britain, and they had heard who he was. I was surprised to learn that he was not a King; he seemed to be that very rare creature, a professional soldier of pure Roman birth, and he led a band of mercenaries in the service of the Roman rulers of the north. This was very odd indeed, for most true Romans despise soldiering, especially as a mercenary, and their comitatis are filled as a rule with Christian barbarians or unromanized Celts from the backwoods. Even in Italy, in the days when we still had occasional news from there, the generals were barbarians, and the last Roman military leader I had heard of, with the exception of Count Ambrosius, had been Count Aetius in Gaul.

If it was strange that a Roman should take up warfare as his profession, it was even more strange that he should make a success of it. The Romans can drill, though as a rule that does not help them very much against a proper Saxon charge; their great strength is that they can read and write, and so keep proper lists of rations and numbers in garrison, and reckon the time it takes to build a fortification; that was why Anderida was about the only first-class fortress which had fallen to a Saxon assault. But in the field their troops usually attempt some complicated manoeuvre and tie themselves in knots, before they are broken by the German charge. This new man must have found some trick of tactics that was too clever for thick-headed Germans, and I wished I could speak to a survivor of his great victories. All my recruits from the north were full of unlikely stories about his prowess, but they could not tell me exactly what he had done to defeat the barbarians. I could only hope there was no reason why he should bother about the south country. In any case I would get more sense out of Cynric when he returned; I had trained the young man myself, and he knew the necessity of getting accurate information about possible enemies.

By the end of September my army was formidable in numbers, and composed of very good material. I must have had five or six thousand free and unattached comrades, besides two thousand peasant spearmen from my own dominions. Such an army had not been seen in Britain since Constantius conquered the land from the usurper Allectus more than two hundred years ago; no combination of the ruler of Corinium and the King of the Dumnonians, with all the petty princes they could gather to help them, should be able to meet us in the open field.

In the first week of October Cynric arrived, with a splendid little war-band. He had spent all my treasure, so that there was not an ounce of gold anywhere on his person; but he had done his duty so tactfully that none of the neighbouring Kings were annoyed at losing their best men, nor so eager for the new expedition that they wished to come in person. I gave him two nights' rest, and announced that the great army would set out the day after to-morrow. October is perhaps rather late in the season to start a campaign, but my men were enured to the British winter, and I hoped to catch the Romans off their guard. Of course, they must have heard rumours of the mighty host that I was gathering, but they would expect me to start next spring. The year's harvest would be gathered, but not yet eaten, and I would find food wherever I went.

Before we set out I had a long talk with Cynric about the new menace from this Roman general in the north. As I had expected, the dear boy had exerted himself to get accurate news, and he gave me a rational account of what he knew. In the first place, the man's name was Artorius, although the Celtic peasantry who spoke no Latin called him the Bear, which is Art in their language; Cynric thought this would be a valuable clue to his family and upbringing, but it left me no wiser than before. I suppose my grandfather had known all the honestiores of Roman Britain, and he could have placed anyone as soon as he knew his family name; but in my boyhood the country was already falling to pieces, and neither my father nor I had ever been north to the country round the Wall. I could say it was not a south-country name; neither the King of the Dumnonians nor the King of the Demetians belonged to such a family, nor had they married into it. This was all to the good; Artorius would not be allied by blood to my foes, and I hoped he would stay in the north, where he had been so successful. It appeared that the Roman slaves in Kent had heard about him in the queer way that rumour circulates among the poor; they were loyal to their Jutish masters, for they would still be slaves whoever ruled in Cantwaraburh, but they were proud that a man of their blood had done such great deeds.

The story was that this Artorius was an honestioris, who had made the long journey to the city of New Rome or Constantinople; there he was supposed to have learned the military art from the drill-masters of the Emperor's guard. Then he had come back to Britain with a holy mission to cleanse the land of all barbarians. His bands were not exactly mercenaries, though they expected pay from the Kings they defended; they would only fight in what they regarded as a just quarrel, against heathens. That was simple enough, but I was puzzled to know why Artorius had been so often victorious. There Cynric could not help me; the slaves said that it was because his cause was just, but I knew that was nonsense; I myself have triumphed over a good many just causes. The only scrap of gossip that Cynric had been able to pick up was that Artorius and all his men were mounted, and made a habit of turning up suddenly when the Saxons thought they were many days' march away. That again seemed a likely thing to happen. A properly-trained Roman soldier would have maps of the country, and would plan where to strike; with a band of mounted men he could always outmarch and outguess the barbarians, who did not know the short cuts. But Roman bands often turned up unexpectedly; as a rule they gained nothing by it, for the Germans beat them when the clash came. This Roman must have some other secret if he defeated the Saxons every time he met them. It did not matter very much; he was safely up in the north, and perhaps I would get more reliable news before he came south.

It was about the middle of October when we marched. We were by far the largest barbarian army that had ever been seen in Britain, five thousand well-armed comrades and about three thousand peasant spearmen. The men were divided into little groups under their chosen captains, but these never numbered more than twenty to fifty men; otherwise the whole army acted in one mass, without any large tactical divisions. It was really too large a force to be under a single command, and things would have been easier if I could have split it into three or four legions; but that would have put too much power into the hands of the legionary commanders, and we might have faced a civil war when it came to dividing the conquered lands. Also you must remember that I could not send written messages to my subordinates, and had to carry everything in my head.

I had never been farther west than Corinium, nor farther north than Ratae; but I had a fairly clear idea of the general shape of Britain. I thought that with this great army I might conquer the south and west at least as far as Deva, which was famous as an impregnable fortress. Thus there were three states to be overcome, the Kingdoms of Dumnonia and Demetia, and the territory of Corinium, which still called itself a municipality. The last was my first objective. The Romans would naturally expect me to attack the Dumnonians, my nearest neighbours. I hoped by a swift march and a surprise attack to find Corinium badly garrisoned, with its walls in a poor state of repair. Accordingly, we marched northwest as fast as we could move, and only plundered the deserted villages on our immediate line of march.

Each man carried food to last three days, but we had no baggage column. At that time of year every village should contain a good supply of corn, and there was no danger of starvation. Many comrades rode ponies on the march, but I did not bother to send them out as scouts; Saxon scouting parties are always too busy looking for plunder to remember to send back information, and in any case I did not fear a surprise attack by the enemy; our men marched well closed up, and a force large enough to attack us with any hope of success must be seen a long way off.

We had about sixty miles to go, and on the fourth day we approached the walls of Corinium. So far the campaign had been nothing but a picnic; the villages we marched through were evacuated at our approach, and the coloni, of course, carried off their valuables with them; but they could not move their corn at a moment's notice, and we found plenty to eat. We had seen a few Roman scouts, but in three days they could not gather an army fit to meet us in the field, and there had been no fighting.

The great question was whether the citizens of Corinium would man their wall, or whether they would take to flight. I sent some horsemen close to the walls, and they came back to say that the gates were shut, and that arrows had been shot at them.

A great many barbarian leaders would have marched past the town and gone off to plunder the valley of the Sabrina. But I was determined to try a siege, if I could hold my men together and get them to obey orders. The real bother was that now I would have to divide my troops; we must send one-half out foraging while the other tried to destroy the wall, and we should also in theory have pickets a day's march away to give us warning of the approach of an army of relief. But you cannot deploy barbarians as though they are disciplined troops, and I knew that any pickets I sent out would soon drift away in search of booty; also Cynric was the only subordinate whom I could trust. The best I could do was to divide the army into two halves, one to forage under Cynric and the other for close siege-work with me. I promised that the two divisions would change places every week, so that each man should have his fair share of plunder and fighting, but I would stay permanently by the city.

The men accepted this decision without too much grumbling, and I went to have a close look at the city wall. What I saw did not encourage me, for it was in excellent repair and the garrison seemed numerous and confident. Of course, we could take it in the end if we went on trying long enough; but I had very little control over my followers, and they might get bored and insist on going somewhere else. I set them to making wicker hurdles, so that we could get close to one of the city gates and try the effect of a battering-ram; that was all I could do for the moment, and I went back to our camp rather disheartened.

My original plans had been vague, except that of my three chief enemies I would attack Corinium first. Once the city had fallen I could advance to the mouth of the Sabrina, a central position between the Dumnonians and the Demetians. Actually I intended to march next against Demetia; then the Dumnonians would find themselves isolated. But all this depended on the speedy destruction of Corinium, which I had not expected to be held against the mighty army I had brought.

After working for several days at the hurdles we made a safe avenue leading to the largest of the city gates. It was more difficult to construct a good battering-ram, for there were no tall trees in the immediate neighbourhood, and we were not equipped to transport one from any distance. During this time I spent most of the daylight hours as close to the wall as I could get with safety, and I came to a very disturbing conclusion. There were plenty of armed men in the garrison, perhaps more than I would have expected to find in a town of that size; but the interior seemed to be deserted, and I never saw women or children. Presently there was no doubt at all; the useless mouths had been .evacuated from Corinium before we began our siege, and the place was held by a picked garrison of Romans from all the west.

In these circumstances was it worth while going on? The valuable plunder must have been taken away, and there would be plenty of food for the garrison. We could not hope to starve them out, and it was very unlikely that they would leave part of the wall unguarded for us to escalade. If we did take the town, with heavy loss of life, my men would be disappointed when they found no gold and the army might go home. I had to decide by myself, for even Cynric was too barbarous to understand all the factors of the problem; but eventually I came to the conclusion, some time in November, that we ought to raise the siege.

At the end of the month it was obvious that we would never get a big battering-ram up to the gate, and I gave the order to march. The army was thoroughly bored, and delighted to be moving. I had observed a first-class road leading northwest, so we followed it towards the river Sabrina and the border of Demetia. On the second day we reached the river, only to find the passage blocked by another strong city, which I believe was the well-known town of Glevum. The citizens were not expecting us, and the place was full of women and children; but it was quite impossible to take it by assault, for immediately behind was a long bridge over the broad and unfordable Sabrina. This meant that the Romans could get reinforcements and supplies in safety from the far bank, while we could only attack from one side. Nevertheless I halted my army, and we sat down in a threatening posture. I hoped the Demetian army would come out to drive us away.

We kept our Yule outside the walls of Glevum, with the hostile town of Corinium cutting off our line of retreat; but I was longing to fight a decisive battle, and I was deliberately tempting the enemy to come out. As a matter of fact, it was quite good country to spend a few months in; the winter climate is mild, and the whole left bank of the river was covered with prosperous farms and villas. This part of Britain had never been raided by Saxons, although most of the villas showed signs of burning from two generations ago, when the Irish were still pagan and their pirates came to all the shores of Britain. We got excellent food from these villas, and some of them had their own vineyards.

For a small body of settlers our situation would have been ideal. We would have begun to plough, and after a few years the Romans would have accepted the loss of their fields, as had happened many times in the east. But we had come to conquer Kingdoms, not to win farms; it was absurd that just because we were in overwhelming strength we could not do as much as three shiploads of pirates.

In the spring of 516 I led my men southwest to the mouth of the river Sabrina, merely for the satisfaction of saying that we had crossed Britain from sea to sea; then we returned. We would see if the Dumnonians were any more eager to defend their farms than the cautious Demetians.

I had a pleasant surprise, for the southwesterly road led to the famous health resort of Aquae Sulis. This had never been a large city, even during the most prosperous days of the Empire, but wealthy invalids had made offerings to the Healing Gods, and the temples and baths were the most elaborate and luxurious in the whole island. It was unwalled and completely undefended, although the Dumnonians had barricaded some of the stone buildings as a frontier post. They evacuated it when we approached, and my barbarians had the run of the lovely carved and sculptured palaces round the spring. Of course, there was no valuable plunder left, except the bronze clamps in the great stone walls of the temples; but the baths themselves were in working order, and I lived for the last time in a real Roman house, with plastered walls, clean stone floors, and a properly weather-tight tiled roof. I even washed myself clean again, and tried to persuade Cynric to do the same; he enjoyed swimming in the great bathing pool, but no

German will take the trouble to wash unless a Roman has built a bathing-place for him.

When we had finished wrecking Aquae Sulis we were at a loose end again. Now that the weather was getting warmer my troops rather enjoyed their holiday, and although we had found no plunder we were all living well on captured beef and corn. It is curious how quickly any particular campaign becomes a habit; we had wandered about the open country for so long, eating food that our enemies had harvested, that we would have been surprised if we had suddenly been compelled to fight a stubborn battle. We hung about Aquae Sulis for some weeks, until all the food in the immediate neighbourhood had been gathered. I had no idea what to do next, and was wondering whether to look for an unguarded ford over the river Sabrina, when in May, after we had been in the field for more than six months, I got word of a Roman army.

It seemed that our enemies were afraid to do anything obvious, for their army had not come to drive us away. Their plan was not the defensive but the counter-offensive, which works among civilized states but is usually a waste of time against barbarians. In other words, the army of the Demetians was now on the headwaters of the Thames, threatening the homes of the Saxon settlers by that river. Everyone clamoured for a bloody battle as soon as possible, and next day we began our march to the northeast, looking for the Roman army.

The great expedition had dwindled after six months in the field, even though there had been no fighting to speak of. A few lucky warriors had found plunder worth taking home, many of the peasant spearmen had gone off to plant their spring corn, while the winter had brought the usual number of deaths from disease. All the same, we must have been about four thousand strong when we marched out for the great battle that would decide the fate of Demetia as a Roman Kingdom.

We had another look at the walls of Corinium, but the garrison was still there, and they lined their defences without flinching when we made as if to attack; they had been isolated in enemy territory since the autumn of the previous year, and they showed more determination than was usual among the Romans; we took it for granted that they had heard of the victories won by Artorius in the north, but it did not worry us. We would deal with them after we had won this battle.

From Corinium we took the road to Calleva. By now it was too late to rescue the squalid villages on the banks of the Thames, and I thought the Demetians would be moving southward, to pillage the farms of my country. It is sixteen years since all this happened, but I remember every detail; these were very important events for the future history of Britain, and I will describe them as well as I can.

On the third day from Corinium we had swerved north to get in touch with any fugitives who might be hiding in the thickets by the Thames. There is a great range of chalk hills south of the river; I do not know the local name for these hills, but one of them bears a great Horse, cut out of the chalk long before the Romans came to our land; it is known as Mons Badonicus, a name that is likely to be remembered. It was about midday, and we were marching eastward along the plain to the north of these hills. We had plenty of corn in our wallets, and a small herd of cattle; some of our mounted men had been sent up to the sky-line, to see if the enemy was near, but when we halted for dinner they naturally came back so as not to miss their meal. I ought to have sent others up there at once, to give warning of any attack, but we had been in the field for so long without meeting the enemy that I had grown slack, and in any case we all thought we could beat off any charge the Romans could make. That was what we had come there for. We were lying on the grass as we ate, and most of the men had taken off their helmets. But when we heard the trumpets on the hill-top we had time to spring to our feet and close our ranks. My men were veterans of many a raid, not the sort of people to lose their heads because the enemy appeared when they were not expected.

Cynric had been eating beside me, and there was no time to send him off to take command of the right wing, the usual place for the heir to the war leader. Our best comrades at once formed up round him, while I took my place in the second line, since I was too old for hand-to-hand fighting. All this time we could hear the noise the Romans make before charging, but we could not see them, for the curve of the hill-side hid the summit from our view.

Then they came down the hill, and shouts of dismay and astonishment rose from the Saxon army. For they were charging on horseback! Line after line of mounted men galloped towards us. I suppose there were really only a few hundred of them, certainly less than a thousand, but horsemen take up a great deal of room when they are in line, and they seemed to overlap our right wing and extend right down to our centre. They carried long lances and big shields, and from the way they were riding I could see that they must be using stirrups. Of course, both Romans and Germans ride on the march, if they can afford to keep a pony; Cynric and I had both been riding before we dismounted for our meal. But when the alarm came not a man of ours made a move to where the ponies were tethered, for none of us dreamt of *fighting* on horseback.

It is probable this was the first cavalry charge that had ever taken place in the south of Britain. At school I read Caesar's *Commentaries*, and he makes it clear that the barbarians of his day used chariots drawn by little ponies, while a hundred years ago the Romans depended entirely on their heavy foot. Artorius and his band were equipped as cataphractarii, the famous mailed horsemen who defended New Rome. No wonder they had won great victories against the German swordsmen of the north. I have read that drilled pikemen are safe against cavalry, but even that was written before stirrups were invented.

I suppose I had half a minute to make up my mind, while they were thundering down upon us. I could see that we would lose this battle, for the line was already becoming unsteady, and a thin spray of shirkers ran towards the woods in our rear. My first impulse was to order a general retreat, but there was no time; I could not get the order round the whole army before the clash, and once we started retiring our formation would break up in a mad dash for safety. If we stayed where we were the battle would follow a pattern that was very familiar in the songs of the poets; first the cowards would flee, then the ordinary sensible men, including the poets themselves; but the heroes would refuse to give ground until the last of them was slain. A very good poem can be made about such a battle, but the trouble is that the leader of the host is expected to die on the field; I knew that Cynric would fight it out, even if I told him to escape, and of course, since I was nearly sixty-five years old, I should not get away myself. This was the end of all my planning.

I was just bracing myself for the oblivion that wise men hope for, or the unpleasantness that the outraged gods will have in store for me if they really do exist, when I had an inspiration. No leader can get undrilled barbarians to manoeuvre, especially when they see the enemy charging, but there are two commands they always understand; one is to retreat, and that was useless for lack of time; but the other is to attack. Naturally the best warriors in the army had been sharing my dinner, and they were still clustered round me. I yelled as loudly as I could, and began trotting up the hill-side at a steady double.

Just before the collision I stole a glance over my shoulder; not a blow had yet been struck, but already my army was dissolving; some comrades were trying to form the shieldring for a defensive fight, a great many had already taken to their heels, and those who looked to their leader in a crisis were climbing the hill.

When the charge met us it was not as bad as I had expected. I know nothing about cavalry and how they ought to behave in battle and I have never ridden a horse in a charge; but I imagine that it is difficult to stop the silly creatures once you have started. Anyway, for a moment I saw a horseman rushing towards me, the head of his lance growing larger and larger; then the point had glanced off the smooth surface of my little red shield, the sky seemed to be full of flying hoofs, and I picked myself up to find that they were all galloping away. Artorius had a second line, and I suppose their duty was to spear those of us who were lying on the ground, but in the excitement they had got too close to the front, and their horses seemed to jump over us as we lay flat. In short, that first charge scattered the army as a fighting force, but did not kill many men.

When the only hoofs I could hear were in the distance, I stood up very cautiously, and continued straight up the hill. Cynric was also unhurt, and so were many of my companions; by the time I reached the top I was at the head of quite a considerable body of shaken and frightened troops. It is a very sound rule, when you are caught in an ambush, to go straight for the attackers; they have usually made elaborate arrangements to cut off your retreat, but never expect you to push farther into the trap.

On the crest of the hill, as I had fully expected, I found
the earthen rampart of one of the old hill-forts that are
dotted all over that part of the country. We bustled inside
it, and I set every man to scarping the grass-grown banks
with sword and bare hands. I could see on the plain below
the Roman cavalry chasing our fugitives towards the
distant woods. It was these fugitives, who turned their
backs on the enemy, that were killed in great numbers; the
Roman poets sang afterwards that Artorius had accounted
for nine hundred and sixty men, and I believe that is a
reasonable figure. If the Demetian infantry had been with
him he would have destroyed our whole army; but he had
attacked with only his own war-band, and the story goes
that the King of Demetia, seeing us marching eastward, was
quite glad to let us continue in that direction; he kept his
men a mile away, and Artorius attacked against his advice.
If this story is true, and it is the best explanation of the
very incoherent series of actions, the Demetians missed a
great opportunity of settling the Saxon menace for good.

My army did not use ensigns or standards, though they
are not unknown among the Germans. I have never been
in favour of anything of the sort for barbarians, since
the usual difficulty is to persuade them to retreat from a
lost fight, rather than to rally them for another charge. On
this occasion, I should have been glad of some mark to
show the scattered survivors where to assemble; as things
were, the best I could do was to send down swift runners
into the plain, to round up any fit men they found
wandering about.

For a full hour we were unmolested on our hill-top. I
had time for a consultation with the leading warriors, and
we made up our minds to stay where we were for at least
the rest of the day. With spears we might have formed up
in close order for a fighting retreat to the shelter of the

woods; but the peasant spearmen had naturally been the first to fly, and the better warriors, who preferred death to dishonourable flight, carried only swords. That meant we could not hope to repel cavalry in the open plain, and must hold out behind our ramparts until something turned up. Holding out until something turns up is an important branch of the military art.

I had begun my march that morning with rather more than four thousand men; about a thousand had been killed in the charge, and others had found shelter in the woods. I tried to count with my eyes how many I had left, for to number them would have been thought very unlucky. As far as I could make out we were nearly a thousand strong. The fort in which we found ourselves was on the edge of a plateau; it was not a Roman work, but an old town of the barbarians before the Romans came to Britain, and the ramparts curved to take advantage of the ground. Roughly two sides were protected by the slope, which a man on foot could barely climb without using his hands; on another side the ground fell, but more gently, and the fourth, the shortest, faced the level plateau and was protected only by the bank and ditch. The whole circumference was rather too long for my force to man, but the attack would obviously come along the level ground, and the other faces needed no more than a few sentries to guard against surprise.

My comrades had recovered from the shock of meeting such an unheard-of thing as a charge of heavy cavalry; they were more angry with the enemy for having scattered them unprepared than disheartened by their defeat. I was confident they would beat off an assault on our rampart, especially as they were working really hard to scarp the bank. Saxon warriors of the upper class are usually reluctant to dig, but they will do it if the enemy are very near and the work can be counted as part of the fighting. What I dreaded most was that the enemy would settle down to blockade us. Of course, we had no food at all, for our baggage was still lying on the plain below; however, Saxons pride themselves on their endurance of hardship, and I knew that they would fast without grumbling for two or three days. Worse than the lack of food was the absence of water; it is unusual to find a spring inside these old ramparts, which is one of the reasons why the Romans built other forts down in the plain. In consequence, we had not a drop of anything to drink, and the nearest water-supply seemed to be at the bottom of the valley to the north.

This was our weakest point, and it worried all of us; but I cheered up the men by telling them that after we had beaten off the first attack the Romans would probably wait for reinforcements and we could escape when it grew dark. I myself did not think this very likely, since Artorius was a skilled general; but it put them in the right frame of mind for hard fighting, which is to have something to look forward to at sunset.

In mid-afternoon the Roman cavalry came back from the pursuit; they were trained and disciplined soldiers, and their general had collected them into a well-ordered formation. I saw no point in trying to hide, and they soon spotted our sentries on the sky-line. They wheeled in excellent order and climbed the plateau to the eastward, before they sent out scouts to have a look at our position. Just at the same time the Demetian foot came out of the woods that lay between us and the Thames. Then they held a council of war, for there was a lot of milling about before they finally drew up in close order on the level ground, and advanced towards us. The well-drilled cavalry marched forward at a walk, with the whole levy of the

Demetians cheering and yelling in a disorderly mass behind them.

I was now able to have a good look at these horsemen who had so completely upset the balance of power in southern Britain. I don't know why I had taken it for granted from their first appearance that they were the war-band of Artorius; but our whole army thought the same, and of course it was perfectly true. Every man was mounted on an enormous charger, much bigger and stronger than the ponies that run wild on all the moorlands of ravaged Britain. The riders were completely covered with metal armour, not only the metal and leather cuirass worn by the wealthy members of the Roman comitatus, but leggings also of the same materials; they carried long lances and big round shields, with heavy broadswords like the Gothic spatha hanging from their belts; and they sat on deep saddles that rose into peaks before and behind to protect the rider's bowels. The big iron stirrups were unusual; these troopers sat up straight and rigid, and seemed to be much more firmly attached to their horses than a Roman nobleman, lounging on his pony's back to save his feet on a long march.

I turned to Cynric, who was standing beside me. 'We can't face these men in the open,' I said. 'You know that when a horseman rides into you the right thing is to strike at his thigh, just above the knee; but they have thick armour on their legs, and your scramaseax would bounce off. They must dismount to get over this rampart, and on foot we can go for their throats with our seaxknives, but I don't see how we are to get away. It looks like the end of the conquest of Britain.'

The dear boy was always cheerful, and he thought it his duty to see that his leader did not give way to despair. 'Never mind, Father,' he answered. 'We shall find some way of dealing with them, if only we can find water. I want to get out of this battle alive, if I can without dishonour, for I think I know the way to defeat them if we meet again. I shall make my men carry axes; no horse in the world could bear the weight of armour thick enough to withstand axe-blows. Those chargers must have been brought in from overseas, for none like them are bred in Britain. Artorius will not be able to keep up the breed, and when they go back to their ponies they will have to take off their armour.'

I had trained my son always to take long views, and to think of the welfare of the Cerdingas after we were dead.

The Roman cavalry realized that our rampart was impassable to horsemen, and they remained in the background while the Demetians advanced. I suppose they thought we might be so demoralized by our recent defeat that our line would give way if briskly attacked; otherwise it was a ridiculous manoeuvre, for I had enough men to hold the one face that the lie of the ground made it easy to attack, and I doubt whether their numbers were much greater than ours. Certainly the well-armed comitatus of a petty Roman Kingdom would not contain more than a thousand men, and the rear ranks must have been filled up with untrained and half-hearted peasants. A few minutes' fighting showed that our position on top of the steep rampart was impregnable as long as my men did their duty, and the Romans retired in good order, with hardly any loss on either side.

Shortly afterwards darkness fell on the first day of the Siege of Mount Badon.

We were all ready for sleep, but first I held a council of the leaders; more to find how my men were feeling, and what fight they had left in them, than because I thought any of these barbarians would suggest anything useful.

They did not. Most German legends have sad endings, and a great many of them finish with the hero trapped in his hall, and an account of the gallant end he made. This was such a good parallel to our present position that all my best warriors were resigned to death, and their chief worry was the fear that there would not be a single survivor to tell the poets exactly what had happened. I am bound to admit that they were not as depressed as I should have been if I had given up all hope of escape, and they would fight bravely until thirst or the sword made an end of them; but they could not be bothered to think out plans for the future. Even Cynric was exalted and full of noble sentiments, so that his brain was not working clearly.

I sent them off to get what sleep they could, and sat on alone. I had now been living among barbarians for forty years, and the daily beastliness of their behaviour no longer jarred upon my nerves, but on these occasions, when what was needed was a cool brain rather than the courage of a bull, I realized how solitary I was. I was the only man inside the rampart of this obsolete hill-fort who could use his head for anything better than ramming it into an opponent's belly.

I tried to put myself in the place of the Roman commander. That at once gave me grounds for hope, for I saw that the enemy were undergoing all the disadvantages of a divided command. Artorius was a skilled soldier, and a man of new ideas with the drive and determination to carry them out; but he was no more than a captain of mercenaries, and Kings would not take his orders. If he was disregarded, or better still, insulted, after the great victory he had won with his band alone, he might get in a huff and march his cavalry away. The second point in our favour was that the whole valley of the Thames was a devastated march. We were not in the territory of any Roman King, there was no population of industrious peasants from whom the besiegers might get food, and it was no one ruler's indisputable business to drive us away. We had no food, and no water, but if we could hold out time was on our side.

I spent the night going round the sentries, since it was too cold for a man of sixty-five to sleep without a fire. Most of my men got a little rest, and perhaps the chill of the night was really a good thing, since it made it easier for us to bear our thirst. The enemy stayed quiet on the other end of the plateau; they had no reason to risk a night attack, when the drill and discipline their troops possessed would be wasted in the darkness. I remembered that the day always began in a Roman camp with a stand-to at dawn, and I thought that Artorius would keep up the custom; but they would not assault our ramparts until the sun was fully risen.

There was a stream in the plain to the north, and the slope was too steep for cavalry to charge uphill. If we all ran suddenly down there we might get a drink before the enemy changed their formation to attack downhill, and that would be another day gained. Unfortunately we had no water-jars, to fill with a reserve supply, but then we were merely living from day to day. Shortly before dawn I roused Cynric and told him to get the men under arms.

A ring of hostile sentinels stood round, as I had expected; but on three sides the slope of the ground prevented them from seeing into the camp. Just before dawn they were nearly at the end of their watch, and as we had kept quiet during the night they were bored and no longer alert. In absolute silence we crept over the rampart and shuffled down the hill-side; no war cries were shouted, and the men kept their swords in the scabbards. The little party of scouts made no attempt to dispute the passage of nearly a thousand men, and soon we were filling our empty bellies with cold spring water; we were already climbing the slope when the cavalry thundered down to the stream, but they did not pursue us up the hill-side. Of course, the infantry should have rushed the camp while we were drinking; but these Romans do not react quickly to the unexpected, and perhaps they feared a trap. We were inside before they marched forward in good order to the assault.

Then I lay down in the sun and went to sleep.

In the evening I awoke refreshed, and Cynric reported that the fighting had ended about midday. Nowhere had the enemy looked like getting over the rampart, and very few of our men had been killed with the sword; but in the afternoon the Romans had brought up huntsmen with bows, and their arrows made things very awkward for our sentries. It was a day and a half since any of us had tasted food, and soon we would be too weak to fight.

I took over for the night, while Cynric had a sleep. This really did seem like the end at last. We might fight our way down to water once again, although now the enemy would be expecting it; but we could not get anything to eat, and death in battle was better than starvation. I did think once or twice that there must be dead bodies in plenty on the plain where we had first been surprised, but I doubted whether my men would eat them even if I ordered it; also we had no firewood, and I don't think even I could nibble at a human corpse raw and undisguised.

All that night I brooded over our very unpleasant position. What was so maddening was that I knew the various Roman commanders would be on bad terms with one another after the failure of the assault; in these cases an allied army always thinks the other contingents have not done their fair share. If we could hold out for a week they would quarrel among themselves. There was only one thing to do; we must attack their camp, and win food from our enemies; we should probably be killed in the attempt, but that was as good a death as any, and I should take great care that I myself was not made prisoner. But first of all I would try the effect of doing absolutely nothing for a whole day; my men would not be too much weakened if they merely sat behind the rampart, and it might make the enemy careless.

I did not sleep that third day of the siege. For one thing I was in the grip of hunger-pains, the first cramps that come while a starving man is still active, before his whole inside feels dead. It reminded me of my youth, when I had led the Regnians through the Forest after the defeat of Count Ambrosius. The recollection cheered me up, for then I had brought them back safely in the end, and I told the story to Cynric as an antidote to despair. I found that I was more comfortable moving about than sitting still thinking about food, and I spent most of the day walking round the rampart; I was troubled to find that the men were beginning to lose heart, and some of them reproached me for leading them into a trap. But not one of the discontented had spirit enough to murder his chief and assume command, though little parties tried to desert; it was interesting to watch the efficient way in which the enemy dealt with them. The scouts raised the alarm, but did not try to hinder them; then when they reached the plain the Roman cavalry rode them down and butchered them to the last man. Otherwise the enemy contented themselves with sending forward archers to worry the sentries on the rampart. No one in Britain normally uses the bow as a weapon of war; these short, stiff hunting-bows, meant to cripple a stag at very close quarters, would not penetrate our shields, and they were afraid to come close.

The enemy withdrew to their camp for dinner, and lit a large cooking-fire where the smell would drift over our fort, to remind us how hungry we were. It only annoyed my Saxons, instead of making them despair; they are people of sudden moods, and if you can only get them boasting about the toughness in adversity for which they think they are famous, they will endure anything with surprising good temper.

Shortly before sunset we had a stroke of good luck, which I think we had deserved by our steadfast conduct. A terrific summer thunderstorm blew up, with sheets of rain. The water drained into the ditch of the fort, and we baled it out with helmets so that everyone had a good drink. My men perked up at once, saying that Seaxneat, their great ancestor, had persuaded Thor to come to the rescue.

On the morning of the fourth day of the siege I felt light-headed from hunger; as I walked round the rampart, leaning on a strong young man, I realized that this was the last day on which my army would be an effective force. The men were lying about half asleep, and admitted that their swords felt much heavier than usual. We had passed the stage of craving for food, and stuffing grass or rubbish into the mouth to go through the motions of eating; now we were growing weaker every hour, but peacefully, without any pain or discomfort.

I had a look at the Romans. Their foot were drawn up on the plateau, listening to orders at the morning stand-to. The cavalry were down in the valley, encamped by the stream where we had snatched our drink on the second day of the siege; it was a sensible move to put them on the low ground, for it would take them some time to descend the steep slope of the plateau. They were not parading, as

Roman troops usually do in the early morning, but fussing over their horses in the dilatory manner of troopers. We had drunk well last night, and our clothes were still wet from the storm and the dew; so we were not in the least thirsty, but food we must have before nightfall.

Cynric was all for a sudden attack downhill, which might have killed a few horses before the cavalry got mounted. At first sight it seemed a promising move, but on consideration I realized that the Roman foot would be on our tails before we could begin eating. But I saw something new in the camp on the plateau; previously the Romans had been sleeping round fires in the open; now their encampment was dotted with large pavilions, such as Kings and rich comrades bring into the field when the army is to sit still for several days. It was an allied army that faced us, and evidently they had not appointed a supreme commander; for these big tents of leather and canvas were pitched without order, straggling at all angles to one another. They were guyed with a tangled web of ropes, since the servants feared the high winds of that exposed ground. I have noticed repeatedly that in the last forty years the lower classes among the Romans have become extraordinarily clumsy and awkward in any task that needs mechanical skill; movements of population have broken down the traditions of apprenticeship. Nothing is ever properly fastened to anything else, since the design is too ambitious for the workmanship; in fact, in some things they are worse than barbarians, who stick to the methods of their ancestors. A Saxon ship is small and dangerous, but its tackle is fitted to its purpose and kept in good order; a Roman ship is bigger and more imposing, but it always leaks, and the ropes are tangled. So in this case the Roman camp was a mass of cordage and flapping cloth, and they were busily laying out more ropes as the wind rose.

It occurred to me that all this mess ought to form a very good barrier to a cavalry charge, if only we could get inside the camp of the besiegers. When I had explained my plan the men were eager to attack. I made them rest all morning, for the enemy waited for hunger to do its work and showed no sign of advancing; I also inspected every man, and made them leave behind any bulky plunder that they had hung on to after our first defeat. I had to let them keep their gold and jewels, otherwise there would have been a mutiny; for most of them thought they would die before to-morrow's sunrise, and they wanted to take a little wealth with them into the next world.

We waited till dinner-time, when we could smell the food cooking in the Roman camp. The enemy knew that we would not be thirsty after the storm of the previous night, and they expected us to go on quietly starving behind our fortifications. We crept on our bellies to the eastern side of the hill-fort, so that the scouts would not see that we were massing for an assault, and poured out silently in a body just as the main force of the Romans was sitting down to dinner.

Nobody could expect me to charge in the front rank at my age, and I was well embedded in the centre of the column. I suppose we were still about four hundred strong, out of the thousand who had taken refuge in the hill-fort; a certain number had been found dead every morning, of exposure and starvation, and others had attempted unsuccessful escapes. A few were too weak to join in the charge, and Cynric arranged that they should have their throats cut with as little pain as possible. Every living man joined in the attack, for I had no intention of returning to that ill-omened hill-fort. Our formation was more or less a solid square of men, and my darling Cynric was in the front rank, with the best and strongest of the remaining warriors. Men vary a good deal in their endurance of hardship, and while some were dying every day others were still fit for battle. It did not take us long to reach the edge of the hostile camp; the main body of the Romans were unable to get into line of battle before we arrived.

I have often arranged for the feeding of troops in the field, in the close presence of the enemy. You can make what rules you like about every man remaining armed and fully equipped, but they always will insist on undoing their swordbelts, and unless you watch them closely they leave their swords by their bedding. These Romans carried more spoons than swords; also they were composed of two different contingents, presumably Demetians and Dumnonians, and the two commanders did not agree on where to offer battle. Half of them ran back to form up in the open, while the other half ran towards us to bar the way to the tents. Just as we reached them Cynric raised the howling wolf-like war cry of the raiders and my men leapt into the camp, all teeth and claws.

In less than five minutes we had swept through the tents, and there was the magnificent Roman stew waiting for us, bubbling in great copper cauldrons; Cynric, with a few chosen companions, made a front among the tangled guy-ropes of the tents while we speared out the meat on the points of our seax-knives; then other warriors, with their mouths full of scalding beef, relieved him while he took his turn round the fires. It was the sort of well-drilled co-operation that I had thought would be impossible for a barbarian army, but I had explained it to them beforehand, they knew each other, and every man regarded himself as a hero, who had survived unimaginable hardships.

The Roman foot rallied to the east of their camp, and arrayed themselves in very good order before they dared to advance. I was not particularly frightened of them, for Germans ought always to beat Romans in fair fight on level ground; the Demetians evidently thought the same, or they would not have allowed us to wander all over the most fertile part of their land during the previous winter. But I dared not order my men to come out from the shelter of the tents when the cavalry of Artorius were climbing the hill and preparing to charge us.

We all gulped down some hot beef, and it made me feel twice the man I had been in the morning. I walked among the comrades by myself, no longer leaning on a borrowed shoulder, and did my best to push them into a close formation. But no matter how close we stood, or how well we prepared to meet the attack, it was certain that our short scramaseaxes would be no use in keeping off a charge of horse. At the last minute, but just in time, I broke up our solid array into little clumps, each covered by the guy-ropes of one large tent. I calculated that when the horsemen charged they would divide into different squadrons; about the only way we could hope to do them any damage was to hamstring the horses from behind when they were brought to a halt.

Soon Artorius led his cavalry to the attack, while the Roman infantry looked on from a distance; evidently there was friction among the allied commanders, which was what I had expected when I laid my plans. It must be a difficult situation when the leader of the best troops is nothing more than a mercenary general, while the foot are under the orders of two co-equal Kings who have frequently fought one another in the past. We must hold this attack or face extermination, and we just managed to do it; one group of about fifty men was broken up and cut down in detail, but the rest stood firm. A single rope stretched low above the ground was enough to bring the horses to a halt, and then the riders could only poke with their long lances at the foot opposed to them. Our little clumps were dotted about in such a manner that as soon as the Romans came to a standstill they found Saxons in their rear, and the tail end of a horse is very easy to deal with; a good cut with a sharp sword just above the hock, and that horse has finished with warfare for ever. After less than an hour's fighting Artorius drew off his men, with the loss of many of his irreplaceable foreign horses.

It was now quite late in the afternoon, and the Romans showed signs of settling down to besiege us in our new position. Apart from the excellent dinner we had found ready cooked for us, there was a store of biscuit in the captured camp; but although we now had food for several days, in other respects we were worse off than we had been in the old hill-fort. When the enemy had recovered from the shock of our sudden change of position they could send forward their archers to shoot us down one by one. I summoned a council of captains.

I always made a point of consulting the captains before every fresh move, for my men were not bound to me by any tie of blood or allegiance; they were my partners in a scheme for the plunder of Roman Britain, and if I issued orders that they thought silly they would just appoint another leader. But I had been trained to marshal my arguments convincingly, which is the most important branch of a Roman education, and I got my way merely by arguing them down. In this case I told them that we could not stay where we were, for we could not repel another attack; we must be in the woods by daylight. Some of the captains were rather too exhilarated by our unexpected victory, and wanted to offer battle again in the morning; they thought it a marvel that foot had been able to beat off a charge of horsemen; but in the end I persuaded them. It is very odd that cavalry have now acquired so much prestige that it is accounted almost a miracle if foot can withstand them; the ancients regarded them as nothing better than scouts and skirmishers. Perhaps the introduction of stirrups has made them more formidable.

That night was overcast, with driving rain; certainly whichever god controls the weather was on the side of the barbarians, which ought to be an argument in favour of Woden; but the Christians always find a way out by saying that Jehovah is punishing them for their sins, so that a careful man cannot make up his mind. About midnight we crept down the steepest part of the hill-side; of course, the Roman sentinels saw at once what we were doing, and we heard their main body standing to arms in the old hill-fort. But the cavalry had to saddle up, and the foot were in no mood to hinder us when we were headed away from their territory. By dawn we were encamped in the middle of a marshy and extensive wood to the north of Mount Badon. I led my men eastward through the thickets of the Thames valley to the borders of the Cantwara, and then southwest to my own land, without ever venturing into the open country. Artorius sent mounted scouts who kept in touch with our column, but the Dumnonians and Demetians went back to repair their burnt-out villages. By the end of July 516 I was back in Venta.

I have related the story of this campaign at some length, for it was of great importance for the future of Britain. When I set out with the largest army of Germans that had ever been assembled since the original landing of Hengist, we had all expected to conquer the island right up to the Irish Sea. It would have been a good thing for the country as a whole if we had been completely successful, and Britain had become a land of German rulers, instead of remaining torn by unceasing warfare between the two races as it is at present. The intervention of Artorius prevented that, and perhaps the next best thing would have been for him to chase us right out of the land. But Artorius was not a King, and I suppose the Kings would not back him with their full force; he was just strong enough to perpetuate the condition of affairs as he found them, with Germans in the east, Romans in the west, and all the fertile midlands the theatre of incessant war.

I reached Venta with about two hundred men, out of the seven thousand who had marched out in the previous year. But, of course, all the others were not necessarily dead; some had gone home before we fought our battle, and after the cavalry charge in the plain the woods had been full of little parties of routed men, many of whom escaped alive. The Roman coalition was breaking up under the strain of victory, so much more trying to good relations with one's allies than defeat; the horsemen did no more than ride over the open country where we had been used to keep our sheep. We retired south to the woodlands; we had to eat more bread and less meat, but otherwise we were not much worse off than we had been before we attempted the conquest of Britain. The horsemen of Artorius went away in the autumn, and they have never come back.

Artorius does not come into this story again, but he was a very interesting figure, and I will set down the little that I know about his end. At first his war-band had been composed of noblemen who thought it a sacred duty to defend Britain against the pagans in return for just enough pay to buy their food; but, of course, when his army won famous victories it attracted a very different class of warrior. His followers grew discontented, and at last one of his captains raised a sedition against him; I have heard that the rebel was also the lover of the leader's wife, and that may have been the case; but I always doubt that sort of story. Poets often pretend that the chief motive of a striking action is a love-affair, but in my experience greed causes more trouble than adultery. Anyway, for whatever reason, there was a civil war inside this band of heavy cavalry, and eventually it split up. Artorius himself was not slain in the fighting, but went into hiding after a defeat; he is believed to be living as a hermit in the west, and the poorer Romans hope that he will one day raise another war-band and rescue them from their oppressors. Of course, all the big foreign horses are dead by now.

I made up my mind to be content with what I had salvaged from the wreck, and to see that my little state prospered from its own resources, without relying on the uncertain plunder of hazardous raids. I was too old for serious fighting, anyway. It may have been a blessing in disguise that we had lost the open chalk-land of the north, for those deserted hill-forts encouraged a wandering uncivilized way of life; now our farmers live very much as they did in Germany, make iron weapons and tools from the ore of the Forest, tell their children the traditional tales, and go regularly to the annual law courts. If we are not getting any more civilized, at least we are not slipping back.

It seemed strange at first that I had gained renown from my defeat; but that is part of the peculiar Saxon way of looking at things. In their hearts, the Saxons believe that life in general is hostile to mankind, and that all true stories have an unhappy ending; they reserve most of their admiration for the hero who can face disaster without losing his head. Their poets spend more time composing songs about disasters than they do on such banal subjects as victories, and the Siege of Mount Badon quickly became the most celebrated occurrence of the century. I was much admired for the courage and resource I had shown in escaping with a remnant of my army when things looked black, and no one ever reproached me for being surprised by a charge of heavy cavalry; no man in southern Britain had any reason to suppose there were heavy cavalry in the island until Artorius appeared.

My state, though smaller, was now more compact and easier to govern. I had as much power as the King of the South Saxons, and Cynric pressed me to declare myself a King. But I had too much of the Roman respect for success to celebrate a great defeat in this way, whatever the Saxons may think about the superiority of heroic failure. I compromised in the end by promising my very dear and patient son that I would ascend the throne immediately I won a victory; I thought it very likely I would never fight again, and I certainly was not looking for any more campaigning, but it satisfied him for the moment.

We had peace for two years, which was longer than I had expected, since the Romans should have been attempting to throw us right out of Britain. But the King of Dumnonia had died suddenly, and the complicated civil war that ensued absorbed all the energy of the Roman Kingdoms.

At the Yule feast of the year 518 I heard definitely that Artorius and all his followers had taken service under the King of the Otadini, north of the old Roman Wall; that meant that the Romans were content with what they had already done in the south, and that the remnant of my territory was secure. But my informant also passed on a rumour that the new King of the Dumnonians intended to find plunder and occupation for his comitatus by an incursion into the German farms by the Sea of Vectis.

I was on the whole quite pleased with the news. I was going to be sixty-eight that year, and I could no longer personally use my sword in the front rank of the battle, but I wanted to lead one more campaign before I handed over my power to Cynric; I enjoy the excitement of planning a war, I was quite confident that we would not be beaten, and I hoped to win a victory of such importance that I could take the royal title without making myself ridiculous in my own eyes. I was determined not to lead another invasion; the Romans had been gradually pressed back, with plenty of opportunities for the faint-hearted to accept slavery or emigrate to Gaul, and those who still maintained their independence in the west were very prickly people, better left alone. But if they invaded us we should have the inspiration of fighting in defence of our families, and they would be weakened by the natural desire of all warriors to avoid death until they have spent their newly-taken plunder.

I had hardly any real professional warriors in my following. The not very numerous survivors of Mount Badon had mostly moved on to more warlike leaders when they found that I had accepted my defeat, and even those who were content with my leadership had soon discovered that I had no gold left after that disastrous campaign. All I had now was a guard of ten men, since a war-leader needs a sentry and a hangman always in attendance. There was also a great mass of peasant farmers, slow-moving spearmen, who did not enjoy fighting and were not very good at it, but who could be counted on to resist any one they saw destroying their crops. It would be a strange sort of campaign, where for the first time the Germans might be inferior as warriors to their opponents. I would be defending my country with armed peasants against professional comrades. I had to think myself back to the old days when I helped to guard the Regni against the fathers of my present followers.

I would never have reached the position I now hold if it

had not been for my excellent Roman education. Not that my school masters taught me very much about warfare, for they were men of peace, and anyway the Roman army has been rather under a cloud for the last hundred years. But they did teach me to think. They were always posing dilemmas, chiefly in the realm of law and theology, but still dilemmas that I had to think myself out of without relying on precedent. A barbarian has an inherited bag of tricks, often very useful tricks that make him formidable in war; but when he is faced with a new situation all he can do is draw his sword and shout his war cry. I sat down like a Roman and puzzled my brains for the best way to meet the coming invasion.

With Cynric and a few elderly farmers I wandered all over my country in the early spring. Of course, none of my men understood even the idea of a map, but it is astonishing how an illiterate man can carry things in his head; soon we could discuss together the lay-out of the country as though we had been born in it, and our fathers before us.

The Dumnonians would naturally invade from the west by marching along the coast. Their object was to damage the crops as much as possible, in the hope that our farmers would find it did not pay to till the soil in that neighbourhood; our best farms were in the south, actually along the shore of the sea, and it was here that they would do most harm. But there was one slight disadvantage in using this line of approach; the invaders would be marching across the grain of the country, instead of following the line of a river valley. Southern Britain is not mountainous and our farmers had thinned the forests, so that nowhere was the land physically impassable to an army, but the rivers themselves might check the invasion. Many little streams run south into the Sea of Vectis, and the tide comes far up them twice a day; sometimes they are fordable, and sometimes too deep to cross. Naturally there is a road along the coast, made in the days of the great Emperors. However, even the Emperors did not bother to build stone bridges over these tidal streams; they contented themselves with paved fords, easy to cross at low tide, and impassable at high water.

Briefly, my plan was to divide the hostile army, by attacking while it was crossing a ford, and delaying the rear till the water rose and cut it off from the van. It is not the sort of trick one would expect from barbarians not native to the land, and the Dumnonians would not be on their guard against that sort of thing. Cynric and my other counsellors agreed that the plan was worth trying, and by May I had stationed reliable men at each ford, charged with calculating at what hours the stream would be impassable each day in the future. It is a thing that all fishermen have to understand; simple men, who do not bother their heads as to the reason for this strange ebb and flow, do it better than educated philosophers.

This was an ambitious piece of tactics, that needed more absolute obedience and a more carefully planned time-table than was generally within the scope of a barbarian army; luckily my troops were slow and patient farmers, who are easier to command than the fiery heroes of the war-band. I went very carefully over the ground and found a place that just suited my purpose. Here the old Roman way ran along the coast, and a paved ford, wide enough for six men abreast, had been built on the actual bar of the river-mouth, while upstream wide bogs lay on both banks and made it very difficult to cross away from the road. I brought my captains to this place, and plotted on the actual ground exactly what each contingent was supposed to do when the enemy came.

In late July the invasion started. The Dumnonians had about four thousand well-armed men, besides a great crowd of unarmed peasants to carry their plunder. Their main body marched east along the coast road, while detachments scoured the country to the north. I had sent our women and children to shelter behind the fortifications of Venta, which was a very unpopular move; the Germans quite genuinely fear to be shut up in old Roman cities, partly because they know they are not good at the constant vigilance needed to defend the walls, but even more because they think that the ghosts of the previous inhabitants will be able to do them harm. I had a reputation as a very wise war-leader, especially careful of the lives of my followers, but even so a number of stupid men refused to expose their families to these supernatural dangers, and made them hide in the woods; as though there were not dead men buried under every tree in Britain. The Dumnonians caught enough of these superstitious people to encourage them to persevere in their plan of campaign, and it had the added advantage of showing to the survivors that I knew better than they did. My stolid farmers retreated before the enemy's advance in accordance with the agreed plan, even when they saw Roman raiding parties carrying the heads of their wives. These agricultural Germans are very attached to the idea of having a wife and family, but they are remarkably free from any silly devotion to the individual woman who shares their bed; they knew that if we led the Romans into a trap there would be plenty of girls in Germany to console the widowers.

In the thick country by the coast it was easy to get a close look at the invading army. I myself had a very good pony, and with a well-armed bodyguard it was safe for me to hover in front of their advance guard and inspect them thoroughly; I was now too old to get away on my feet in an emergency. It appeared that the new King of Dumnonia cherished old-fashioned views on military affairs, as was natural in one who hoped to revive the sway of Rome; he seemed to have a comitatus of five hundred mailed swordsmen, and a main body of rather more than two thousand spearmen of the lower class; these were equipped with leather tunics and caps, and seemed to have some idea of the old legionary drill. I peered at them very carefully, remembering how formidable had been the drilled troops of Count Ambrosius, but they did not march as though their training had become second nature, and a great many of them did not carry swords. I thought their King had made a mistake. Spearmen without swords are no use against the savage close-quarter fighting of the Saxons, and he would have been more formidable if he had brought fewer men and those better armed.

The Dumnonians killed every human being they could catch. In my young days an able-bodied Saxon slave was a valuable possession, but Britain is now such a distressful country that a slave can run away over the border whenever he wants to; it brought home to me the appalling decline in civilization that has taken place in my lifetime, for without slaves to do the rough work no man is really free.

Towards the end of August the Dumnonians approached the right ford from the right direction, the west. We had been waiting a very long time, but in the end things fell out just as I had planned. They halted for the night about three miles away, and in the morning resumed their march along the road. High water was about midday, and they evidently intended to ford the stream before they halted for dinner. I placed my army in position among the dense thickets by the mouth of the little river.

The invaders had been in our country for nearly two months, and I had taken care that parties of our scouts should always be close to their vanguard. Now they had grown careless after eight weeks without a fight, and although they knew that there were Germans in the nearby woods, they did not realize it was our whole army. Two hours before high tide their van was on the eastern bank, and the main body was beginning to wade the stream, which was up to their thighs and increasing every minute. I was lying under a bush about three hundred yards away, with a keen-eyed young comrade beside me, since I cannot see as clearly as I did forty years ago. Half the comitatus, with their King on his pony, came first, with the other half of their best men presumably in the rearguard; the common foot formed a long line in the middle.

When the first of the common foot had reached the bank I blew my war-horn, and my men rose up and charged whooping towards the ford. I had discussed with Cynric and the captains exactly where we should place our ambush, and we had decided against having more than one hiding-place; in consequence I had only eight hundred men, to cut the enemy column and hold the ford until high water; but Cynric with two thousand more a mile away would march towards us when he heard the noise of battle.

Two lusty young men pulled me along by the arms; I have always been against the use of standards in a really fierce fight, for good men get killed saving them for sentimental reasons, but I thought that, just this once, I would myself act as a living banner for my army. We pushed back the Roman line until a solid wedge of our men formed up with their backs to the ford. The sea was immediately to the south, and no enemy could come at us from that side; but on three sides we were beset by superior numbers. It was a very awkward position for the first half-hour, and I wondered whether we could hold out until the tide was full; however, it was impossible to run away, and in a predicament like that the Saxon usually fights his best. I stayed in the very middle of our square, and never had a Roman within reach, though I drew my sword to make it look as though I was fighting like a hero; in the distance I could hear my son advancing with the rest of our forces. Soon the rising waters gave us protection, and the fighting became easier. Standing where I was, protected by a devoted bodyguard but seeing everything that went on, I became very interested in the battle; in a sense it was the first battle I had seen, for when you are fighting yourself you cannot watch more than your immediate opponents.

At first the Dumnonians did not realize exactly what we planned to do; as the tide rose they recognized the danger, and I saw their King rallying his comrades to cut a way through while the ford was still passable. They very nearly succeeded; one warrior killed the guard who stood in front of me and aimed a blow at my shield; I took it squarely, though it beat me to my knees (the last blow that I have ever taken in battle), and then young Wulf, who stood beside me, threw himself at the man's ankles and pulled him to the ground. Then Cynric with our main body broke the line of spearmen, and a wedge of his best comrades linked up with our battered square; the ordered ranks split up into little groups fighting without coherence, and the enemy began to flee towards the woods.

Naturally the common foot, who had no hope of posthumous fame, did their best to get away alive; but just as the battle broke the King of the Dumnonians was wounded in the leg by a dying Saxon, and when the King could not get away most of his comrades made up their minds to die with him. The other half of their army, on the opposite bank, shouted and made war-like gestures while the battle was still evenly balanced, though of course they could not come to the assistance of their fellows. As soon as they saw that their King was down, and that it was a Roman defeat, they fled westwards as fast as they could. We crossed the river when the tide permitted, and recovered a great deal of our own property, though we could not catch many fugitives. However, we marched in a body to the borders of our land, and challenged any foe to face us in arms; then I was carried back to Venta in a litter, for I was bruised all over, and the excitement had made me feverish.

Such was the great victory of Cerdics-ford, a very famous fight and the subject of many well-known songs.

VII

519–531

KING OF THE WEST SAXONS –
THE HAPPY ENDING

Our great victory called for a celebration on a really large scale, to make sure that it was properly remembered. It is at these victory feasts that the poets sing their epics, and thus they are made known to the warriors in the hall; no Saxon is educated unless he knows a great many songs about the famous deeds of his ancestors. My head was already so full of the Roman learning I had been taught as a boy that I found it very difficult to remember these poems, and I have always had to conceal the fact that the only one I know is the verse account of my ancestors back to Woden; but illiterate men remember everything that they hear sung, and Cynric knows an enormous selection.

Since we had to give a victory feast that would inspire the poets, Cynric suggested that at last the time had come for me to assume the dignity of King. Henceforward the throne would be hereditary, in any of my descendants whom my men should invest with the honour; Cynric is my only son, so he must succeed me without danger of civil war, but if my family increases as it should the Cerdingas will in future have plenty of candidates to choose from. That, of course, means civil war, sooner or later; but then the Empire, when it was flourishing, saw civil wars nearly every time an Emperor died; every monarchy must face this peril, and as a matter of fact in a well-established state it does little harm, and ensures that a fool or a weakling does not hang on to power until he has injured his subjects.

It was important that everything should be done in due order. The initiative was supposed to come from my followers, who would be so overcome by my greatness when they saw me sitting in my hall, feasting after I had led them to victory, that they would offer me hereditary honours. My dear Cynric arranged all this with the captains of the war-band; I would give them magnificent presents in return for their loyalty, so they were delighted to play their part. Any war chief can always get himself proclaimed King, if he values the title, unless he has a comrade unrelated to him by blood, who hopes one day to succeed to the leadership.

There were the remains of a good basilica in Venta, which had once been the capital city of the tribe of the Belgae. Someone had set fire to it, and the roof had fallen in, but no one who has lived many years in Britain objects to being rained on at a banquet. There the feast was held, and I had got hold of some fermented honey, very potent, to mix with the beer. At the right time the captains raised the cry of 'Long live our mighty Cerdic, King of the West Saxons,' and everyone joined in the shout, without any grumbling that I could see. To give the occasion the sanction of religion my dear Cynric had fetched in an aged prophetess, a very holy and tiresome woman; she was not only frequently inspired by Seaxneat himself, the founder of the Saxon race, but also had the good sense never to threaten level-headed men who were not afraid of her; she reserved her curses for the superstitious, and on this occasion had agreed beforehand to do nothing more than wish me luck.

She drank a good deal of fermented honey, and then danced on the table until she felt the god take possession of her. She put the prophecy into verse, as these holy people do, and in fact the convenience of scansion often dictates what they will say next; but the gist of it was that my descendants would reign over the West Saxons for more than two hundred years, that in a time of crisis they would defend all Britain from a dangerous invader, and that then they would rule the whole island, Germans, Celts, and Romans, for countless ages, until the great War of the Gods brings the world to an end. The interesting thing is that she seemed to believe it herself, and certainly no one has ever prophesied such good fortune to any other German King. I like sometimes to toy with the idea that she really could foretell the future, and that it may all come true.

After that someone produced an old Roman shield, of the large square legionary kind, and Cynric thoughtfully put a cushion inside, for old age has made me thin and hard seats cause me great discomfort. My faithful followers took me outside where all the peasants could see me, and I was carried round on the shoulders of the chief captains. That is all the ceremony of enthronement that the Germans use; although they are very much guided by the advice of their priests in the affairs of daily life, they regard government as a wholly secular matter, and there is no religious rite of coronation.

So at last, after more than forty years of striving and the commission of several rather discreditable murders, at the age of sixty-eight I found myself as independent as any man on earth. I was even more lucky than I deserved; for the method of life that I had been forced to plan for myself would normally have left me without a single friend that I could trust, but because Cynric chanced to be a very honourable man I knew that I could depend on my son. I don't know how he had come by his sense of filial piety since I had killed my father and his mother had plotted to murder her husband; but I suppose there have to be a few honourable men on the earth at any one time, otherwise human life would come to a stop.

My only regret is that the need for independence forced me to live among barbarians. Of course, I should have been much happier as the King of a civilized state, but Romans are cleverer than Germans, and I should have had to face more strenuous competition. Now, in my old age, I begin to think more of my comfort and less of the joys of unfettered power. I would give a very large weight of gold to lie for a whole day in a real bath, with fine towels and plenty of hot water, or even to eat a well-cooked meal prepared in a clean kitchen. I know that I shall never enjoy these simple pleasures again, no matter how much longer I may live.

Curiously enough, I never missed very much the pleasure of reading and writing, which I dreaded to give up when I cast my lot among the barbarians. I find the excitement of politics is quite enough to keep the mind occupied, and in idle moments I can listen to the endless stories of the poets. Success can only be bought by giving up something, and the exchange is one that I am willing to make. I do not count the unfortunate deaths of my father and my brothers as something that I had to pay, for I was lucky enough to be born without the silly handicap of natural affection. I try to persuade myself that I only like Cynric because he is likeable, and not because he is my son; although here I may be indulging my fancy.

Now it is the autumn of the year 531, and last summer I celebrated the eightieth anniversary of my birth with fitting splendour. The Kingdom is in very good shape, there are no awkward problems outstanding, and the dynasty is as secure as any German dynasty can be. I cannot expect to live much longer, but it is quite certain that Cynric will succeed to my throne, and he has a large family of sturdy sons to come after him. I know he will rule with prudence, and his children have been well brought up; after three generations the Cerdingas will be a habit, and the West Saxons will be used to obeying them. I have hinted to Cynric that perhaps it would be a good idea if his younger sons met with fatal accidents, so that their eldest brother has no rivals of equal blood; I am afraid he did not realize what I was driving at, and I could not bring myself to advise the murder of his children in so many words. These things can be done, but they cannot be said. Cynric has all the more obvious virtues, and his filial piety has enabled me to associate him in the supreme command without any fear that he would try to displace me; but he is not very quick in the uptake. I console myself with the thought that if he had been a keen student of politics I should probably have had to take steps against him years ago.

I see no pressing external dangers to the Kingdom of West Saxony. All Gaul and the West has collapsed into chaos, and the nearest Emperor is at Constantinople. He still has the best army in the world, but if he ever marches west he will want to conquer Italy and Spain before he thinks of our remote island. The barbarians on the Continent are having a splendid time; they live in the half-ruined cities on the labour of great multitudes of well-educated slaves. They also ought to be content with what they hold, and there is no reason why they should cross the sea to lay waste our muddy fields. No man can really foretell the future, but I shall be very surprised if my grandchildren see hostile fleets in the Channel, apart from the pirates who come and sail away again, as they have done since history began.

That leaves only the other Kingdoms of this island as potential dangers, and here my confidence is based on more accurate information. The South Saxons and the Cantwara dwell on our eastern borders, and they show no signs of wishing to extend their power at our expense; in fact, my private opinion is that those states are going downhill. South Saxony is a very small Kingdom, cut off from expansion by the Forest, and lacking good harbours on most of its cliff-bound coast; Aella was a great man, and while he lived he kept round him an excellent war-band, but he has been dead for many years now, his people find it a great bother to hack their way through that enormous Forest every time they want to go raiding, and gradually they have settled down as farmers and shepherds on the open spaces of their chalk hills. They are the most barbarous of all the barbarians in Britain, and I think it is more likely that one day my successors will conquer them than that they should ever menace our independence.

Kent will always be an important state, for it contains the best harbours facing towards Europe, and there is still traffic across the narrow seas. The Cantwara were lucky enough to settle in the country as the friends and allies of King Vortigern, and thus they were able to subdue a large population of civilized coloni without a war of extermination. In consequence, they are moderately civilized people, making good metal-work and dwelling in the remains of Roman cities; although I believe none of them can read, so that their culture is bound to decay with the passage of time. They would be formidable now if Cynric were so foolish as to attack them, but they are not very numerous, their prolific royal house has already started to wage civil war for the throne, and they seem to be content with their present boundaries. If Cynric treats his fellow-Kings with respect, and arranges some method of settling disputes under a treaty, there is no reason why the West Saxons should not live in peace with them for ever.

The Kingdom of the Marchlands is more of a danger. It lies to the north of the Thames, and seems to have no boundaries at all, as indeed its name implies. All the tough scoundrels from the rest of German Britain drift there to win plunder in the never-ceasing wars. The Marchmen have the finest war-band in the island on the rare occasions when it is united, but they lack an undisputed royal house; often their civil wars end in a draw, with different Kings setting up separate thrones. They may one day produce a mighty warrior whom all their fighting-men would follow willingly; and then it would be well if the King of the West Saxons makes an alliance while his help is of some value; but at present it is their habit to win one village from the Romans every spring, and spend the summer fighting among themselves to decide which King it shall belong to.

I had almost forgotten to mention the Kingdom of the East Saxons, north of the estuary of the Thames; that is because they hardly come into this story at all. Most of their land is flooded by the tide twice a day, and the Romans were always too sensible to live in such a country; these barbarians settled there without fighting, and they have lived obscurely ever since, though they sometimes dispute with the Cantwara about the ownership of the ruins of Londinium. I cannot imagine they will become an important Kingdom.

Farther north are a number of little pirate settlements, right up to the Great Wall and beyond it. Most of them consist of no more than a fortified harbour, with a few cultivated fields immediately outside; they will probably coalesce into a powerful Kingdom one day, after a lot of warfare between their different Woden-born war chiefs, for there is no real Roman state to face them on the west. Loidis is a miserable group of villages, surrounded by forests and desolate moors, that only remains Roman because it is not worth conquering. But all that is far in the future, and West Saxony should be strong and established long before a threat arises in the north of Britain. By the way, these northern states are not composed of true Saxons; the pirates there call themselves Angles, after a tribe that used to dwell in the northern Angle of Germany. Actually they are of mixed race, as all pirates must be, and I do not think there is any racial antagonism between them and the Saxons.

I know that mighty warriors sometimes arise in the most out-of-the-way places, and it is always possible that a great conqueror might be born in the Island of Vectis, for example; but it is no use laying plans to meet that sort of contingency. By all the laws of probability West Saxony will be independent for the next hundred years, and no one can plan further ahead than that.

You will notice that I do not take into account the possibility that the Romans will recover the lands they have lost. In my opinion the Roman power in Britain has sunk so low that the decay cannot be arrested; sixty years ago they had all the prestige of unbroken success; if they had been worthy of their ancestors they would also have had the advantage of drill, discipline, and sound equipment. I wonder what would have happened if a single Emperor had taken control of the whole island, and preserved the wholesome division of society into honestiores to fight and administer the laws, and humiliores to provide them with food and money. But my generation was brought up to hate the very name of an Emperor of

Britain, since Constantine III abandoned the defence of the Wall to lead his troops on a wild-goose chase in Gaul. Then every city set up its King, with all the absolute military power and dislike of alliances with his equals that the office implies. When the great wars came the Romans had worse weapons and less training than the shaggy barbarians from across the sea.

The curse of the Roman Kingdoms is a disputed succession. In the old days the Emperor Septimus Severus had made it a rule, with few exceptions, that military commands should be given to 'new men' without ancestors, and the honestiores lived on their rents or took employment in the civil service. The idea was that great nobles with troops under their command might be dangerous competitors for the throne, but it had another result; when Britain was thrown on her own resources by the barbarian invasion that swept through Gaul the nobles who took command had no military training, and there was no tradition of obedience to their families. The Saxons have their useful division into Woden-born, common freemen, and laets who are not quite free; this means that in any Saxon Kingdom there are only a few possible competitors for the throne, and a civil war usually ends when all the Woden-born, except one, have been killed or driven into exile. But among the Romans, now that the division into honestiores and humiliores has broken down, every able-bodied man is a possible King, and every petty captain is tempted to fight for his own hand.

The result is that no Roman ruler can trust his army, and they dare not set up even civil judges to look after things in separate districts. Everything has to be done by the King in person, and only too often the King is the most bloodthirsty and unlettered savage in the realm; civilization decays at the top. Count Ambrosius, the last man who tried to revive the old Roman discipline, has been dead for many years; and Artorius has not been heard of since he fought that battle against his rebellious comitatus.

So I expect that the Kingdom of the West Saxons will prosper in peace, until my descendents feel strong enough to enlarge their boundaries. We are well placed for that; as I have often pointed out to Cynric, we have only to make a push as far as the river Sabrina to drive a wedge between the Dumnonians and the Demetians; but perhaps the Marchmen, who expand every year, will save us the trouble. As soon as the Dumnonians are isolated we must march west with all our force, for it would be fatal if a war-like German state were established to the west of us. Once we rule from Vectis to the Ocean we shall be as strong as any state in Britain, and may one day bring the whole island under our rule. But who is 'we'? I am writing as though I were immortal; why should I concern myself with the fortunes of my remote descendents?

The odd thing is that I do, in spite of all the arguments of common sense. When I was a boy my greatest wish was to live as an independent ruler, and to fulfil that desire I have committed every crime that is hateful to gods of men. Now I find myself planning for the future like the abbot of a monastery. I hope that my grandchildren will bear sway in Britain for countless ages, as the old prophetess said; and I even like my own family, as persons. Cynric is good and law-abiding, and he is bringing up his sons to stand together against the outside world; if they follow his advice, there is nothing they may not aspire to. A united family of brothers and cousins would be something unique in both worlds, Roman and barbarian.

It is a far cry from the tough young man plotting in Anderida how to supplant his elder brother, to the benevolent old King making wise plans for his beloved grandchildren. But if I have travelled a long way, on an unexpected road, there have also been great changes in my surroundings. I was born into a world where the Roman order seemed destined to endure for ever, all the more because we had got rid of the drain in money and troops caused by the efforts of our previous rulers to succour or overthrow the central government in Italy. We seemed to have taken the best things in European civilization, and rejected the tyrannous central organization of the Empire.

But you cannot choose the best out of two worlds in that way. We light-heartedly broke with the Emperor, thinking that all the honestiores of Britain would then become little Emperors on their own. Too late, we discovered that Rome really gave us something in return for the gold that left the province, and that it was something we could not replace from our own resources. It is hard to say when we first realized the barbarians were too strong to be withstood; at first everyone blamed the incompetence of King Vortigern, and only waited for a wiser King to arise, who would drive the Saxons into the sea. As late as the campaign of Count Ambrosius that hope did not seem absurd, and nobody dreamt that even the plains of the midlands would follow Kent in a few years. Artorius is the only Roman who made a single-minded attempt to fight the barbarians, because they were heathen barbarians and for no other reason; he found, if the stories are true, that his men would not follow him on this holy enterprise, but insisted, to the point of mutiny, on fighting for their own profit. All the other Roman Kings fought each to defend his territory, always looking over his shoulder to profit by the difficulties of his neighbour. They wasted their strength in the unceasing civil wars that were caused by the absence of a recognized royal line, and attacked their fellow-Christians in the rear. They deserved to lose their land, and they have lost it.

But I must admit that I am rather sorry; I would have preferred to be a Roman ruler. I have a tidy mind, and the endless boasting and circular arguments without which barbarians cannot decide the simplest matter drive my nerves to frenzy, though I try to conceal it. I often think with regret of Anderida, now a desolate ruin; and even that comfortable spot was not a real city, but only a fort built to withstand barbarians. What must Londinium or Eboracum have been like in their prime! Yet I realize that I am as foolish as Vortigern; you cannot combine civilization and independence. If I had lived under the full sway of Rome I should have been a rich landowner, constantly harassed by the tax-collector, spied on by informers if I played any part in local politics, and yapped at by bishops if I amused myself on my estates at home. Certainly I should not have been my own master, as now.

One can get used to filth, and I no longer mind very much when I see a louse swimming in the stew on my table (most of my followers eat on the floor). I am resigned to hearing every night the raucous songs of drunken warriors, and to listening patiently to long and badly-expressed speeches before taking the simplest decision. I sleep on straw, and when it rains I get wet. But I would like to talk to a well-educated and intelligent man before I die, and I know that is quite impossible.

There is one other thing that worries me, especially when I lie awake at night. Suppose all that nonsense that my brother Paul used to preach is really true after all? In that case I shall certainly burn in Hell for ever and ever. But it was fun while it lasted.

Note

Cerdic died in his bed in the year 534, and was succeeded by his only son, Cynric. From him sprang all the Kings of

Wessex, who later became Kings of England. Through Matilda, the Queen of Henry the First, the present royal family of Great Britain are Woden-born Cerdingas.

NOTE ON AUTHORITIES

The theme of this book is that Cerdic Elesing, founder of
Wessex, was really a Roman of Britain, bearing the Celtic
name of Coroticus. I did not discover this theory for myself;
it is to be found in Sir Charles Oman's standard History, and
other historians have played with the idea. There is one
strong argument against it: the Saxons took their pedigrees
very seriously, and had great reverence for chiefs who were
descended from Woden (there must have been some way of
checking a claim to this descent, perhaps by the recitation of
a metrical pedigree in archaic poetical language, as I have
described in this book). How could a Roman of Britain be
descended from a Nordic god? Oman can only suggest that
Cerdic's *mother* was a Roman captive, with sufficient
influence to name her son, who would, however, like all
Germans, trace his descent from the father only. I claim
credit for spotting Fraomar King of the Buccinobantes, who
was actually brought to Britain as I have described; he and
his tribe were absorbed into the population, but most
gentlemen remember the names of their ancestors a century
ago, and if he left descendants they would not forget the
distinguished stock from which they sprang.

In art there was certainly a Celtic revival in the fifth
century, and probably in names also; although Gildas, a

hundred years later, always calls himself and his fellow-countrymen 'citizens', and it was a long time before the Welsh admitted that their connection with the Roman Empire had been broken. St Patrick, also a 'citizen', addressed a letter of remonstrance to a certain Coroticus, a Christian who was ruling Christian 'citizens' in the neighbourhood of Dumbarton about the year 450. This is confirmed by the Irish annals, which say the tyrant was turned into a fox by the prayers of the saint. It shows that the name, which is the same as the first-century Caractacus, was current in the fifth century. Celtic philologists deny that Coroticus could become Cerdic, but Ceredigion, the land of Ceredig, became the County of Cardigan.

The story of the Coming of the Saxons is told only in three very unsatisfactory documents: Gildas, Nennius, and the Anglo-Saxon Chronicle. About the year 540 Gildas wrote an incoherent sermon, addressed to contemporary Welsh Kings, in which he refers to certain historical events; he mentions Ambrosius Aurelianus, whose grandsons were ruling when he wrote, and tells of a great defeat of the Saxons at the Siege of Mount Badon, 'near the mouth of the Severn', though he does not say who was besieging whom. The site of Mount Badon is unknown, and I have put it on White Horse Hill for my own amusement.

Nennius probably wrote about the year 685, according to Sir Charles Oman. He tells of Hengist and Vortigern, and mentions Mount Badon as one of the victories of Arthur, whom he calls Dux Bellorum, not King. Oman suggests that Arthur, a real person, may have been the leader of a band of heavy cavalry, equipped in the fashion of the contemporary east-Roman cataphractarii. The only weakness of Sir Charles as a military historian was that he knew very little about horses, and he did not realize the difficulty of keeping up the breed of large cavalry chargers in a land overrun with raiders, where wild moorland ponies could always get access to the mares. Without incessant selective breeding any race of horses reverts to the pony type, and I suggest that this was the reason why Arthur's effort failed, when his original stock of big horses were dead.

From the Welsh side, the crux of the matter is this: if Constantine III left Britain in 407, and the land returned to its allegiance to the Emperor Honorius in 410 (though cut off from Italy by barbarians in Gaul), how did Vortigern achieve his hereditary kingship by 450, as all accounts agree that he did? Here again Oman suggests an explanation. Cunedda, hereditary King of the Otadini, a tribe of Britons north of the Wall and therefore outside the Empire, was brought by Stilicho to North Wales, to expel Irish 'Scots' who had conquered the local inhabitants. This would introduce the institution of Kingship among the helpless provincials, left without any government at all, since the Diocletian reorganization had abolished the self-governing 'civitates' of the earlier Empire. But the setting up of these new Kingdoms, which appear about this time in the Welsh genealogies, must have been accompanied by stresses and discontent, as I have described.

On the Saxon side we have the Chronicle, purporting to give an account of the invasion. It was only written down at the instigation of King Alfred, four hundred years after the events it relates; but it is based on tradition, and my own opinion is that it can be trusted for genealogies and the relative order of events, though perhaps some of the dates were sprinkled in much later. Polynesian genealogies, e.g. in Hawaii and New Zealand, go back more than four hundred years, by oral tradition only, and then agree with one another in the most gratifying manner. Savages do remember what their ancestors were called, and how long they lived.

I have taken one liberty with the Chronicle. Cymen, Cissa,

and Wlencing are named as the sons of King Aella of the South Saxons, but I thought my hero would not follow a leader who had three stalwart heirs, and I made them his captains. This is the only occasion where I have not followed my sources. Otherwise I have stuck to the Chronicle, even in its dates, and attempted to find some plausible explanation for the most unlikely incidents it records. Natan-leod took some explaining away, but he fits in quite neatly.

The Chronicle is rather too busy in explaining why places bear the names which in fact they do; Portsmouth is called after a certain Port, and the Isle of Wight after a certain Wihtgar, though we know they really kept their Roman names, Portus and Vectis. I have devised an explanation for Portsmouth, and the same magical pilgrimage would do for Vectis; this was in the original version of my book, but I cut it out for reasons of space and because it was a reduplication.

The Chronicle is not interested in women; only fathers are named in the genealogies. Cerdic's love-life is entirely my own invention. So is his connection with Anderida; but the capture of that place made a great impression on the compilers of the Chronicle, who relate that every Briton was slain. They do not tell of the fall of any other Roman fortress in the early years of the Conquest, which suggests that most of them were evacuated without an assault, as I have described in the cases of Silchester and Chichester.

That brings me to the only other class of evidence I have used: archaeology. The picture given in Collingwood and Myers' *Roman Britain* is not quite what we would expect if the Chronicle were accurate; early Saxons turn up in very unexpected places, for example on the headwaters of the Thames, and brooch-types show one well-travelled route of invasion, from the Wash through the Fens and by the Icknield Way to Salisbury Plain, which left no tradition at all, possibly because it did not lead to the foundation of a

Kingdom. But those Saxons in Oxfordshire had to be fitted in somewhere, so I have made them the mercenaries of Ambrosius, and related how they presently coalesced with Wessex, thus forgetting the story of their own arrival in this country.

Archaeology also gives some vivid details of the decline of the Roman cities; the column from the town hall of Corinium, which fell across the main street and lay there until grooves were worn in the stone, was found on the site; so was the statue of Mars at Silchester. Many cities walled up their gates in the last days, which shows not only fear of raiders, but also that wheeled traffic, and therefore trade, had come to a stop. But most of them did not end by bloody sack and burning; apparently the citizens just could not earn a living where they were, and went away. As villas became self-supporting, and as the arts in general declined, there was no economic justification for city life, which is always a little unnatural in an agricultural country. This agrees with the literary evidence from Gaul, where in the fifth century every gentleman of independent means lived in a country house; two hundred years earlier he would have lived near the forum of the biggest city he could find.

To sum up: I have used all the evidence there is for the Coming of the Saxons, and, with the exception of the sons of Aella, I have used it accurately. But where there is no evidence I have not scrupled to invent. Yet everything I have written could be defended by historical argument, though not all historians would agree with my interpretation.

All Orion/Phoenix titles are available at your local bookshop or from the following address:

Mail Order Department
Littlehampton Book Services
FREEPOST BR535
Worthing, West Sussex, BN13 3BR
telephone 01903 828503, *facsimile* 01903 828802
e-mail MailOrders@lbsltd.co.uk
(Please ensure that you include full postal address details)

Payment can be made either by credit/debit card (Visa, Mastercard, Access and Switch accepted) or by sending a £ Sterling cheque or postal order made payable to *Littlehampton Book Services*.
DO NOT SEND CASH OR CURRENCY

Please add the following to cover postage and packing

UK and BFPO:
£1.50 for the first book, and 50p for each additional book to a maximum of £3.50

Overseas and Eire:
£2.50 for the first book plus £1.00 for the second book and 50p for each additional book ordered

---

BLOCK CAPITALS PLEASE

name of cardholder ....

address of cardholder ....

....

....

postcode ....

delivery address
(*if different from cardholder*)

....

....

....

postcode ....

☐ I enclose my remittance for £ ....

☐ please debit my Mastercard/Visa/Access/Switch (delete as appropriate)

card number ☐☐☐☐☐☐☐☐☐☐☐☐☐☐☐☐☐☐

expiry date ☐☐☐☐   Switch issue no. ☐☐

signature ....

prices and availability are subject to change without notice